By T. Davis Bunn

The Gift
The Messenger
The Music Box
One Shenandoah Winter
The Quilt
Tidings of Comfort & Joy

The Dream Voyagers
The Presence
Princess Bella and the Red Velvet Hat
Promises to Keep
To the Ends of the Earth
The Warning
The Ultimatum

By Janette Oke & T. Davis Bunn

Another Homecoming
The Meeting Place
Return to Harmony
Tomorrow's Dream

99B

Sacred Shore
Copyright © 2000
Janette Oke & T. Davis Bunn

Cover by Dan Thornberg

Published by Bethany House Publishers
A Ministry of Bethany Fellowship International
11400 Hampshire Avenue South
Minneapolis, Minnesota 55438
www.bethanyhouse.com

Printed in the United States of America by
Bethany Press International, Minneapolis, Minnesota 55438

ISBN 0–7642–2247–3 (Paperback)
ISBN 0–7642–2249–X (Hardcover)
ISBN 0–7642–2248–1 (Large Print)
ISBN 0–7642–2246–5 (Audio Book)

**The Library of Congress has cataloged the hardover edition as
follows:**

Oke, Janette, 1935–
    The sacred shore / by Janette Oke and T. Davis Bunn.
      p. cm.
    Sequel to: The meeting place.
    ISBN 0–7642–2249–X
    ISBN 0–7642–2247–3 (pbk.)
    I. Title. II. Bunn, T. Davis, 1952–   1. Canada—History—To
1763 (New France)—Fiction.
PR9199.3.O38 S24   2000
813'.54—dc21
                                              99–006839
                                                CIP

This book is dedicated to
one who was
a special friend
and enthusiastic reader

Laura Lohmeyer

who, at age sixteen, is now in His hands.

JANETTE OKE was born in Champion, Alberta, during the depression years, to a Canadian prairie farmer and his wife. She is a graduate of Mountain View Bible College in Didsbury, Alberta, where she met her husband, Edward. They were married in May of 1957 and went on to pastor churches in Indiana as well as Calgary and Edmonton, Canada.

The Okes have three sons and one daughter and are enjoying the addition of grandchildren to the family. Edward and Janette have both been active in their local church, serving in various capacities as Sunday school teachers and board members. They make their home near Calgary, Alberta.

T. DAVIS BUNN, a native of North Carolina, is a former international business executive whose career has taken him to over forty countries in Europe, Africa, and the Middle East. With topics as diverse as romance, history, and intrigue, Bunn's books continue to reach readers of all ages and interests. He and his wife, Isabella, reside near Oxford, England.

$\mathcal{P}$rologue

Catherine stood within the shadows of the kitchen and watched her daughter pass before the open window. She glanced at the delicate face framed in dark hair and knew instantly where Anne was going. Catherine began to call out to her, to tell her that it was time to prepare dinner. But she held back. Though it had always been difficult to allow Anne to be alone at times like this, Catherine knew with a mother's instinct that she must give her daughter these moments on her own.

Her daughter. Catherine moved closer to the window to watch the slender figure continue down the village lane. Anne was headed for the cliffside, a high promontory with far-reaching views. Just beyond the village borders, the sparkling blue Bay of Fundy joined with Cobequid Bay. When Anne was still a young child, she had taken to walking out there with her grandfather,

9

and she had selected an ancient tree trunk as her favorite spot. Catherine had joined them on several occasions, and she knew Anne still went to sit there and be alone with her thoughts.

What is she thinking of today? Catherine wondered as Anne moved out of sight. A child no longer, she was now eighteen, with a quiet yet joyful nature. Even so, there were moments like these when the stillness seemed to gather about her like a shroud. Then her features became as grave and inscrutable as an elderly woman's, and Anne would wander off on her own.

Catherine could not help but ask herself again if they had done the right thing. Should she and Andrew have told her early on about her heritage? About being born to a French family, then being exchanged for Catherine's own infant so she could be taken to an English doctor, and then losing contact with her birth parents after the tragic French expulsion—was it right to subject a young child to such truths? Was it proper, as she and Andrew had with great soul-searching concluded, to tell Anne these things while she was still young and able to accept with a child's loving trust? At moments like these, when Anne's features became etched with the quiet sorrow of pieces missing from her life, Catherine could not help but wonder.

Other memories too painful to ponder tumbled through her mind, and instantly Catherine returned to her dinner preparations, the motions as natural as breathing. There were more questions she dared not ask. Not any longer.

Chapter One

Before Charles Harrow set foot upon land, he already loathed the place. Halifax was, to his mind, loud and ugly and utterly unappealing. Nothing about the scene seemed inviting at all. The sun rested on the western slopes and shone upon the town rising in dirty, unkempt stages from the harbor. Jostling throngs filling the harbor square were forced to thread their way through bleating cattle and shouting soldiers. From every corner rang hammers and saws and shouts intermingled with the mewling of the animals. The workmen's dust was so thick it reminded him of the storm at sea they had recently endured. Charles sneezed into his handkerchief and wished himself back in London, away from these untamed and uncivilized colonies. The fact that a whim of fate had forced him here left him furious. He was not accustomed to doing anything other than exactly what suited him most.

"As I live and breathe, there's the *Pride of Weymouth*," cried the captain, moving up alongside him at the rail. "Look at her resting there at anchor, calm as by-your-leave. I never thought we'd see her spars again."

Lord Charles, eighth earl of Sutton, released an explosive breath. It would do no good to bemoan his fate again. He had survived the journey; he had made the crossing. He snuffled and made rejoinder out of courtesy rather than interest. "Your son is on that vessel, am I right?"

"Aye, if he didn't wash overboard like your two servants. The lad shipped as midshipman, against his mother's wishes. Eleven years old and the youngest of my brood. I'll rest easier once I learn I don't have to go back and tell the missus he was lost at sea."

Charles Harrow sighed heavily and squinted over the bustling capital of the colony known as Nova Scotia. Halifax was a city that threatened to burst its own seams. *My servants.* The older man had been with Charles since he was a child, since before his father had died and passed on to him the estates and the money and the power. The old servant had been like a second father, so attached to Lord Charles he could not think of letting him make this journey alone. And now he was gone, buried in the heart of a storm Charles had thought would cost them all their lives.

As though reading his thoughts, the captain confessed, "There were moments when I thought we all were headed for Davy Jones's locker."

Charles turned to the captain, noting more gray in the man's beard than there had been at the beginning of their voyage. "It seems strange to look at our rigging and not see icicles long as my arm."

"Crossings to Halifax this early in the season remain rare for good reason. But you made it, sir, and arrived here while the hills remain topped with white." The captain offered the glimmer of a smile. "That's something for you to tell your grandchildren."

My grandchildren. Charles Harrow ground his teeth at this unwelcome reminder of why he had made the perilous journey. "I must be off," he muttered.

"I'll have a couple of seamen carry your gear." The captain offered a stiff bow. "Whatever it was that sent you over, m'lord, I hope you're successful."

"My thanks." Charles Harrow returned the captain's formal bow and started down the gangplank, followed by two seamen laden with trunk and bags.

His first step on dry land in two months

almost sent him tumbling, for a shepherd led a flock of sheep directly into his path. Only the quick hands of one of the seamen saved him from sprawling in the half-frozen muck. Charles waited as his sea chest was hefted from the mud and fleetingly wished there were some way to transport himself back to London.

But there was no help for it. Fate had dealt him a cruel hand, and he was here. Without power or comforts of wealth and home, and even the familiar faces of his two most trusted servants gone. His only hope was to complete his business and—

"Lord Charles? Are you Lord Charles?"

"I am."

The mud-spattered young man whipped off his hat and made a parody of a courtly bow. "Winston Groom at your service, m'lord. I bring Governor Lawrence's sincerest respects. He regrets that he could not be here to greet you himself, but urgent business has called him to the hinterland."

"Of course." Charles pointed at another flock of bleating animals bearing down on them. "Let's carry on somewhere safer, shall we?"

"Certainly, your lordship. This way." The man bowed and scraped in the way of someone awed by Charles's station, seeking to lead and follow at the same time. Winston Groom reminded Charles of an oft-beaten dog. "Did your lordship have a pleasant journey?"

"Don't be daft, man. Crossing the North Atlantic at any time could hardly be call for pleasantness. A passage between March and April was nothing short of dreadful."

"Yes, yes, sir, humble apologies, sir. The *Weymouth* feared you'd been lost with all hands." The young man was dressed in what most likely passed for high fashion in the colonies. His shirt collar was starched and his winter coat fur trimmed, but his clothes were as mud spattered as his boots. "Governor Lawrence will be delighted to hear that you survived the journey."

"Is there a suitable inn in this town? A hostel? A wayfarer's lodging?"

"Indeed, that is where I am taking your lordship." He led Charles and the two silent seamen up onto the elevated wooden walkway. The seamen's clogs clattered loudly over the rough planking. The remnants of hard winter were everywhere: dirty snow remained piled against north-facing walls; tiny icicles still dripped from the walkway's overhang. The distant hills were more white than brown. Horses drawing wagons and carriages along Halifax's thoroughfares still bore their rough winter's coats. Charles picked his way behind the young man across a busy intersection, dodging supply wagons and a trio of mud-drenched horses and two boys leading half a dozen pigs by rope leads. The pigs were the biggest he had ever seen, rude beasts that fit the town perfectly.

Eventually Winston Groom opened a glass-topped door with a flourish and announced, "Right through here, your lordship."

The hotel was so new it still smelled of fresh-cut lumber. But the floor was waxed and there were tallow candles in the chandelier and the owner there to bow him over the threshold. Charles took the first easy breath since stepping off the gangplank. Here at least there was a semblance of civilization.

The owner bowed a second time and said, "Welcome, Lord Charles. We have taken the liberty of preparing for you our finest rooms."

Charles permitted himself to be led up the central staircase, inspected the rooms and announced them adequate. He gave the seamen a silver penny each. When he saw Winston Groom's eyes widen at the amount, Charles had the impression that here was a man who could be bought.

The innkeeper said, "We've got a fresh haunch roasting on the fire, m'lord, and the last of our winter's stock of root vegetables making a fine stew. And bread in the oven."

His stomach grumbled at the thought of fresh food. "I don't suppose you have any fruit."

The hotelier was a sharp-faced man more suited to the counting room than the kitchen. His laugh held the easy roughness of the colonies. "Not for another month, your lordship. Not till the first vessel arrives from the southern colonies."

"Very well, I'll take whatever you recommend." He turned to the governor's assistant hovering by the bed. "Groom, is it?"

"Yes, m'lord. Winston Groom." The spindly man was all angles and hollows.

"Perhaps you'll join me for a private word."

Charles watched as the groom's eyes widened. He was obviously flattered at the thought of speaking confidentially with an earl. "You're too kind, sir."

"Not at all. Not at all." He extended one arm to direct the young man back down the stairs beside him. "Tell me, Groom. You know your way around the colony. Perhaps you've heard tales of another man bearing my name?"

The step faltered, and the young man grasped the railing. "I'm not . . . I'm not certain, your lordship."

He had. Charles was certain of it. "Come, come. A man who holds the governor's confidence must have heard something, surely. Andrew Harrow is his name. Some mention would have been made of this when *Weymouth* reported that I was journeying on their sister ship."

Winston did not respond as he was led across the foyer to a pair of tall chairs by the fire. Charles observed the young man's furrowed brow, the way he started to speak and then cut himself off, the eyes that refused to move in his direction. It was all the answer Charles required.

"Andrew Harrow," Charles continued smoothly, his genial tone making it as easy as possible for Groom. "Formerly Captain Harrow, head of the military garrison at Fort Edward. Resigned after the expulsion of the Acadians. Word has it that he was forced out under a cloud."

"I . . . I may have heard some mention, m'lord."

"Of course you have." Keeping his voice light, his tone airy, as though they were discussing the weather on a kind summer day, Charles turned his own gaze toward the fire, seeking to hide his sudden eagerness. "I understand that my brother went off to the American colonies for a time. He and his wife, apparently. A woman he met and wed there in Fort Edward. Boston, I believe, was their destination."

But the young man's attention had been snagged early on. "Did you say *brother*, m'lord?"

"Indeed, yes. Andrew Harrow is my only brother." It cost Charles dearly to hold to his light tone, but he had no choice. No choice but to hide the shame and endure the dreadful voyage and come to a place he had sworn never to visit. All for a brother who had been the greatest threat Charles had ever known, a man he had vowed he would never see again. How wrong he had been. About so many things. But Charles kept his voice easy as he spoke to the fire. "Andrew studied at a seminary in Boston. I have received a letter from the head of the school confirming that, and the fact that Andrew returned here to Nova Scotia. But since then I have lost track of him."

"Governor Lawrence did mention something about a . . . a former captain who carries your name," Winston Groom acknowledged with obvious reluctance.

"I thought perhaps he had. I *hoped* as

21

much." Casually Charles reached into his waistcoat and pulled out a drawstring pouch of softest leather. He caressed the hide, causing the gold sovereigns within to clink together. "I was wondering if I might ask a favor, young Groom."

"Anything, m'lord." The pasty-faced man's eyes fastened on the pouch and its tinkling music. "Anything at all."

Charles bounced the pouch within his hand so that the weight was evident. "I am here to find my brother Andrew. I need to know where to look."

"Governor Lawrence said he'd heard nothing of the man since the expulsion, m'lord. That was eighteen years ago."

"Indeed." He bounced the pouch a second time. "But a resourceful young man, one with ambition and a desire to better his position, no doubt might have ways and means of finding out more."

"I . . . perhaps . . . yes, m'lord." Winston Groom licked his lips. "I think I might know where to start."

"Then might I offer this paltry sum to help further the search." Charles passed over the pouch and watched in amusement as bony fingers eagerly sought to count the sovereigns through the leather. "I will double that amount if you can determine my brother's whereabouts within the week."

Chapter Two

"Here. Let me get out here."

"I can take you closer."

"No. Please, Jean, stop here before . . ." Nicole let her voice trail off.

But she knew Jean understood when he finished angrily, "Before the village sees you with me."

"Not the village." Nicole kept her tone steady because she did not want another argument. "My parents. And you know if one person sees us together, my parents will know before I reach home."

As her eyes swept over his face, she knew Jean Dupree was incensed by her request. But he did as he was told. He was as skilled with the flat-bottomed skiff as he was with a gun, a bow, a fishing pike, or a net. Jean Dupree was the only man in all of Vermilionville who could compete with Nicole's father at hunting or fishing. Every festival where there were shooting competitions, one or the other man always won. But this rivalry was not why Nicole hid her frequent rendezvous with Jean Dupree. Not at all.

Jean paddled the skiff over to a spot

where the riverbank was clear of undergrowth. Nicole stepped lightly from the skiff's bow onto dry land. She turned and gave him her warmest smile. "I had a wonderful time with you today."

Thankfully, the smile worked its magic, and Jean's anger faded as quickly as a summer squall. "Tell me."

"Oh, Jean."

His brow furrowed, but this time in play. "Tell me, Nicole."

"I love you with all my heart," she said, the French words rolling lyrically off her tongue. For a moment she believed them.

"And now tell me you will be my wife."

The words were there, ready to be spoken, finally out and said and the step taken—after putting him off for almost six months and enduring countless arguments because of this. But as she opened her mouth to speak, a veil of warning seemed to drape itself across her heart. Soft as the Spanish moss that hung overhead, quiet as the call of doves on the bayou. But it was enough to still her speech before she had begun. She closed her mouth, and her face must have betrayed her anguish.

Jean was a man of great passion and strong moods. His anger could flash like summer lightning, his eyes cloud like dark thunder. But now he did not look angry. Only weary. And this was the worst of all. "You must decide, Nicole."

"Soon. I promise." Yet this time it was not enough. The words had been said so often they held no strength for either of them. "Jean, I am afraid of your friends," she finally forced out through lips stiff with her inner turmoil.

She had said this before as well. But not often. For to challenge his friends was to challenge Jean Dupree himself. Yet again there was no anger. "I am what I am, Nicole."

"Yes, and it is Jean Dupree I love. Dearly." She reached for a low-hanging branch so she could ease closer to the bank. "My Jean has a soft side and a large heart. He laughs and he sings and he loves me."

"My friends sing."

"Yes, but all their songs are of blood and battle. They sing of vengeance."

"You hate the English as much as I do. As much as any of us."

She wondered why she was even trying to explain. Nicole knew he was not going to change, that he would not give up his friends, even for her. A blade of sunlight pierced the tangle of branches overhead, falling green and golden upon the Vermilion

River's slow-moving surface. Nicole had the sudden impression that she was not saying all this again to change Jean at all. Instead, she was saying it to explain why they must part.

The sudden pain was so strong that it was a physical wrench in her heart. She leaned over farther still to plead, "Jean, your friends are dangerous. They rob the newcomers, French and Spanish and English alike. No, don't argue, for once, please, I beg you. Listen to what I am saying."

And for once he did. As though he too sensed a shift in the sultry late-April wind and knew that change was soon in coming. He laid the paddle across his knees and remained silent. Still. Watchful.

"You are two-natured. My mother has said it countless times. I argued with her because I always thought she meant you were weak. But that's not it; I see it now for myself. You are truly as she says, Jean. You have a very good side. You have a great heart and a smile to match. You are strong and good and would make a fine husband."

He watched her with the stillness of a hunter. His entire being seemed focused upon her as she stood on the bank. "But?"

"Yes. But there is your other nature as well." She took a breath. "I say this because

I love you, Jean. You have a dark side."

This time he did not shout and leave, nor did he deny what before he had refused even to hear. "No one who has lived through what I have could survive without a dark side."

"My father has." She said this simply, not in condemnation but in the sadness of acceptance. Nicole was forcing herself to see all the reasons why her parents had refused to consider a courtship of their daughter by the dashing Jean Dupree. "My father and my mother both. They trekked for eight years before finally coming here. You know the story as well as I do. We were some of the first Acadian settlers to arrive in Louisiana. When we came, there was nothing. Less even than when you arrived. No, please, Jean, don't argue. Not this time. I beg you."

Her heartfelt entreaty must have broken through to him because he said, "Say your piece."

The air seemed stifling, as though she were locked in August heat and not an April afternoon. Nicole struggled to find the breath to continue. "If you stay with your friends, they will change you. When you are with them, your dark side comes out. And I do not love you then, Jean. I fear you. You seem to drink in their evil and anger and love of danger. When I see you with them, I think you are able to do anything."

He nodded solemnly. "I can. With them, anything is possible. Even a revolt against the English."

And there in the words was the reason why her father was right, and she was wrong. Nicole looked at the only man she had ever loved and said with the sorrow of a broken spirit, "A man who plots revolt is not a man I can marry."

His body stiffened as though she had reached across the distance and slapped his face. But again there was no anger. Only the careful watchfulness of a hunter stalking prey. "I will think on what you have said, Nicole. Only tell me once more."

This time she shook her head sadly and turned away in silence. As she walked away she brushed tears from her eyes at the sound of him calling her name. But she did not turn back. For if she had, she knew her will would have snapped. She would have rushed to him and flung herself into his arms and let him take her away. Anywhere, so long as they would remain together. Even if she knew it was wrong, knew that it would end in tragedy. Her love for him was that great.

Nicole pretended not to hurry as she walked the white-sand road back into town. And then she wished she had not turned away. Wished she had given her promise to Jean, turned a deaf ear to her parents' warnings, and done what she longed to do.

Then her step faltered, for there upon the trail leading into Vermilionville she realized that just like Jean, she was a person of two natures. She was strong and certain and willful and brave. Yet she was also weak and frightened and lonely and aching. If that was so, how could she ask Jean to refuse one side of his nature? How could she expect him to be what she herself could not be?

Such lingering regret was not like her. Nor the inability to make a decision and stick to her course. But as she entered the village and hastened toward home, her heart keened like a lonely hawk, circling far overhead, searching for the man she had sent away. A man she had denied for reasons she could no longer recall.

Jean Dupree was the most handsome man in all the southern Acadia province. She thought this because it was true. She had seen her own impression reflected in the gazes of all the local girls, lasses who would never have resisted his urgings. Jean was tall and strong and darkly beautiful, his looks so powerfully attractive they would almost have been effeminate on someone less virile. He suited her perfectly. Even her mother admitted as much, and her mother disliked Jean Dupree so intensely she would not permit him into her home. Nicole herself was tall with red highlights to her hair and eyes green as the Vermilion's water. No one in all Acadia had eyes like hers. Nor the will to match. For Nicole was not only headstrong, she was willful and impatient with the weak meanderings of most men. Only Jean was strong enough and man enough to have won her heart. A heart that now felt as if it were being squeezed to nothing. She sighed as she turned down the lane to her home. Only Jean.

She shooed the chickens back before opening the front gate, then was fastened to the spot by a sudden impression. She gazed up at the red-brick chimney rising from her home's north wall and had a fleeting vision of its being painted white. A white-painted chimney was the Acadians' way of proclaiming that within that home resided an available maiden on her way to being an old maid. Hunters and fishermen treading the bayous would pass word on to other outlying clans, and soon enough the men would appear, silent and often hostile from living too long alone. The swamps and bayous worked strange effects on those who lived solitary existences, painting their beards the dark gray of Spanish moss and twisting their bones like contorted tree limbs.

Some families painted their chimneys as soon as the daughter reached her eighteenth birthday and remained unwed. When Nicole had turned eighteen three months earlier, she had heard someone jokingly ask her father whether they should mix up the lime-wash and prepare the rags. But her father was head of both the village and the outlying clans, and he had the strength and position to say that no, his daughter was slow in choosing, though she could have had any young man in the village. Henri Robichaud had added that she was too special, too precious, to let go easily, and she could stay home as long as she wished. He had spoken with such conviction Nicole had almost believed him.

"Nicole?" Louise, her mother, appeared in the kitchen window. "Do you wish me to do all the work of dinner myself?"

She collected herself as best she could. "I thought I saw some new eggs."

"We have enough for today. Come inside. I need you."

"All right." She cast a final glance at the unwashed chimney and repressed a shiver. She climbed the stairs, her mind sadly chanting one word in time to her steps. Over and over her mind and heart intoned the name of Jean.

Louise worked alongside her daughter and knew Nicole had been with Jean once more. Against her express orders, her daughter had visited the man Louise had forbidden to step over the threshold of their home. Louise pounded and kneaded the dough she was preparing, working her ire into the flour. She knew there was nothing to be gained from saying anything more. Nicole was a child no longer. Almost a head taller than Louise, her determination halted any further conversation. And then there was the matter of her beauty. Just the previous week Louise had seen it happen. Together the family had attended the Plaquemine festival. Louise had sat beside her husband and watched every young man at the gathering follow her lovely Nicole wherever she moved. Yet this same beauty was also a barrier, for Nicole's loveliness was matched by a strength that cowed men twice her age. She was headstrong and intelligent and unwilling to hide either trait.

Louise picked up the rolling pin. Her

anger left the dough flat as a sheet. Why would she not accuse her daughter of defying her specific orders? Louise folded the sheets over and over, then began stamping out circles for biscuits, rapping with the strength of hammer blows. She knew she remained silent because she feared what Nicole might do. If Louise gave the ultimatum that swelled her chest almost to bursting, Nicole could very well turn and walk from their home without a backward glance. She was that headstrong a daughter.

In her heart, Louise often wondered what Nicole would have been had she been shaped by different circumstances. Forced, with family members, to flee like chased rabbits from place to place, eking out an existence from the forests, or working dawn to dusk for enough poor food to be called an evening meal, often dodging shouts and even hurled stones of village children, being eternally unwanted. Those early years had stamped an indelible mark upon their souls, one the serene life they now enjoyed along the bayou could never erase.

Louise began placing the biscuits on the baking tin. A quick glance at Nicole halted her movements. "Daughter, what's wrong?"

Nicole did not respond. She leaned over the vegetables she was meant to be washing, her tears falling silently. A more tragic sight Louise had never seen. The daughter who never wept, who never showed anything but willful strength, was now stooped like an old woman. Nicole seemed unable even to tremble. She did not cry aloud, did not sob, did not speak. She stood with her shoulders bowed and body unmoving. She looked more than sad. She looked tragic.

Hastily Louise wiped her hands on her apron and rushed over. She put her arms about her daughter and hugged her with the will to draw this sorrow out into the light. "Tell me, Nicole. Tell me *now*."

"Jean has asked me to marry him." The voice that spoke was a full octave below that of her mother's. A voice full of defeat and woe. "I love him so, Mama."

Louise bit down on the angry retort that pressed her stomach into a hard knot. Jean was not good enough for Nicole. But saying that now would do nothing. So she held her daughter close and trembled with the struggle to hold back her thoughts.

"I know what you're thinking. That Jean is a bad man." The tears came faster now and finally the sounds of weeping. "But he's not. He has . . . pain and angers and rages, just like all of us. But he is also strong and gentle and good."

The desire to dispute this pressed up so hard Louise coughed to keep from speaking.

Nicole shrugged out from the arms that held her and turned her tear-streaked face. "I always thought that if he loved me enough, he would be the good man I know he has inside him. But today, today . . ."

Louise bunched her apron up in her hands and could only whisper, "Tell me."

"Today we talked like we have never talked before. And I told him he had to give up the friends, the ones Father hates so."

"Your father hates no man."

Nicole conceded with a tip of her head, then hurriedly amended her words. "The ones he thinks are so dangerous. Jean said he would think on it."

This was enough to shock Louise to stillness. First that her daughter would be so perceptive, to see the need to extricate her beloved from the threat of such companions. And second that the headstrong and dashing Jean Dupree would love Nicole so much as to be willing to consider such a change.

But Nicole was not finished. "He will not do it. I know him because I love him, and I know he will not do it. He will not, and because of this I cannot marry him. I *must* not." The sobs seemed almost to choke her, and the effort of trying to breathe and speak must have debilitated her physically, for Nicole collapsed into her father's chair at the head of the kitchen table. She bowed over her hands, leaning down until her hands and her face rested upon her knees. Her voice was muffled, but the words were clear. "I love him, but I must not marry him. I must not. For the children I will never have, I must not."

Louise only realized she was crying as well when the figure who appeared in the doorway wavered in and out of focus. Her husband of twenty-one years seemed to swell and recede as he approached. Henri Robichaud rested one hand upon his daughter's shoulder and the other reached toward his wife. She moved into his embrace and was comforted by his strength. As always. Henri did not smile and laugh so easily as he had when they were younger, but his strength remained unvanquished both by the years and all the hardships they had endured. Here in her husband's embrace, Louise Robichaud could be weak, could be uncertain, could be threatened by doubts and sorrow. Henri would keep her safe and strong. Henri would know what to do.

"My two beautiful ladies," he murmured. "The jewels of my life. Look at you now. Both of you crying is enough to break my heart. I think it must be a man that is the cause of so many tears. Am I not right?"

Through spates of tears, Nicole managed to give a brief explanation. When she had ended the telling she whispered, "I wish I knew what to do."

Henri spoke in a tone to match his daughter's. "Have you prayed of this?"

"So much," she sobbed. "So often."

"Ah, wait and hear me now," he said, stroking Nicole's hair. "I know you have prayed for Jean to know a change of heart and be your man. But have you asked God to show you His *will*?"

Louise clutched her husband's homespun shirt, grateful for his strength and his calm. The storms of life had etched their way deep into his face and his soul, turning what once had been deep smile lines into creases that folded more easily downward. But his quiet and gentle nature had only been increased, his wisdom solidified.

Nicole drew a deep breath. "I think so."

"You *think*." The work-scarred hand stroked their daughter's hair with impossible tenderness. "You *think*. Something this important, don't you think you should *know*?"

She looked up then, her tear-streaked gaze as open as a child's. "But I want him. So much."

Louise's mother-heart lurched at the depth of honesty and of sorrow in the admission.

Henri said, "I know you do. And if I know this, in all my impossible worries as a father and an imperfect man, don't you think our Father knows as well?" Nicole gave a tiny shiver of a nod, and he went on, "Don't you think God would give him to you if he was indeed right? Yes? So perhaps the wisdom you showed in your talk with him today was God's hand at work in your life. Did you think of that?"

"Yes." The words were soft as a spring wind through the year's new leaves. "Not in those words. But yes. I thought that."

"Then you also know what is God's answer here to your dilemma, yes?"

Her tears spilled faster once again. "I think that is why my heart aches so."

Henri's arm around Louise tightened instinctively, and Louise knew their hearts yearned as one over their grief-stricken daughter.

That night, as Henri lay beside his wife, he spoke to the dark. "Our Nicole is no longer a child."

"In truth, perhaps she never was." Louise's breath was soft against his cheek. "I was just thinking about the time after Jacques was born."

Some memories were so heavily laden with emotion that they were rarely spoken, as though the story's power did not fit comfortably into words. It was all Henri could do to murmur, "I remember."

The truth was, he would never forget. They had been expelled from Acadia, the province now called Nova Scotia, in 1755. Nicole had been a mere infant, a bundle of joy and hope in a time so bleak it scalded Henri even to remember it now, sheltered here within his own home on his own land in a region that had at last welcomed them with open arms.

After the expulsion and the voyage they had finally been deposited far down the eastern coast, at the port of Charleston. The few French colonists had helped as they could, but times had been hard, and the Acadians had survived by hiring themselves out as laborers when work could be found, scrounging harvested fields or forest floors and streams when it could not. Henri had fished and farmed, just as he had at home, only it was on someone else's land. His family had lived in a lean-to behind the owner's barn. They had lived thus for the two longest years of Henri's life.

Upon leaving the ship initially, most of the Acadians traveling with them had scattered. Henri knew now this had happened at almost every colony and outpost where the Acadians had been deposited. Some had begun endless treks across oceans and continents, searching for clan and families dispersed without record. They spent years and lifetimes chasing rumors and tales, staying in one place only long enough to gain the money to travel on. Others returned to France, only to find themselves unwelcome visitors in their own homeland. Those without families moved west and became trappers and scouts in the wild frontier lands. Others traveled to the Caribbean and South America.

Two years after their arrival, the band of Acadians who remained near Charleston had pooled what money they had and bought a small plot of land. Days they had worked for the people who housed and fed them; evenings they had worked for themselves. For four years they had struggled, earning a reputation as being silent God-fearing families who worked hard at anything they turned their hands to.

Two children had been born to Henri and Louise during that time, first Josef and then Jacques. Three weeks after Jacques was born, Louise had been stricken with fever. It was planting season, and evenings Henri returned home so exhausted he could scarcely walk, much less take care of a wife and three small children. Almost seven, little Nicole had taken over the duties of her mother. The neighbors had helped as much as they could, but planting stretched everyone to the limit and beyond. Henri had felt his soul blistered by the sight of his daughter tending two infants and a sick mother, remembering the hardship that had scarred his own early orphan years. Here he was, leader of a clan that had been scattered to the four winds, reduced to watching his daughter repeat a life he had struggled to put behind him forever.

For her seventh birthday, Nicole had asked for a bigger pot and a new broom. Hearing those words spoken by a small child had sent Henri staggering from the house. He had walked back to his field, and there over the tiny seedlings he had vowed to take his family to a better place. A place of hope and plenty. A place where they could find peace and grow and be welcome.

"I remember," Henri repeated softly.

"Nicole was never really a child," Louise

repeated. "She was more my youngest friend."

His eyes burned from the words and the love behind them. "You are a blessing to all the family, my dearest."

Her voice carried the smile his eyes could not see. "What a strange thing to say when we are speaking of hard times and a child growing up."

"She has grown into the beauty she is," Henri replied, "only because of you."

A week and more went by before Henri judged the time to be right. For Louise, she was content to leave the decision to her husband. Henri's habits were well-known, the caution he showed toward most decisions learned from a hard life and years of leadership. He waited and he watched as Nicole left behind the tears and learned to live with the hollow point of sorrow in her gaze and her days.

Twice Jean Dupree came by the house, ignoring Louise's command for him to stay away, drawn by the mournful love that shattered his own gaze as well. The first time Nicole walked with him a brief way, going through the village so she remained protected by company and watchful neighbors. The second time she refused to descend from the porch, saying only that there was nothing more to be said unless he accepted the need to make a change. Jean had shouted words the entire village had heard, then raised clouds of spring dust as he had stomped back to his boat. His tirade echoed long after his skiff had disappeared down the bayou. Louise had remained standing upon the balcony, bowed by the weight of soft tears.

Four nights later, the boys were asleep early, planning to be up and away with the dawn for crayfish. Louise and Henri sat on the broad front veranda, made large enough for the entire family to sleep out of doors in the heavy heat of July and August. Nicole came and joined them, moving silently to the chair by the railing, seating herself and rocking gently, saying nothing. This alone spoke volumes, for seldom was Nicole without a song or a smile or a tale from village life. Henri sat enclosed by the gathering dusk and the quiet, hearing the night birds and the cicadas herald another spring on the Louisiana delta.

Louise shifted in her chair, the quiet creaking a wordless agreement to Henri's own decision. So when he spoke, he knew it was for them both. "Nicole, there is something I need to tell you. Something that has been a secret for many years."

Again there was the sign of a troubled heart, for secrets were one of his daughter's greatest joys. The only way to keep anything from Nicole, be it words or a gift, was for her not to know the first hint. Otherwise she would weasel and wile until she knew it all. Yet tonight she said nothing, and the moonlight shone upon a dark head that did not even turn to meet his words.

Henri asked, because he had to, "What are you thinking, daughter?"

"I was wondering," she said, her voice a velvet whisper, "if God really exists at all."

Louise caught her breath there beside him, but even before Henri could reach out a hand to keep her from protesting, his wife stilled herself and settled back into her chair. Henri waited through a pair of calming breaths before asking, "Why do you say that?"

"Because I've been praying so hard my heart feels twisted like a washrag. And I have had no answer, no peace, no calm. Nothing but silence. God can't exist and be quiet while I am feeling such pain, Papa. So I am beginning to think He does not exist at all."

The matter-of-fact way she spoke rendered him unable to do more than reply, "He exists."

"I know you believe. I know you find

44

great solace in that. And I am happy for you. Really. But you asked what I was thinking and I told you." She could have been discussing a new family arriving from downriver, her voice was that flat and calm. "God cannot exist and remain silent. Not when I need Him more than I have ever needed anything in my entire life." A faint tremor entered her voice, quickly stifled. "Except the one thing I can't have."

Louise started to move then, yet Henri's hand halted her before the chair creaked. He cleared his throat and tried again. "Sometimes God is quiet because He wants us to draw closer and listen harder."

His daughter did not respond for a long time. When she did, it was to say, "What did you want to tell me, Papa?"

It was his turn to hesitate. Henri closed his eyes to the night and the two women he loved and prayed for wisdom, for direction, for the right words. For him too God remained silent, but here and now it seemed the silence held a rightness, a harmony. As though God felt no need to speak, since Henri was moving as he should. Henri opened his eyes. As if in confirmation, Nicole slowly turned about to face her parents.

So he took a great breath and said aloud, "Daughter, this is not easy to tell. Perhaps it should have been said long ago. I did not know then and still cannot say today whether my decision was wrong or right. But now . . . now you must prepare yourself for what I fear will be a great shock."

Chapter Three

"I am *what*?"

"Shah, my love," Louise chided, fingers to her lips. "Your brothers."

Nicole lifted from the chair as though pulled by invisible strings. "But I don't . . . I can't be." Her voice trembled through the darkness of the veranda. "I've always been . . ."

"You are ours—but you are also another's. Parents who loved you dearly. Who must have died a thousand deaths since we left Acadia."

"I am *English*?"

"You are our child," Henri responded. "You are our mourning dove. That is what you must remember."

"But I *loathe* the English!"

Louise leaned forward, stretching out one hand toward her daughter. "Unless you wish for all to hear and know, my child, you must speak more softly. The night has ears."

"The English are the ones who banished us from Acadia!" Though she spoke more quietly, the words carried no less vehemence. "They drove us like cattle. For *years* we wandered!"

"Yes, and now we are here. Now we are home. We have found another Acadia. Now you are an adult. Now you must know." Henri was repeating himself, but he continued to speak because he hoped his voice would carry the more important message of calm and strength and love. "Understand me, daughter. You were not given to us. You were placed in our care only for a few days. Your mother agreed to this exchange of babies because our own child was ill and close to death. Your mother's closest friend was an Englishwoman named Catherine. She knew a French baby would not be given medical treatment. She did this out of Christian compassion. But while the Englishwoman was taking our baby to the doctor in Halifax, the British soldiers expelled us. We could not leave you behind. Nor did we have time to seek our own child. Your mother . . ."

"My mother," Nicole repeated, caught by that single word. "Who *is* my mother?"

Louise's hand no longer had the strength to reach out. It dropped limply into her aproned lap. "That you should ask such a question, my child, breaks my heart in two."

Nicole started forward, and the movement brought her face into the moonlight, revealing features contorted by shock and anguish. Her own hand froze in midair; then she spun away from them and nearly tumbled down the steps in her haste.

Louise softly cried the words, "Go after her, Henri."

For once his famous strength seemed unable to heed his call. "What shall I say to her?"

"Whatever comes to your heart. But go."

Henri moved down the steps and along the garden path and out into the village lane. Ahead, his daughter's silhouette staggered like one stricken by a disease. He continued to follow, but the closer he came, the slower he walked. He found himself unable to move up alongside her. This beloved daughter whose heart was twice broken in such a short span of time.

Nicole broke the invisible barrier by asking, "Are there any other truths I don't know?"

"The truth," he said softly, weak with relief that she was still speaking to him. "The truth, my beloved Nicole, is that you are the reason we could bear the anguish of that terrible time. You gave us joy when we thought it was gone forever."

She glanced back at him, her face a silver wash of moonlight and tears and new sorrows. "But I was just a baby."

"Yes. A baby who needed us. And we needed you. The truth, my blessed daughter, is that we do not believe baby Antoinette would have ever lived through the expulsion. We do not know if she even survived at all. The truth also is that it was this same Englishwoman who led your mother and me along the pathway to God."

A quiet voice hailed them from one of the porches. Henri did not respond, and the voice did not call again. It was the way of folks in the bayou, to offer invitations but not to insist. At one time or another, all had found a need to walk the darkness and struggle with the unseen.

For a time their footsteps were the only sounds in the night. Henri continued when they had moved beyond earshot. "The woman Catherine and your mother used to meet in a meadow up above our village of Minas. Her husband was the officer in charge of the garrison at Fort Edward."

Nicole spun to face him. "An *officer*? An *English* officer?"

Gently Henri gripped his daughter's arms and pulled her to him. "One of the finest men I have ever known, and I met him but once. We could not speak together, for he knew no French and I no English. But I knew him through his wife, through the love on her face and the concern they shared together when baby Antoinette became so ill. They said . . ."

Nicole pulled from his grasp, and Henri fell in step beside her. The night seemed to press in from all sides, so full of memories and heartache that the air itself seemed too heavy to breathe. Henri worked his chest like bellows and found the strength to say, "They told us there was nothing they could do about the madness sweeping the English. Nothing except help to save this one French baby. It was their act of peace, their small voice crying against the wilderness of war."

"Oh, Papa." Her face was luminous in the moonlight.

"All you need to know about your English parents, Nicole, is that they are the finest people on God's earth." The night seemed reflected in his daughter's eyes, like starlight upon the Vermilion waters. "Though we have had no word from them in eighteen years, still I count them among my closest friends."

Nicole began walking again. "You wrote them?"

"So many letters. Through every contact we could muster. We even asked the family I worked for in Charleston to write on our behalf to the garrison commander at Fort Edward, and even to the military chief in Halifax. No answer was ever received. None. We are certain the letters did not arrive. We have heard the same from so many others of our people. Letters sent and never answered. It is an additional price we still pay to ensure our banishment."

"English," Nicole whispered. "I am English."

"You are both," Henri prompted. "You are French, more Acadian than most of those who claim the right by blood. But, yes, your first parents were English. *Are* English, as I can only hope your father survived."

"You think he might have died?"

"Of one thing I am so certain I know this in my bones, daughter. Andrew Harrow would never have taken up arms against the peaceful villagers of Minas or anywhere else. What may have happened to him for disobeying such an order, I am afraid to even guess."

"Papa, why did you not tell me all this until now?" The pain in her voice carried far more weight than the words themselves.

Henri sighed deeply. "Yes, my beloved

Nicole," he began, "you have every right to wonder about that." He paused for a moment. "In those earliest days of our banishment, only a handful of our closest family members knew at all. And the danger from the English did not cease when we were expelled. So your English roots were a carefully guarded secret. The danger of this becoming common knowledge was not simply to us but to our whole clan. During our years of wandering, the danger continued."

Henri paused again to search Nicole's face. "When we settled here, your mother and I were also settled in our hearts. God had given us a peace and an acceptance of His will that led us to feel He would show us the right time and place to tell you." With his tone as gentle as he could make it, Henri finished, "And we believe that has happened."

Henri could hear Nicole's deep sigh. She did not speak but turned to walk on.

They continued to where the village ended and the lane joined the trail north to Opelousas. Silently they turned back. Before them the houses glowed with candles and fires, the lights soft and yellow and welcoming. Henri felt his heart swell with thanks for the gift of a place to call his own. He murmured, "Home."

Nicole sighed again beside him and

whispered a word of her own, disbelief still edging her voice. "English."

Chapter Four

The ball in Halifax was intended to be in his honor. Charles had no choice but to attend. He stepped from the governor's carriage, nodded in response to the honor guard's noisy salute, and climbed the steps to the governor's mansion. The house was a rather grand affair relative to the rest of the colony, stone and stalwart. So was the ball, full of swirling gowns and powdered wigs and loud talk and shrill voices that probed at him constantly. Charles danced with the older ladies only, avoiding flirtatious glances from women half his age.

When the musicians paused, Charles forced himself from circle to circle, restless and impatient. It had been four days since his arrival, and still no word had come from Winston Groom. Four days he could ill afford to spend waiting and wandering about this unkempt outpost.

One of the officials' wives approached with a veiled smile. For the life of him, he could not recall her name. "Lord Charles, would you be so kind as to accompany me for a breath of air?"

"Delighted," he replied with a bow. In truth, he did not mind. He had been expecting such an emissary to be sent. His presence all the way from England was too great a mystery. But perhaps this bit of digging for information could work both ways. With any luck, he might discover some yet unknown piece of his own.

The woman waited until they had stepped onto one of the small upstairs balconies to say, "You have the entire colony abuzz, Lord Charles."

"No doubt." Through the windows of the double-doors, Charles watched as the sentry stepped over to stand duty directly in front of them. Clearly this was a calculated moment, one intended to politely wrest some truth from him. So he made known that he was willing to speak openly by responding, "With unrest brewing in the American colonies south of here, I am certain to be raising all sorts of rumors and concerns."

"You must forgive me, m'lord, I am but an addle-headed woman." She had a sweet voice and a winning smile that belied eyes hard as agate. "I know only one way to speak, and that is directly."

He gave a second bow. "I am at your service, my lady."

"Tell me, why are you here?"

"I have several reasons. One for public propagation, the other strictly private."

"Oh, you mustn't worry. I am very good at holding secrets." The smile came easily to her. "I shall only tell those who truly must know."

Despite himself, he liked her and her direct manner. "Then I shall entrust you with both. The first is, His Majesty was kind enough to grant me deed to lands south of here."

"Yes, indeed. And where, may I ask?"

"Along the westerly borders of Massachusetts Colony."

"Forgive me, sir, but Halifax is a circuitous route to take to Boston. Especially when it means braving late-winter storms in the North Atlantic."

"Yes. But if I am to manage one colonial estate, why not two? I hear there is land to be had near Halifax."

"That there is. Half the land once tilled by the Acadians still lies fallow, though more settlers arrive every day from Scotland and Wales. Even Europe." The gaze turned piercing. "Not to mention those fleeing the coming troubles in the American colonies."

Charles understood perfectly. "The king

did not send me to spy upon his subjects here, my lady. Nor does he question your loyalty."

She relaxed a trifle. "Do you know, Lord Charles, I almost believe you."

"I am no more comfortable with convoluted conversation than you, my lady. A worse diplomat or spy the king could not have chosen. Believe me, if he were to ask my opinion of the loyalties in these parts, my response would be, I have no opinion at all."

Below them, on Halifax's central avenue, a mule skinner cracked his long whip and shouted so loud both their glances turned downward. Charles counted sixteen slow-moving mules pulling a wagon piled so high with bales he could almost reach out and touch the top. When he turned back, he found the woman's gaze had turned more kind. The lady asked, "And the second reason?"

"The second." He could not help but sigh. "I have a brother. My only living kin. The last I knew of him was from this region."

For once the lady's practiced demeanor faltered. "I may have heard something . . ."

It was his turn to smile. "Come, come, my lady. We promised one another honesty."

"You are right, of course." She bowed her acceptance. "There have been rumors of this also swirling about since your arrival. Something to do with a former captain of the King's Own Regiment, one who resigned his commission only because he was threatened with court-martial and disgrace."

Though the news was old, still to have it spoken of aloud pierced his soul. "All true, I fear. I have had agents inquiring after Andrew for several years now. He did indeed resign. Eighteen years ago. It happened just after the Acadian expulsion."

A cloud flitted across her features. "A horrible time."

"You were here?"

"I had arrived the year before." She shuddered lightly. "I shall carry the sound of those pitiful screaming women and the smell of their burning fields and homes to my grave."

"Andrew left the army. He went to seminary in Boston. The head of the seminary believes he returned here."

"A minister," the lady murmured.

"I must find him."

The corseted lady found her smile once more. "Rumors are that England's most eligible earl braved the North Atlantic in winter because he wished to take a colonist as a wife."

Charles could not repress his own smile.

"Hardly. I have been married twice, and lost both ladies to illness. I have no wish to know a further such trial."

"That news will drive our maidens into mourning," she said archly.

"Why—" His question was broken off by the sound of scuffling beyond the balcony door. Charles recognized the figure trying to make his way past the sentry, and hastened to open the door. "Let the man pass."

"But the general himself—"

"Let him pass, I say. He means no harm. He is known to me."

The sentry stood aside, and Winston Groom hurried out. He looked quickly at the woman standing by the balcony railing and gave them both a sharp bow. "M'lord. Lady Brighton."

Charles demanded, "You have news?" Winston glanced hesitantly at the lady, his shrewd eyes shifting. Charles barked, "Never mind her. Tell me, man! Do you have news?"

"Better than that, sir. I have found your brother."

Charles took a deep breath, his hand going up unconsciously to his brow as though wiping away long days of anguish. When he spoke, it was one emotion-fraught word. "Excellent."

He started from the balcony, then halted to demand, "Is he married?"

"He is. As you said, to a local woman." Groom was clearly very proud of ferreting out such information. "Her father—"

Impatiently he waved further commentary aside and demanded, "Do they have children?"

Winston Groom looked puzzled, shifted from one foot to the other, then answered, "One child. A girl."

Charles stifled a blast of disappointment. A girl. He had hoped for at least one son to have been born to Andrew. Well, it could not be helped. He moved for the doors, ignoring the curious stares. "Then there is not a moment to be lost."

Henri sat at the borders of the gathering. It was a strange position for the clan leader to take, but he had never been comfortable where all eyes might rest upon him. Whenever he could, he preferred to sit back and let the talk swirl around him. Henri spent most of such times whittling kindling wood into toys for the village children. He had practiced his art over many such nights, carving for hours as his peers talked and argued. After setting out the main questions, rarely did he speak, until it was time to decide and act. And then often Louise would speak for him, directing the flow of discussion or cutting off someone who went on too long.

Henri had long ago discovered two important facts about such gatherings. The first was that for many elders, having a chance to speak their mind was their primary concern. The second was that the less he spoke, the more people listened to what he had to say. Besides, much of what he learned was wisdom garnered from people who did not think he was listening. This night he was whittling a wagon and a high-prancing horse. Over the twenty years that he had been clan leader, his whittling had grown from something to keep his hands busy into work that some called art.

Responsibility for his people had fallen on his shoulders the year before the expulsion. But the folk he now called clan had little or no connection to those Acadian villagers. Most of the original clan remained scattered to the four winds. Henri eventually had accepted leadership of all who gathered around him, all who did not wander further to seek comfort and loved ones elsewhere. It did not matter where they had called home before the expulsion. These Frenchmen were his people, by right of origin, time, and hardship.

The fifth year after their expulsion, word had arrived to the group of Acadians in Carolina that the Spanish had taken over control of the former French colony of Louisiana. It had mattered little to the local citizens of New Orleans, as France and Spain had been allies for centuries. But the other news that had spread through the Acadian clan was extraordinary, the first ray of hope since their tragic departure.

The new Spanish rulers recognized that outside a tiny sliver of Mississippi River borderland, much of their province remained utterly untamed. They had sent out a proclamation that swept around the entire globe—to Africa, South America, and all the colonies. Any Acadian who wished might come to the Louisiana delta and receive seed and tools and land. Spanish ships were ordered to stand ready to transport all who decided to come.

And come they did. Land-hungry Acadians flocked in from everywhere, shipload after shipload, desperate at long last for the chance to call someplace home.

Here and now, eighteen years after the

expulsion, they still were arriving, their journeys delayed by the need for money, or simply because they had been so lost it had taken the welcome news this long to reach them. Eighteen years.

Henri paused in his whittling and listened as the talk moved on from illness in Plaquemine to crop rotation. Their village of Vermilionville planted mostly cotton, sugarcane, vegetables, and indigo. The demand for indigo dye was growing, and one elder suggested giving over all available land to the crop. Henri was against it. The village had finally become self-supporting. They grew almost everything they needed. They even had their own blacksmith and weavers. But the elder was voted down before Henri felt the need to argue against him. He returned his attention to the tiny wooden horse's tossing mane.

In truth, it was hard to concentrate upon anything this night except his daughter. Nicole had remained distant and withdrawn since their discussion a few nights earlier. She refused to be drawn out on anything. She did her work and drifted about the house like a wraith. To stand helpless as his passionate and spirited daughter faded to sorrow and shadows left Henri feeling as though he had used the carving knife on his own heart.

Out of the darkness there came the sound of pounding feet. The meeting halted in midflow as Guy, Louise's brother, raced up the stairs to pant, "A letter has come!"

Instantly the entire gathering was on their feet. Letters arrived once or twice a year, if that, so the fact that one had arrived was enough to stir the entire assembly. One of the elders demanded, "From where?"

Guy waved the stained and crumpled parchment over his head, his face taking on an excitement that mirrored his voice. "Acadia!" he called loudly. "A letter has come from *home*!"

Chapter Five

Winston Groom returned to the carriage and announced, "We've arrived, m'lord."

"Excellent." Charles alighted from the high-wheeled conveyance and could not hide his dismay at the sight. "What did you say was the name of this town?"

"Georgetown, m'lord." Groom took a deep breath. "I say, this is quite the lovely place."

Charles glanced over and decided the man was not being sarcastic. He turned back and tried to put aside his dismay at where his brother had chosen to live. Where his niece had been raised. Here, as far into the back of beyond as Charles could imagine.

The carriage had halted upon a rise, where hills fell in gradual waves to the distant waters. The village below contained perhaps a hundred houses, clustered within a shallow valley and surrounded by vast groves of trees. Charles asked, "With all this land, why on earth must they crowd together so? Are they serfs?"

"Not hardly, m'lord. My guess is they own all the land you can see, right to the water's edge." Winston Groom sounded envious. "They build their houses close together because it is safer."

"Ah. You mean Indians."

"No, m'lord. Winter."

Charles thought back to the voyage and the winds and the cold. One night the halyards holding the sails had frozen so hard one had snapped with the sound of shattering glass. "I understand."

"Governor Lawrence offered every able man who would settle these parts a hundred acres, a plow, an ax, and two bags of seed." He inspected the vista for a long moment, then added, "Two more years I have in service, then this is where I'm headed. The air is free here, m'lord." He took a deep breath. "Free."

"Yes, well, you have been most helpful." Charles pulled out the second pouch of sovereigns. "I will go on alone from this point."

Winston Groom clutched the pouch of gold to his chest. "But the governor ordered me—"

"Tell Governor Lawrence I am most grateful for his hospitality and the kind gift of his transport." From the carriage's rear gate, Charles untied the horse he had purchased in Halifax and swung into the saddle. "I wish to meet my brother alone."

"But the road back to Halifax can be most perilous to a man traveling by himself, m'lord. You should really allow—"

"I seriously doubt," Charles offered in parting, "that I shall make the return journey alone."

The closer he drew to the village of Georgetown, the more dismayed Charles became. Even though on closer inspection the village was not disorderly. Far from it. He owned many such hamlets within his own estates, and few if any bore such an air of quiet dignity and careful maintenance.

Though unadorned and stark, everything was well constructed. The apple groves were weeks away from budding, but the vast stretches of trees appeared carefully tended. The houses themselves were sturdy and snug, built of stone and thick local timber. The animals he saw were shaggy with winter coats, yet healthy and clearly well fed. The lanes were bordered with tall posts, no doubt to mark them after hard snowfalls. The entire village seemed strong and patiently ready for the coming spring.

But visits through his own holdings had shown Charles clearly the kind of people who settled and raised offspring in this kind of bucolic setting—strong, boisterous, hearty souls who were best left on the land. Not at all the type of person he required.

A farmwife ensconced on a wide front porch halted in her industrious weaving to watch him pass. Charles doffed his hat and received a pleasant good-day in return. He started to ask her where Andrew lived, then decided to head straight for the church. But he truly dreaded the coming encounter after so many years, after so much hostility between himself and his brother. So many years of quarreling and struggle, especially after their mother had passed away. In truth, he had always feared his brother. Andrew had been a strong and handsome lad, clearly his mother's favorite, and a threat to Charles's full inheritance. But Charles had won in the end, gaining both the riches and the title. And yet here he was, hat in hand, having set out across the North Atlantic to search for a brother he had not heard from in over twenty years.

His jaw clenched in frustration and his heels dug into the flanks of his horse. He might as well finish what he had begun.

The church steeple was the tallest structure in Georgetown, taller even than the highest trees. The building was whitewashed and as sturdy as all the other structures, set in a clearing bordered by fields and the descent to the Bay of Fundy. If Charles had not been so on edge, he probably would have found it attractive in a quaint sort of way. As with the rest of the village, there was no sign of wealth to the church, no stained glass or ornate decorations. Yet there was also none of the poverty and filth he always associated with English villages of comparable size.

Charles hitched his horse to the gatepost and mounted the church steps. He hesitated there, drawn to stillness by all the anguish that plagued his nights, by all that was hanging on this meeting. He glanced up to where the village lane joined with the road to Halifax. The surrounding hills still bore stained drifts of late snow, the air still held a wintry bite. By this time his own English gardens would be in full bloom, the air fragrant and full of birdsong. Charles had a fleeting fierce desire to leave this humiliating encounter behind, just ride away and take the next ship back to England and home.

Angrily he turned away from the road and the hills and the sunlit day. He had no choice. None. He struck the door latch with his fist and was sorry to find the church unlocked.

It was not his clergyman brother who stood startled by his sudden appearance. Instead a young lady with broom in hand, her eyes round with surprise, faced him and asked, "Can I help you?"

"I . . ." Charles found his anger fading as fast as it had appeared. What to say to this young woman? "I . . . I was riding by and found myself wishing to enter the church."

To his own ears, the words were feeble. But she seemed to find nothing unusual in them. She offered him a polite curtsy and said, "You are most welcome." She backed up a pace, but her eyes did not leave his face. "Have you visited Georgetown before?"

"No. Not ever."

"I thought not. I know everyone here, and most of their relatives and friends." She gave a genuine smile. "It is a pastor's lot to be involved in the lives of all around us. Even the outsiders we come to know at least by sight."

"Yes, I suppose you must." Charles sat down in the nearest pew and studied this woman intently. "You are related to the pastor?"

"I am his daughter. My name is Anne."

His heart leapt with the urge to blurt out his own identity. To ask of his brother's welfare. But he bit down on the question and fought to keep his voice even. Controlled. "I'm honored to meet you, Anne. Miss Anne."

She smiled shyly, nodded an acknowledgment, and resumed her sweeping. "And I am glad to find a gentleman who is willing to take time from his day to stop in God's house. Time with the Lord should not be left only for the Sabbath, do you not agree?"

"Yes," Charles managed to affirm after a moment of hesitation. "I suppose so." He draped both hands over the pew in front and leaned forward, watching her as she moved gracefully at her task, his thoughts far from the exchange about church attendance. He could scarcely believe his good fortune. This was no rough-hewn village lass. Anne Harrow was raven-haired, lithe, and slight, somehow holding to a fragility more suited to a formal parlor than a primitive country village church.

Dressed in homespun and a small lace cap, with no jewelry or adornment whatsoever, she was evidently poor. Yet she possessed the calm demeanor and confidence of a true lady. Charles felt his heart race with anticipation. Perhaps fate's hand was finally turning toward him.

"Excuse my chatter," she said, starting to move away. "You no doubt wish for solitude."

"You are not disturbing me at all," he quickly assured her. An idea took shape in his mind. Perhaps he did not need to go hat in hand to his brother at all. It was possible he could avoid the need to beg him for anything. He could speak his piece here and now to this newly discovered niece and present his brother with an accomplished fact.

Anne walked over to put her broom in the corner. "My sweeping can wait. I should leave and permit you to speak with God in peace."

"No. Wait. I . . . I wish to speak with you."

She showed quiet surprise. "With me?"

"Yes. You see, I . . . well, I come from England."

"England." She clasped delicate hands before her. "Oh, I have always dreamed of seeing England. My father comes from there."

"I know." He was making a terrible job of this. Charles tried to swallow down his nervousness. "Would you sit here for a moment? Please. This is important."

She hesitated, her dark gaze wary now. When she did nod and move forward it was to slide into the pew opposite his own, sitting on the very edge. "What could be so important about a village church that it would interest a gentleman from England?"

"It is not the church. It is you."

Her eyes widened. "Me?"

Charles nodded. "I have traveled all this way to find you. And I must say, my dear—"

But Anne was already on her feet. "Perhaps you should reserve further speech for my father, sir."

"No, wait! I beseech you, Anne Harrow, hear me out!"

She halted midway to the door. "How did you know my family name?"

"Because it is my name as well." Charles rushed on, hurrying now to say what he had planned for months and months. "I am your

71

father's brother. Charles, the eighth earl of Sutton. Has your father not spoken of me?" When there was no reply, only a shocked look on the girl's face, he hurried on. "I am wealthy, my dear. I don't know how else to tell you. Rich beyond your wildest dreams. I am also childless. My second wife died last autumn, leaving me no heir. I have braved the North Atlantic in late winter because I had to find you. I want—"

"No . . ." Anne's feet seemed unable to move in time to her body. She stumbled against the last pew, caught herself, stumbled again. "I must . . ."

"I want to take you away from all this, give you the kingdom! I mean just that!" He started toward her, then stopped midstride, fearful of driving her away before he could say it all. "I will make you a proper lady, introduce you at court, give you everything you have ever dreamed of owning and more. It is all yours, Anne. Titles, land, riches, everything!"

Her hands scrambled over the door, found the latch, and flung it open to flee down the steps. Charles stood with one hand outstretched, listening to her footsteps grow distant down the village lane. In his heart he knew he had bungled everything. Smacking a fist into his hand, he chided himself for his impatience and insensitivity. After coming so far and enduring so much—he had totally mismanaged the encounter. Now he would need to start over and attempt to rectify the damage he had done. He was used to having his own way without question or resistance. But now he had frightened Anne half to death. It would be a long, slow road to trust. He uttered a curse under his breath, then turned to leave through the still-open door.

Chapter Six

It seemed to Henri that all Vermilionville spoke of nothing except the letter. That was hardly a surprise, as it was the first message received from Acadia since their arrival. Some, mostly the young and unmarried, spoke of it with a sense of adventure and yearning. Others, mostly the old and weary, spoke of it with dread. Should they trust it, should they listen, should they respond to its invitation? As Henri walked alongside his horse through the village to his fields, he spotted another boatload of people arriving at the town dock and shouting questions to the first who passed. *Where was the letter?* It was not enough to hear the news. They wanted to see it for themselves, make sure it was real. The letter awoke passions and memories like an August brush fire, bringing Acadia from the realm of a distant memory to the here and now.

Henri Robichaud, for one, was not sure how he felt about it at all.

"Henri!"

He slowed and waited for Louise's brother to hurry over. Henri had always liked Guy. Some men followed because they were too weak to lead. A few, like Guy, did so because of genuine affection and a willingness to trust someone they respected. Henri's leadership had survived several very hard times because of Guy's unquestioned loyalty.

Because it was Guy, Henri was able to growl, "Why didn't you burn that letter before you opened it?"

Guy responded with a sunburnt grin. "I've been asking myself the very same thing."

Henri turned back to the lane and the fields up ahead. He shook the reins to start the horse plodding along once more. "A stick in a beehive wouldn't cause as much commotion."

"Emilie and I were up half the night."

"You and everyone else in this village." He waved a hand at the empty fields ahead.

"Here it is the second week of planting, and not another soul at work."

The letter had been a copy, one of six, sent to all the corners of the earth. It had been penned by Guy and Louise's cousin, a young man who had vanished on the night of the expulsion and had not been heard from since. He had kept the message very brief, for he was not much at writing and it all had to be said again and again. He did not know where his family might be, so he was sending copies to the places where he had heard Acadians were gathering. He and his family had been shipped back to France. Life there had been terrible. The big landowners distrusted them, because for generations now the Acadians from the new continent had owned their own land. No serf in France was a landowner. The nobles loathed the prospect of Acadians traveling from place to place, spreading discontent among the villagers. Many Acadians had finally left France for other places—Switzerland, Africa, the Caribbean. His own family had been planning to travel to Louisiana when Governor Lawrence had issued an edict from Halifax, inviting any and all Acadians to return. All they had to do was take the oath of loyalty to the Crown. Guy's cousin had done so and was now there again with his family.

Life in Acadia was not easy either, he admitted. Much of their original land had been resettled by new colonists from Scotland and Wales and the American colonies. But it was possible to return, and several new Acadian settlements had been established, all of them far from Halifax and the meddling English. If they wanted, come. There was land and the prospect of a free life again.

Guy asked what everyone had asked one another the entire night long. "What do you think?"

"The oath of loyalty to the British crown was something I could not sign twenty years ago. And what can they offer that we do not already have here?" Henri did not like being made to give his opinion, not like this. If it had been anyone except Guy, he would not have spoken at all. But Guy was more than a friend, more than family. He was a trusted ally. He deserved an honest reply. "The man spoke of land. Well, I have land already. Forty acres. I have two boats, a house, horses, a market for my crops."

"You have a home," Guy agreed quietly, and for some reason the words seemed to make him sad.

"We all do. Not a single family in our village goes to bed hungry. Not in all of South

Acadia country, so far as I know." Henri spoke with quiet pride. What the Spanish offered newcomers was a foothold, nothing more. But through his leadership and example, the village had prospered enough for him to declare, "We have enough to offer every new family a roof and food and tilled land and seed and tools. This is our home now, Guy. We have made it our place in the world."

"And you have done wonders," Guy agreed. "No one could have done better."

But Guy's tone made Henri tug on the reins once more, slowing his horse to a halt. "What are you not telling me?"

"Henri," Guy started, then stopped for a deep breath. "Henri, Emilie and I have talked long and hard. We are going to go back."

The words bit like a knife. "Not you. Not my wife's brother. Not my own dear friend."

"We are going," Guy repeated. "I must. Part of me is still there. I must find it again. Put myself back together." His message was clear. The decision was made. No amount of argument would change his mind.

Henri stared silently into Guy's face and saw the resolve in his friend's eyes. He clamped his mouth against the rising objections, flicked the reins, and walked on alone.

He entered the fields, stopped by his plow, and could not help but glance back. Guy was still standing in the middle of the dusty village lane. Henri raised his hand in a mournful wave, then turned to hitch his horse to the plow. His gut churned with concern over how many others would follow Guy and leave Louisiana.

Three nights later, at a gathering attended by all the village and most of the surrounding settlements, animated discussions brought family after family face-to-face with the reality of how good life had treated them here. They felt safe, finally, hidden among the bayou swamps. Yes, the work was hard, the insects ferocious, and the summers were terrible. But for every negative point brought forward, another of the same family had something good to say. Food was plentiful. They were among friends. The Spanish authorities were only too pleased to have them settle and remain. The land was deeded them for all time. They had houses, fields, boats, villages, friends. This was home. Not Acadia. What once had been was no longer. This was home.

Guy's stubborn silence told the group he was not convinced. Eyes watched him with grudging admiration, others with heads shaking their disapproval.

But the next evening, the elders, including Henri, voiced their formal acquiescence to this: Guy and his family would travel north. They would send back a report. The following spring, any others who wished might follow. Guy and Emilie they knew and trusted. Their word was solid. What news they sent back could be believed. As talk swirled, bemused glances were cast toward Guy. Most of the others were relieved to have a solid reason for not uprooting their families and leaving behind all they had carved from the bayou wilderness, all because of a stranger's letter that had taken almost a year to find them. No, better to wait and hear the firsthand account from one of their own.

That night, after the elders had departed, Henri sat alone on his veranda, scarcely able to believe this latest difficulty had passed so easily. He listened to the sounds of his family preparing for bed, to the night gathering in close and warm about him, and wondered if he could trust this peace. A shadow coalesced in the darkness, and a familiar voice said, "Am I still welcome in your home?"

"Always," Henri said, saddened anew by the coming loss. "Though what I will do after you depart, Guy, I do not know."

"You will do what you have always done," Guy replied, walking up the stairs and seating himself. "Lead your people, farm your land, provide for your family, dispense wise counsel when it is needed."

"I can still remember the gathering when they said I was to become the new clan leader," Henri said, his voice reflective. "Papa Belleveau was still strong and healthy then—and wise. So very wise. He had a bad cough that winter, and it was enough for him to insist that the elders choose a new leader. Not long after, the British expelled us." Henri studied the darkness and found himself confronted again with his own weaknesses and lack of answers. "He was the kind of man who could see what was not yet formed. He looked around corners, that man."

"I remember my father very well," Guy said comfortably. "He was a man like many others. With strong points and weak ones. Plenty of both."

"I wish I had his wisdom."

Guy pulled his chair up close enough to settle one hand upon Henri's shoulder. "The winter before Papa died, he and I were together one night. That was just after Emilie bore us our second, you remember?"

"Like it was yesterday," Henri replied, missing the old man afresh.

"He said choosing you as clan leader was the best thing he had ever done. No one else could have kept the clan together. No one." The hand rose and fell one time. "Papa said something else that night. He said that he had often envied your strength of faith. Whenever he thought back to his choice of you as leader, he felt sure that God had spoken directly to his heart."

Henri sat back in his chair. The air stirred through the cypress, whispering and speaking in the tongue of bayous and still waters. Henri took a deep breath, and another. "I will miss you, old friend."

"And I you."

They sat in silence for a few minutes, then Henri stirred and spoke quietly, wanting these words to be heard by no one else. "There is something you can do for us. That spring, after I was chosen to be leader, Papa Belleveau entrusted me with some valuables that he had been collecting and saving from English eyes and ears. I buried the treasure on a hillside over Minas, up where my Louise used to meet with a friend."

The chair next to him creaked. "Treasure?"

"There were some gold coins, clan heir-looms, a jeweled crucifix. Two heavy sacks. I remember how I sweated carrying it up the hillside." Henri studied the silhouette of his friend. "I want you to take what you need to get started and bring the rest to us here."

"But, Henri—"

"This is our home. This is where we are rooted now. I do not think so many others will follow you back to Acadia. The future may prove me wrong, but I don't think so. The clan's wealth and heritage should be with us here."

"Henri . . ." Guy stopped once more, then proceeded as gently as the night. "I do not know if we shall be returning to the bayou. Emilie and I have talked. If it is as the letter said, we will stay in Acadia." When Henri did not reply, Guy continued, "If we so choose, to whom should I entrust this treasure for the voyage back?"

The sound of a light footstep behind them made the two men turn as one. A voice cut through the night and Henri's heart. "To me."

Chapter Seven

After that disastrous encounter in the church, Charles had not pursued Anne. Instead he had taken a room in the village inn. He needed time to think through the approach he should now take, and also to recover from the humiliation. He was not accustomed to being so thoroughly rebuffed.

The next morning was a strange mixture of seasons, the sun already warming and yet the wind biting. Charles followed directions he had received from the innkeeper, offering no explanation to the man's probing look when he asked after Andrew Harrow.

As the village's broad lane passed beneath the largest elm he had ever seen, a thought occurred to him. In return for Charles's help in making peace overtures to the French court, King George III had recently deeded to him a vast estate in the frontiers of the Massachusetts Colony. Of course. He could offer this to his brother in exchange for Anne. It was perfect. The new estate was a quarter the size of Nova Scotia—how could the man reject such a proposition? Even so, Charles had to fight the urge to turn and stomp away. He hated to plead for anything from anyone. The idea of lowering himself to beg from his brother, of all people, was infuriating.

Charles marched up the road, each step only making him angrier. Charles knew exactly how his brother would be—superior and haughty, rubbing Charles's nose in the fact that he was the one who in the end had come to plead. Charles tasted bitter gall, and knew he would have no choice but to endure. All the battles, the years of secretly hating and fearing his brother, all threatened to boil over.

Footsteps hastened down the lane toward him. Even before the figure could be seen clearly, Charles knew it was Andrew. He stiffened in readiness for conflict.

It had been twenty-two years since their last meeting, when Andrew had stomped out of their ancestral home and left England, vowing never to return. Even so, Charles recognized his brother instantly.

Andrew was lean, hardened by his life. The years in this untamed land were stamped deep on his features. The hair was graying, his clergyman's clothing simple and frayed. All this Charles saw, but did not see. He stood there with fists clenched, ready for whatever combat would erupt. But his body and mind were frozen by two swift images. They had to be swift because when Andrew caught sight of him, he rushed forward in a flurry of steps. The first image was the cry Andrew gave upon seeing him. The second was captured in the tears and the smile upon Andrew's seamed features.

Charles's confused mind was certain he had made a mistake; he could not have heard what he thought Andrew had cried. But the words were repeated in a voice that sounded almost strangled. "Charles, oh, thank God, thank God."

Then his brother embraced him with arms hard as iron, and said once more the words that left Charles utterly paralyzed. "Thank God!"

Andrew led his brother back up the lane, warmly welcoming him and saying how sorry he was over not being there for his arrival in Georgetown. Andrew explained that he had been away visiting an outlying hamlet and only returned to the news this very hour. He had rushed out to find him the moment he heard.

When they approached the manse, the door opened and Andrew warmly introduced his wife, Catherine. She bade Charles welcome. But her expression was cautious, her voice so subdued it scarcely could compete with the morning wind. As Andrew seated his brother by the fire, Charles noted that the daughter was nowhere to be seen.

"Are you comfortable, brother?" In his excitement, Andrew's words tumbled over each other. "Will you take something to drink?"

"Brandy, if you have any. If not, ale."

"I'm sorry, brother. We do not have either. Will you settle for cider?"

"Yes. All right. Cider, then."

Andrew waited as Catherine poured the cupful from their kitchen jug, then gave it to Charles. "I cannot tell you what a joy it is to have you appear, brother. A miracle. Truly."

Charles accepted the mug, running a finger over its rough surface. "I confess this is not exactly what I expected to hear," he finally said slowly.

"No, I suppose not." Andrew reached a hand out to his wife. "Come join us, dear."

"I must see to . . . to things," she replied quietly and moved for the doorway.

"Very well." Andrew turned back and settled into the bench on the fire's opposite side. Charles endured the silence and his brother's intense gaze. He knew full well what his brother saw—a man who wore his power and his wealth with careless ease, dressed in clothes that would have cost more than what Andrew probably earned in a trio of hardscrabble years. The frill on his chest was stitched with silver threads, the buttons on his coat solid gold, the buckles on his shoes sterling silver. Charles knew himself to be wide of girth in the way of one used to eating more than was good for him, and doing so often. There was strength, yes, but well padded and sagging with the weight of years and care.

Andrew asked, "How are you, Charles?"

"Tired. It has been a long journey."

"Yes. That I can imagine."

"Two months on the high seas. There were days when I doubted I would ever see land again, I can tell you." Charles drained his mug and set it on the floor by his feet. "Nothing but the most urgent affairs would ever have forced me to board that ship."

Andrew leaned forward and spoke with deep earnestness. "Before telling me of your business, I must tell you something of my own. I have wanted to speak these words for years."

Charles felt his body grow stiff and cold as stone. He knew exactly what Andrew was about to say, here in the privacy of his home. He knew because it was precisely what he would say himself. "Yes?"

The fire's crackle sought to fill the silence as Andrew lowered his head for a moment. He seemed to gather himself, as though intending to leap across the distance separating them. Charles felt a growing dread over returning to the conflict of his youth. So much depended upon this connection. So many hopes, the ambitions and plans of generations to come. Charles steeled himself further, willing himself not to give in to an angry counterattack.

But when Andrew lifted his gaze from the stones ringing the fireplace, the words were, "Charles, I wish to ask your forgiveness."

Charles felt his hold upon himself waver slightly. "I beg your pardon?"

"I deserved your malice. I realize that now. Had I the opportunity, I would have treated you with far more cunning and hatred than you showed me." Andrew's voice sounded taut with compressed passion. Yet there was no anger, no bitterness, no wrath. "Competing with you drove me to scale heights that would have otherwise been impossible. The fact that I could never win, never gain your titles or your power, filled me with a loathing that ate at me like a chancre. I was glad to leave England and the endless undeclared battles behind. Yes, glad."

Andrew leaned back, looking drained. "For all that happened between us, for all I thought, for all I wished I could do to you, I humbly ask your forgiveness."

Charles inspected him with a frankness borne on Andrew's own words. "You have thought of this for some time."

"Years and years," Andrew agreed. "And prayed for a day I thought would never come so I might tell you so. I wrote you. Twice."

"I never received your letters."

"No, mail from the colonies is notoriously unreliable. And after all the time that had passed before I put pen to paper, well, I feared I had left things too long."

"Time and events both." Charles hesitated, then said, "I heard you were drummed out of the regiment."

"I resigned my commission. But what you say is true enough. Had I tried to remain, I certainly would have been court-martialed and most probably hanged."

"Hang a Harrow?" Charles was hotly indignant. "They would not have dared!"

Andrew smiled. "Dared and done, my brother. I deserved no less. I refused a direct order in time of war."

"To what purpose?"

"I refused to round up defenseless Frenchmen and women from homes they had occupied for over a century and send them off to fates unknown." Andrew's features showed the pain of those old wounds. "At least, I would have refused. But the Lord in His infinite mercy saw fit to rescue me in time."

Charles shifted in his chair, uncomfortable at the turn of the conversation. "You speak . . . well, differently."

"My life is now God's." Andrew nodded. "Do you have it within you to forgive me, Charles?"

"Of course, of course." Charles recognized it as the opening he had hoped for, but for some reason found it difficult to press forward. He was unable to hold his brother's frank gaze. "That is . . . well, I come asking for a favor of my own."

"A favor?" Andrew glanced over to the sunlit doorway, empty still of his wife and daughter. "A strange way to describe your request for my only child."

"You heard, then."

"Catherine and Anne tried to tell me when I returned this morning. They both were distraught, but I think I understood what you wish."

"My second wife died last autumn. She left me childless. I have no heir. You know as well as I that our father's only brother died without children. Your daughter is my only living blood kin."

Suddenly Charles could remain seated no longer. He rose and began pacing the room's confines. "I am desperate for an heir. Anne would lack for nothing. You know our land, our holdings, our wealth. There must be an heir to inherit—or it will all be lost. Lost for all time, Andrew. We Harrows cannot let that happen. We cannot."

"There was a time when that thought would have disturbed me as much as it does you, but now . . ." Andrew paused, in deep thought. "It must have cost you dearly to make this journey."

"You have no idea." Charles's pacing turned swifter still. "She would inherit everything. I would hire the finest tutors, present her at court, wed her to the noblest family. She could perhaps marry into the royal line, Andrew. Think of that! Your daughter wed to the court of St. James!"

"I imagine," Andrew replied mildly, "that Anne would have something to say about that herself."

"Of course she would. I'm not a barbarian. She would not be forced into some loveless union. I come seeking an heir, not chattel. It is not merely for my benefit. Think what it would mean to the girl." Charles stopped in the middle of the room. When Andrew did not stir, Charles spun to face him. "I must have your answer, Andrew. I must."

"Come sit down, Charles."

Andrew's calm riled Charles. "Don't play games with me!" His hands clenched into fists. "I have to know!"

Andrew rose. As he stepped forward, Charles had the sudden impression that his brother was breaching barriers formed over years, over oceans, over the world's trappings. Andrew settled a hand on his brother's shoulder. Charles flinched but did not move away.

"Charles, listen to me. I know what you are thinking. I know you are seeking my permission to let Anne go with you. To allow her to leave her home and go to a strange land—filled with wealth and power, yes, but foreign all the same. But that is a decision that, thank God, I will not be forced to make." After a long moment of silence, Andrew finally said, "Anne is not who you think."

"What are you saying?"

"She is my daughter—yes. But she is not of Harrow blood."

"Adopted? But I heard . . . the reports were that you had a child."

"I did. I do." The sigh sounded as though

it came from the depths of Andrew's heart. "But she is not Anne."

"I don't understand."

"Of course you don't." He drew his brother over, and this time Charles did not object. "Come sit down. I will tell you of the circumstances, of the tragedy that has shaped our lives."

Chapter Eight

Nicole sat amidships in the village's largest skiff, willing to let others do the paddling upriver against the Vermilion River's current. Normally she disliked sitting quietly by, as though a woman was not able to handle a boat as well as any man. She could paddle, sail, net, and fish as well as the next. The long pikes used for stabbing the huge catfish in the shallows, no, she did not have the strength for that. But normally when she entered a skiff or canoe, she faced its challenge with the best of them. Not today, however. This skiff held three adults and the pile at her feet—their three guns and the crossbow.

She had asked the other two to come because she had not wanted to say her farewell to Jean Dupree alone. She did not want to risk breaking her decision to leave, find herself turned from the chosen course by his compelling words and convincing smile. Part of her still hoped that he would come over to her side, confess he had been wrong to ever become involved with such evil men, and agree to rejoin the community and her. But when they had arrived at his dwelling, set in a sheltered alcove several miles downriver from the village, it had been empty. Nicole knew instantly that this was the answer to her hopes, and that his decision was already made. Even so, she needed to see him a final time. Because she also knew where he would be found, she was very relieved to have the company of these two men. At her direction they had turned upriver past their village to continue the search.

"Turn in here," she now said quietly.

Guy himself handled the bow, and he turned to look doubtfully back at her. "Are you sure?"

"This is it," Nicole confirmed. "You may trust me on this."

"You have been here before?"

"Many times." There was no longer any need for secrecy. No need for hiding what she had carefully held about Jean.

Guy's oldest son handled the stern, a strapping lad of seventeen, already a head taller than his father. "I have fished down here before. It ends a hundred yards ahead in a small pool."

"This is the turning," Nicole insisted.

Looking resigned, Guy turned the boat and started down the small bayou. They were perhaps ten miles from the village—it was hard to tell exactly. The Vermilion River meandered and backed upon itself constantly, opening into great swampy reaches, splitting time after time into so many bayous only the largest had even been named.

Swamp cypress lined their way, the roots reaching out like black arms and branches crossing overhead, hung heavy with Spanish moss. Cypress and moss—they intertwined every aspect of life here on the Louisiana bayous. The skiff's rope was knit from Spanish moss. The boat itself was hollowed from a single cypress trunk. Even the houses were built with these two materials. Buildings were beamed in cypress because termites and beetles did not devour this wood. The moss was mixed with mud and shaped into wattle, which filled the spaces between the beams. Cypress shingles formed the roof. Nicole looked upward at the sunlight flickering through the branches and the hanging moss. The morning was green and beautiful and filled with the scent of springtime. The water flickered and danced, an emerald mirror that reflected their passage with timeless beauty. She took a deep breath, another, and missed this world already.

Guy seemed to understand her mood, for he said over his shoulder, "I would never have thought you would be the one to leave."

She studied the broad back of her mother's brother, his quiet strength, and knew she had to be honest with him. She was joining her own life to his family's. She was traveling all the way back to the mythic land of her beginnings. There was no one to rely upon, except for Guy and Emilie and their children. A whole world of strangers, and only these to be known as clan and friend.

So she spoke with all the honesty she could muster from a heart torn by the coming departure, by the meeting that waited just up around the bend. "You know the story of my birth?"

Guy hesitated, his paddle poised dripping over the emerald green waters. "I do."

Pascal, his son, asked, "What story is that, Papa?"

"Another time, my son."

In a roundabout fashion, so as not to arouse further suspicion from Pascal, Nicole wondered aloud, "How did they arrange the name change?"

Guy must have understood her perfectly,

for he answered in kind. "There were few of us Minas folk on the boat after the expulsion. Henri and Louise discussed the naming with Papa, Emilie, and me. We simply changed it and that was that. The others were so exhausted and distraught, no one had time to think much over a baby's new name. Perhaps they thought it was a fitting act after what we had endured."

The bayou passed through a gentle bend, widening further in the process. "I have long felt as though I've never had a home," Nicole went on. "For the longest time I thought it was simply because of the time we spent moving from one place to another."

"I know this feeling," Pascal said quietly from behind her. "All too well."

"I thought perhaps I had been so branded by years of wandering that I would never belong anywhere." Nicole surprised herself, both by the secrets she confessed and the ease with which she spoke. "Even before I knew how to put this into words, I felt as though I had never really had any sense of home, anywhere."

With Guy's paddle again suspended in midair, he paused, this time turning to study her. His gaze said he was seeing her not as the child he had known, but as the woman she had become. Nicole went on, "When the letter arrived and you decided to return to Acadia, and then again when Papa spoke with you about the treasure, I felt as though I had finally found a purpose, something to do with my life. I would travel up, I would bring back your report, I would carry the treasure. If I cannot have a home, then at least I can scout for the clan." She took a deep breath at the effort of revealing her innermost thoughts. "Perhaps I will never find a place where I belong, but at least I can still have a life of worth."

"I hope," Guy said quietly, "the future proves you wrong."

She was saved the need to respond by Pascal's saying, "Papa, the bayou ends up ahead."

"No, it doesn't," Nicole answered, pointing. "Between the two trees there."

Both men showed astonishment. "In there?"

Her terse nod was the answer. She felt herself tensing as they approached the pair of giant cypress, both so thick three men could not link hands around either base. The roots appeared to join in a snakelike tangle. But on closer inspection, a sliver of open water appeared between them, scarcely broader than the skiff.

The branches overhead became so intertwined the day grew dim like twilight. The water broadened once they had passed the trees, but the light remained as dusk. The bayou opened farther still, until it was twice the boat's length from bank to bank, almost as broad as the Vermilion in front of the village. But the water here was utterly quiet, the silence broken only by a pair of hunting hawks. Where the Vermilion banks boasted grassy slopes and wild flowers, here the bayou was edged with black mud and roots, the water as dark as the banks. High branches clustered overhead, filtering out all wind and almost all light. The two men looked about in astonishment. This was an unfriendly, hostile place, a world utterly different from the light-filled delta where they lived.

They rounded a gloomy bend, and the water broadened yet farther. Faint sounds carried in the still air, men calling out, and raucous laughter. Guy's shoulders stiffened as they heard a fiddle strike a tune. Nicole understood perfectly. This was not the sound of festivities at the end of a hard day's work.

"Hold there!" A figure rose from his place by a pair of fishing poles, drawing up a rifle and fumbling for the hammer. As one,

Guy and his boy reached and pulled up their own long-barreled hunting rifles. The man froze in midmotion.

Nicole was the one who called out a response. "I seek Jean Dupree!"

"Nicole?" The man squinted across the broad black waters. "That you, *cher*?"

Another figure, stocky and squat, stepped from the gloom. "You know better than to bring strangers out here!" His voice held fierce anger.

"I have nothing to say to you, Daniel!" It pleased her to feel the rush of fury burn so harsh she could not be frightened. She gripped the gunnel with both hands and shrilled over the waters, "You are the reason I had to come here at all!"

"Nicole?" A third man joined them at the water's edge, taller than either of the others. "What are you thinking of, bringing outsiders here?" Jean Dupree sounded incredulous.

"I needed to see for myself!" Tears of rage and sorrow burned hot behind her eyes, but she held them back by will alone. "I could not believe that your love was so small, and your will so weak!"

Jean Dupree glanced at the sharp-faced man standing next to him. "I came back here because you said it was over."

"It is over because you make it so!" She did not care that all the men were staring at her, did not care who heard or what was said later. All the entreaties she had planned to speak, all the last efforts she had hoped would win the love of her life to her side, everything was lost. By choosing to be with these ruffians, Jean Dupree had confirmed that he cared more for the dark side of his own nature than he did for her.

The future they could have had together was ashes in Nicole's heart. "You refuse to see that these men are evil! This Daniel destroys everything he touches! Even his shadow is poison. And he will make you into a fiend just like himself!"

Daniel Lafoe's features twisted into their accustomed snarl. Reaching over, he demanded of the first man, "Give me your gun."

"No!" Jean Dupree stepped between the two of them. "Nicole, go! Leave immediately! You are not welcome here!"

The older man snarled a French epithet. "Get out of my way, Jean!"

"You will not harm her!" Jean Dupree squared off against the smaller man, his fists large as mallets. "Let us be, Daniel. I will make her leave."

The man, obviously not accustomed to

being crossed, muttered, "Better you leave with her." He turned away. "Go and hide yourself in a woman's skirts."

Jean Dupree's voice trembled with controlled rage as he turned back to Nicole. "You were wrong to come like this, Nicole."

"I was wrong to ever become involved with you," she lashed back. "I was wrong to ever think you would be worthy of more than scorn."

His voice became menacing through the gloom. "This is why you came, to push us even further apart?"

"No. I came because . . ." And just as suddenly as it had ignited, her rage was gone. And with it all hope, all caring. Nicole slumped over an empty heart. "I came for no reason at all."

"Go home, Nicole. I will see you—"

"No, Jean. You will never see me again." She pointed downriver, and the two men immediately turned the boat to begin their return. "This is a sorry end to what never should have begun. Good-bye, Jean. Forever."

Chapter Nine

Catherine felt as though she were two people. One stood by the kitchen window, making dinner and listening as Andrew and Charles walked back and forth and argued quietly in the front garden. The other person seemed to be watching herself as she worked. She studied her flour-covered hands, rough and hardened, as though they belonged to another. Two sets of hands filled her vision and her mind. One picked up the rolling pin and pressed the dough upon the table. The other recalled a day some twenty years earlier, as she had fastened a ribbon into her hair and listened to the music of her wedding trilling in the air. It had been a strange day, her wedding—a lively village festival, yet carrying a martial air in keeping with Andrew's position as a British officer. She had walked down a row of saber-wielding soldiers to where her Andrew waited, tall and proud in his uniform. Silver trumpets had heralded the day and the time to come, joyful and foreboding all at once. Catherine sighed over the young girl and all her hopes and fears, and felt the past push hard against her.

Now angry tones drifted in through her open window, forcing her attention upon the present outside her kitchen. Charles nearly shouted, "I fail to see why you resist my decision to go in search of your daughter."

Andrew's tone did not meet that of his brother, neither in hardness nor in volume. Only someone who knew him as well as Catherine would fathom his turmoil. She knew his heart as well as she knew her own. It was for both of them that he answered firmly, "First of all, brother, the decision is not yours to make. And secondly, our daughter is here with us now."

Charles's strident voice told better than words that he was used to having his own way. "You know perfectly well what I mean!"

"Listen, my brother. Are you listening? I don't mean just hearing the words. I mean hearing what I am saying and what I am not saying. You owe me this much, if I am to speak at all. Because it is the only way you will ever understand how much it costs me to speak of this."

Catherine put down her rolling pin and went to check that the pots were not boiling over. She pulled them farther from the flames so they would only simmer. Then she returned to the window. She wanted to give full attention to what was said next.

"All right. Yes," Charles was saying as he heaved a great sigh. "I will listen. Speak away."

"Thank you." Now the two brothers were seated side by side on the bench, positioned so it would catch the afternoon sun. Their garden was the first in the village to lose its snow, the first to bloom. This early spring day was warm enough for the brothers to sit in shirt sleeves. Andrew continued in a voice as controlled as it was quiet. "In the early days, we tried to make connections with the Acadians in every place we knew the boats landed. We had agreed to be conduits for correspondence between those scattered to the winds. Almost no mail ever arrived, I am sorry to say. And what news we did receive was not good."

"Perhaps it was because you did not go through official sources."

"But we did, brother. We did. You have met Catherine's father. John Price was the garrison's notary and a friend of the governor. He used his official position to garner information, which was refused to all but a few. What we learned was, as I said, not good." Andrew paused a long moment, long enough for Catherine to be very glad she had sent Anne off on an errand with Grandfather Price to pick up a ham offered by one of the more distant farms. Andrew finally continued, "Five of the eight ships that sailed from our end of Cobequid Bay were sent to the colony of Maryland. Four of them were lost to a great storm."

"Oh no." Charles's groan held, in a moment, the despair that Andrew and Catherine had felt and fought for nearly a score of years.

"I beg you, brother, don't mention any of this to Anne. Your arrival is causing her enough distress as it is. We have tried to shelter her from as much of this as we could." Andrew paused. "Where was I?"

"The storm."

"Yes. Four of five vessels lost there. Three other vessels from this end of Cobequid Bay, I regret to say, we were never able to determine their destinations. We fear it is because they were lost in storms as well, and the officials prefer to keep all this tragedy secret. There was outrage over the actions they took here, expressed at the highest levels. Every new disaster that befell the Acadians only fueled the fire. We heard that one entire convoy bound for the African colonies never arrived. I am certain the officials would have done their best to keep this also secret, rather than cast yet another dark mark upon their actions."

There was a long silence, one filled with the unspeakable tragedy, then Andrew continued softly, "Four other vessels from neighboring regions were sent to Martinique, a French colony in the Caribbean. We wrote two dozen letters and received only one reply. There was trouble between the colony and the new arrivals. Apparently they were not able to acclimatize and suffered from both heat and disease. Many begged their way onto vessels bound for France."

Charles's own voice began to resemble the quiet flatness of his brother's. "You wrote there as well, I suppose."

"Orleans, Bordeaux, Marseilles, Nantes, Paris. All the cities known to have accepted Acadians. Correspondence was very difficult because of the war. But friends within the church attempted to help with our search. No identification was ever made of an Henri and Louise Robichaud."

"What about asking after your daughter herself?"

"Think a moment, Charles. If you had smuggled aboard an English baby, after everything the English had inflicted on these people, would you admit it?"

"No. Of course. I see."

"You would change her name and declare her as your own." Andrew's voice broke slightly. "So, you see, we do not even know under what name our daughter has been raised—if she indeed is still alive."

This time the sigh was quieter, longer, sadder. "I regret that my coming has brought you distress."

"Much of life is like that, I find—happiness and sadness so intermingled it is hard to know one from the other." Andrew's voice strengthened. "Nonetheless, I am glad you came, Charles. Very glad."

Catherine returned to her bread making. She found herself wondering at her own inner sense of peace. If someone had come to her the day before Charles's arrival and announced that all the memories and wounds from eighteen years ago would be brought back to the forefront, she would have fled in terror. Yet now she felt no pain. Sorrow, yes, but even this was held within by a peace so strong it could not be denied. The calm of her heart made no sense, the harmony almost belied the words she heard spoken just beyond her window. Yet here it was, surrounding her and comforting her.

Catherine placed the dough on the baking pan and slid it in close to the coals. Their dinner would be a far cry from the fine meals Charles no doubt was used to. Yet even here there was no sense of shame or distress. Their life was what it was, and despite the hardship and the absence of many comforts, it was a good life indeed. She had a home, she had a husband and a daughter, she had a purpose that only serving God could bring. She had love, she had contentment. No grand palace or earthly power could compare with her own wealth. Even now, as she brushed flour from her work-hardened hands, she knew a rightness to her life and her place upon this earth.

It was the most natural thing in the world to close her eyes and pray for guidance. The only conscious response she was aware of was the smell of bread and the quiet simmer of pots. And the peace that overlaid everything that day. Catherine opened her eyes and accepted the message. So long as that quiet rest remained, she could face the unknown.

A pair of familiar voices sounded from down the lane. She went back to the window and called out a welcome and a warning both. "Father, Anne, hurry now! Dinner is almost ready."

The first birdsong rang out before the light became strong enough to dispel the sliver of moon. Catherine knew because she was awake and staring out the window, watching the gray wash of dawn take shape upon the eastern horizon. Andrew enjoyed sleeping with the window open. When the snows halted and the hard freezes were defeated by yet another spring, he treasured the return to his mild-weather habit of fresh air in their bedroom. No doubt the result of his years leading troops through all sorts of weather, it was a habit Catherine had found difficult at first, but now she loved it as well—all save that first moment when the covers were tossed aside, the frigid floor was touched, and the chill pounced on her through her nightclothes. Andrew did not seem to notice even that.

She knew he was awake too. Years of loving and lying next to this man had taught her to read the small signs. He was awake, and he was distressed, and he was trying not to trouble her. Catherine closed her eyes and prayed that he would have the same sense of peace she had known the day before. Then she rolled over and murmured, "Tell me what is the worst and most troubling thing of all."

Andrew's eyes turned to her and focused instantly. He studied her a long moment, his expression clear and direct. Without needing to ask of what she spoke, he said, "It is bad enough that one of us is worried."

"Tell me, husband dear. I want to know."

He sighed as his gaze turned to stare at the ceiling. "All the wounds I thought God healed long ago have been torn open again."

Yes, the peace was indeed still there. It was not something she could point at and say, here it is. No, she knew because she could lie there and calmly study the hair emerging from the edge of his nightcap. The dark brown was laced with silver and pewter, matching the fine etching of lines from his eyes and mouth. "My fine, strong, handsome man," she whispered, tucking her hand in between the jawbone and neck. Andrew covered her hand with his own in silent acknowledgment.

"I suppose the most distressing possibility of all," Andrew confessed to the ceiling overhead, "is that if Charles is successful in his search, we will not have regained a daughter. We will find Elspeth only to lose her a second time. She no doubt will become the next Lady Harrow, viscountess and holder of royal charters."

When Catherine did not respond, Andrew rolled back over to face his wife. "These things do not distress you?"

She had no choice but to honestly confess, "Not at this very moment."

"Tell me your secret, then. What do you know that I do not?"

"I only know that God has comforted me. It is such a fragile thing, I fear even speaking about it might disturb the calm." She kept her voice soft, for only thin walls separated them from Anne on one side and her father on the other. "But it is here. I know it without doubt or question. It is the only thing that keeps me from being immobilized with pain."

He blinked once, then reached over and took her hands with both of his. She felt in his contact the strong touch, the years of loving and working together for their God. "Does God say anything to you? Anything at all?" he asked.

"I have asked for guidance. And if He has spoken, it has been with a voice so quiet I have missed it entirely."

"That," Andrew murmured, "I doubt very much."

"I have just one question for you," she continued. "What if our daughter is out there someplace, and what if her lot in life is hard?"

He studied the face inches away from his own. "I'm not sure I would ever want to think thus."

"No, nor I. But what if it is true? We have

heard tales of hardship. What if Elspeth is among those who wander without home or solace?" She had to stop then, for the sudden pain pierced her like a sword. Yet a single breath was enough to still both the pain and the worry, and once again she felt certain that her heart was comforted by an invisible hand. She went on, "What if she has needs that only your brother's wealth can answer? What if God has brought Charles here because Elspeth needs what he can give? Or what if our Father wishes to use her to reach others also, in ways we could not begin to fathom? Would you deny Elspeth this?"

"Never." The reply came instantly. "If I felt God's hand was upon the search, for whatever reason, I would not do anything to hold Charles back. I could not."

Catherine slid forward, closer still, and softly kissed her husband, willing the shadows to be lifted from his features by the strengthening daylight. "There is your answer."

Chapter Ten

Louise and Nicole walked in silence from the village to the family's farthest fields. Land about the village was separated into three tiers. Where the neighboring bayous flowed broad and shallow, the clan had diked the thick mud. Anything would grow in this black earth, anything at all. Moving away from the rivers and the bayous, next came the prized village acreage, not as rich as the bayou silt yet fertile indeed. Beyond this second narrow band began the Louisiana plains. This was strange soil, unlike anything they had ever seen before, porous and loamy. It could rain buckets for days, yet one afternoon of sun was enough to return the land to gray dust. This land was good for growing cotton and indigo and little else. Irrigation ditches had to be rebuilt before each planting, and the crops required constant watering.

With a careless wave, Louise returned the greetings of neighbors working their land. Guy and his family were departing in four days. A ship was heading for the British colonies up the eastern coastline, the same one taking their indigo to the northern mills. The market wagons were leaving with the indigo, taking her brother's family. Ever since the letter had arrived, Louise had prepared herself for a momentous battle with her headstrong daughter. But Nicole had hardly spoken of it at all. She had gone about her business, but with a careful nature that left Louise wondering just how well she knew her daughter.

Louise shifted her lunch basket to her other arm and waited while Nicole spoke to farmwives taking lunch to their own families. She tried to pay attention to what was said, but even her smile came hard this morning. Finally she set down her basket and turned her full attention to studying her daughter, grateful for the bonnet's shadows that hid her gaze.

Nicole spoke with a warmth that was both becoming and unusual. She had never been a haughty child, but she could be very abrupt, as though whatever she had on her mind occupied her totally. Now, however, she opened her face and her smile to the women, sliding the bonnet off her head so that it hung down over her long auburn tresses. Her green eyes sparked with genuine warmth, and her smile was from the heart. The women seemed to come alive with Nicole's attention, laughing and chattering like nesting birds. Louise felt a burning to her eyes, but could not think of why she was saddened by the sight of her daughter being sociable with their neighbors.

When the women had moved off, Nicole turned a questioning gaze toward Louise. "Yes, Mother?"

"I was wondering," Louise said quietly, "what has caused this change to come over you."

Nicole could have denied the change or pretended not to understand. Instead her green eyes opened, revealing depths Louise had never seen before. Her daughter replied, "I am trying, the best I know how, to wish my friends and clan a fond farewell."

Louise rallied all her resources in preparation for the argument that had been boiling inside her for so long, the one that would begin with the declaration that her daughter was not leaving.

Louise saw in her daughter's eyes that she knew the battle was joined. But Nicole did not back away, did not arm herself with that temper famous from Plaquemine to Martinsville. Instead, she simply stood and waited.

The sun and the warm breeze teased the corners of Louise's eyes, drawing from them a wetness she had no intention of releasing. She knew now why Nicole's warmth to the neighbors had sorrowed her heart. They were the actions of a woman. Not a child, not her daughter, not a youth she could command any longer. Louise hid her distress by bending to heft the basket and start down the lane. "We shouldn't keep the boys waiting."

Their trek was marred by a tension that floated with the pale dust. Finally Nicole asked, "What was my name, Mama?"

"Your name," Louise replied with a firmness she did not feel, "is Nicole."

Again there was the disconcerting calm. "What was the name given to me at birth?"

Louise felt the sorrow burn not only her eyes, but her throat as well. "I was wondering when you would ask me that."

"Do you remember?"

"Of course I remember. I would never forget such a thing. Never." To her own ears, her voice sounded as flat and dry as the dusty trail. "Your name was Elspeth. Elspeth Harrow."

They entered the final copse of trees that separated the village and the bayous from the hot plains. The air was instantly cooler, tinted with the fragrance of spring blossoms and new leaves. The silence held them almost to the forest's other side. There Nicole said, "I have to know who I am."

"You are my child. My beloved daughter." Louise felt a heaviness constricting her chest, a lifetime's sorrow pouring forth to be lost in the hot Louisiana sunshine. "You are a precious gift God has given to me."

It was as though Louise had never spoken. "I need to know who I am. I need to know who these British are, the people who sired me, who gave me life. I have spent years hating them."

At this Louise whirled to face her. "Now you listen to me," she said, her voice grating deep with intensity. "You were blessed with the most genuine parents a girl could ever have. Your mama—she was all love. All sweetness. This—this exchange never would have happened if she had not possessed the heart of an angel. She loved and fussed over you like I never saw another woman do. But she knew I loved my little Antoinette in the same way, yet I was watching her die. Before my very eyes she was fading away. That's why she offered to take her to the doctor. Our baby would have died, sure enough, if Catherine . . ."

"Catherine? Was that my mama's name?"

Louise caught herself short. She hadn't meant to let that slip. Now she had no choice but to reply with, "Yes. Catherine and Andrew Harrow."

Nicole quickly said, "I didn't mean I hate

118

them in particular—but their kind. Sometimes I think I don't want to know them. Ever." Louise watched closely as Nicole turned to sweep the landscape with a sorrowful gaze. "I must sort this out," she said slowly, as if speaking to more than Louise. "I must find out who I really am. I . . . I feel that I'm two people. Part of me belongs to all this, and part of me is lost. I have to find *myself*. I must put the two pieces of my soul together again."

"But—"

"I may never learn to forgive them. I don't expect to ever be able to love them. But I must know them. I must. The love I felt for Jean . . ." Only here did the resolute calm seem to shiver and threaten to break. But Nicole stiffened and continued in the same tone as before, "I need to make up my own mind now. I need to meet these people, and to know this other part of my heritage. And, I hope, come to know myself."

Louise was not only defeated by the calm, she was terrified. "I don't know if I have the strength to let you go," she whispered through trembling lips.

"It will be hard for us all." The sunlight filtered through the trees and already beat upon them with the intensity of coming summer heat. Up ahead the boys spotted them and shouted their thirst and their hunger. As the four started toward them, Nicole finished, "So hard for us all."

Chapter Eleven

Louise felt as though her heart were being squeezed in a blacksmith's vise. Nicole, who sat silent and pale beside her, was soon to board a ship that would carry her from their sight to a great unknown future.

It had been useless to try to protest further. Louise knew that from the start, even before Henri held her close and whispered, as he patted her back with work-roughened hands, that they could not, dared not, try to hold this young woman, their beloved Nicole, who also belonged to another set of parents.

The trip itself was not Louise's biggest fear. Oh, she fretted about the perilous sea voyage, but that had not caused her sleepless nights as the wind sighed through the cypress trees. No, it was the thought that once gone, Nicole might never return. Louise could not imagine life without her daughter.

"I've lost one daughter," she had mourned to Henri that dawn. "Now it appears that I am about to lose another."

He had tried to console her, but she knew his heart was heavy also. No matter how hard he struggled to maintain a brave front, his visage reflected her own sorrow.

"We must leave her in God's hands," he finally had answered. "Since we are also in His hands, we will be joined together always, though the distance is a little longer."

"You call *this* a little longer?"

"In God's eyes there is neither time nor space," he had replied, both his tone and his gaze beseeching her to take heed, to hold fast.

She stifled another outburst, knowing it would lead to fury. The dawn was already too heavy with coming loss. She could not bear the load of useless anger as well. Not this day.

Now Louise stood in the shade of high-stacked bales and tried to focus upon the sweltering scene. Dark-skinned laborers loaded the awaiting ship, grunting and sweating in the hazy afternoon heat. Dockside at the Mississippi Delta, there were no trees to block the sun's intensity. No whisper of breeze nor stir of air. Louise found it hard even to breathe.

"Mama, why don't we go over to the shade of that shed?" Wordlessly Louise allowed Nicole to lead her away. Away from the smell of sweat. Away from the barrage of shouts that she could not understand though they rang loud and profane in her ears. Away from the bustle of bodies and the swing of ropes and chains and pulleys and bales and crates and cartons. She shuddered as she walked. Ships brought back too many unpleasant memories. She didn't know how Nicole could even think of boarding one now.

"Sit down here," Nicole was saying, patting a forgotten bale over which she had spread her shawl.

With a sigh Louise managed to settle herself on the shawl. Nicole sat down beside her.

"Where is your papa?" asked Louise, fanning herself in a futile attempt to get some air.

"He went with Uncle Guy to see to the passage."

The passage. Another reminder of things to come. "You're sure . . ."

"Mama, we've been through all that."

It was true. They had been through it, but Louise kept hoping, praying, begging God to make Nicole change her mind.

"When you see Catherine—"

"I may never see her."

"I thought that was why you're going."

Nicole hesitated, as though fearful to look that far ahead. As though she dared not get her hopes centered on such a possibility, lest she be dreadfully disappointed. "We do not know if she's still there. If she is even alive, for that matter."

Louise shivered in spite of the heat. "She's alive."

"How do you know? It's been more than eighteen years. She might—"

"I'd know. I'd feel it." Unconsciously Louise placed a hand over her heart.

Nicole turned her eyes to the hazy sky. Not even a bird disturbed the shimmering haze. There was only the stifling heat and noise and dust and confusion of milling bodies, both man and beast.

The three-day trek from Vermilionville had been grueling. Even Henri had looked exhausted by the time they had reached the mouth of the Mississippi. Guy's young ones, who had begun the journey with all the excitement of childhood, now stood solemnly and mutely upon the docks in a bewildered, weary little group. The youngest child had fretted constantly from the irritating heat rash covering his entire little body. The crying baby wore on nerves already stretched to the limit.

Louise sat beside her daughter and spotted Henri bending his way through cargo and milling bodies and coils of hemp rope. She watched as he approached an officer in the ongoing negotiations to secure passage for the travelers on the boat that rested in the harbor. She could not bear to watch, so she turned her eyes back to where her daughter sat and gazed over the deep-running waters. *We should be talking*, thought Louise. *We should be saying all those things that we'll wish we had said once the boat pulls up anchor.* Yet she could not think of a single comment or question. Perhaps they had said it all. Perhaps they were too fatigued from fighting feelings and the elements and the heat to be able to converse. Perhaps they didn't want to speak—for speaking meant thinking, and Louise was not certain she could bear to think of what lay ahead.

It was Nicole who broke the silence. "Would you like another sip of water?"

The water jug lay near at hand. Louise knew that she should drink. But the water was warm and insipid. What she would give for a cup of cool water from the village well, or a refreshing glass of cider brought up from the depths of the cellar. She shook her head.

"In this heat you should drink, Mama." Nicole lifted the jug to her own lips and swallowed several times. A trickle of water dripped from her chin and she lifted a hand to wipe it away.

Louise, watching silently, suddenly felt moisture on her own chin. But it was not water. It was a tear that splashed a trail down her cheek, followed closely by another. Nicole reached out and took her hand. "What are your thoughts, Mama?"

Louise stirred and blinked back more threatening tears. She lifted her other hand to brush at the wetness on her cheeks. "So many things," she eventually managed to answer. "So many things. Things I have pushed back for so many years. You—your leaving has brought them all to mind again."

Nicole leaned away and showed her mother yet again this strange womanly gaze. One so full of calm and strength Louise could not observe it without thinking that she had already lost the child she loved.

She breathed hard, seeking to press her thoughts into shape. "I wonder what it is like in Acadia. I wonder if the spring still comes to the meadow in such lavish color and brightness. I wonder if Catherine still has that way of smiling that lights her whole face and makes her eyes sparkle. I wonder if her faith is still as strong. If Andrew is still with the army after all those horrid . . ."

She struggled to sort through the tumult in her mind and heart. "I wonder where the others are. If the orchard is still there. If my room is still under the eaves."

She was silent for some minutes. "Most of all, I wonder what little Antoinette is like now. Is she shy and retiring, or bold and self-assured? Does she walk like her papa? Has she learned how to cook, how to keep house? Is she strong and healthy? Does she have a beau? She could even be married—a mother. It is not unheard of.

"Your leaving for Acadia brings all of those questions to my mind once again," Louise went on, looking searchingly into Nicole's face. "I had put them aside for so long and now . . . I wonder. I wonder if she even knows about me. If she knows that her father is a good man. Strong of faith and spirit. She should know that. She should know about her father."

"Mama, please. You are only making it more difficult for yourself."

Louise felt the heat and the coming loss solidify into a burning lump at the center of her being. "You speak of *difficult*. You have never known *difficult*. Not like I have known it. God grant that you never shall. To have your baby—your own flesh and blood—torn from you. To sail away, knowing that she is still onshore. To watch the land fade away in the darkness of night and know that it is too far to swim should you cast yourself into the sea. And that you might never, never be coming back." The tears were flowing unheeded now. Louise made no attempt to check them.

Nicole's gaze darkened and her face flashed with the spirit Louise had taken as natural from her daughter. Instantly Louise regretted her outburst, and tried to swallow away the ache and the irritation. She reached out a hand to her daughter. "But there was you," she said in a softer tone. "There was you—or I would have died. You smiled and cooed and you needed me. The flame of love I had lost was lit again by the new love that you brought to my heart."

But Nicole's eyes did not lose their glint. "I cannot imagine what you have felt, what you have endured," she said, "but you also can't know what I have felt and suffered."

Louise knew the look all too well, the brooding that flashed into sudden anger, the eyes like dark pools. There was a new edge to her voice, yet another sign that her daughter was changing. Growing apart from her. "I never meant—"

"I have been forced to give up the only man I have ever loved. Then I learned that I am not who I always thought myself to be." Her voice sounded hot as the day. "I have parents I do not know. *English* parents. A homeland I cannot recall. I do not know if my family is alive—or dead. If I have brothers or sisters."

"You have us. Your brothers are—"

Nicole stood to her feet in one swift motion. "My brothers are no more my brothers than those men toting the bales," she answered with vehemence. Louise sucked in her breath. "It is true," went on Nicole. "There is no blood tie between us. Why, I could marry Josef and the law would not frown upon it."

"Sit down," demanded Louise. She slapped the shawl beside her. "Sit down *now*."

Nicole hesitated, then seated herself again on the bale.

"Stop that right now." Louise's voice came in tight little gasps. "You may have been—cheated, not knowing your rightful parents. I grant you that. But you have also been blessed."

"Blessed?"

"Yes, listen to me, blessed. You have had not only one set of parents who have loved you, you have had *two*. Two sets of parents who would have died for you had it been necessary. Two. Many do not even have one. Two—do you hear me? Who can boast the same? And yes, I am still your mother. Your brothers are still your brothers, and so they will always be. Don't you forget that. Don't you *ever* forget that."

"And Antoinette?" asked Nicole, tipping her head slightly to one side, but her tone less challenging. "What about her?"

Louise did not back down. "Why, she is equally blessed. She had Andrew and Catherine—and she has us."

"You still love her?"

Louise was shocked at the question. "I still breathe, do I not?"

Nicole's tiny nod was uncertain.

"There you are," came a booming voice, and Henri pushed his way through the teeming crowd and drew near. His eyes sought out Louise, asking questions without words. Louise had questions of her own but was unable to voice them.

"They were able to get passage," Henri announced. "It's not a passenger ship, but the cargo seems to leave room for people to find space and to stir about. There are some empty berths, so they agreed to take the family. They sail at first light. Guy is busy even now stowing their things on board. The captain wants all those traveling with him to be settled on board before nightfall."

So it was happening. Louise turned her attention to a barking dog that someone had tied to the quay. Nearby a sheep bleated. Dust rolled toward them from the mules that brought in another load of bales. Louise heard and saw it all, yet perceived nothing. She brushed at the irritating flies buzzing about her face, then reached out for Henri's hand. With his help she slowly came to her feet and stood mindlessly listening to the waves that lapped against the wooden dockside. Henri turned to Nicole. "You are ready, my daughter?"

Nicole was honest in her reply. "I am, and I am not."

"You will need to board within the half hour." Henri seemed to be forcing out the words. "We will miss you while you are gone. It makes the parting harder, not knowing when or how you will make it back home."

Back home, Louise's heart echoed. *Once my beloved daughter makes this trip, where will her home be?* But she did not voice her thoughts. Nothing was to be gained from asking the unanswerable.

Nicole then spoke words that surprised them all. "If opportunity arises, what should I say to Antoinette?"

Louise felt a lance of sunlight pierce the

marrow of her bones. Yet again there was no answer. All the hope and pain of years seemed to bear down, squeezing more tears from her eyes.

It was Henri who answered for them both. "What a question. Do you not know us at all?" Their daughter's head bowed under the weight of Henri's rasping words. "Speak your heart. You will be speaking our heart as well."

Louise struggled to find her own response within her heart. What should Nicole say for her? How to reduce the distance, to overcome the past?

Henri seemed to read her thoughts, for he went on, "We have longed to see her year by year. We would be blessed to see her even now. But we cannot go back and change what was. Our tears are spent. Time and circumstance cannot be altered. She is their child. There is no way to undo the past."

Was Henri speaking to Nicole? Louise wondered. Did he think she was attempting to change the circumstances of their lives?

Nicole spoke hesitantly now. "But if she wishes to know . . ."

"Then may God give wisdom to you both."

"God?" Nicole spoke the one word with a coldness that made the breath catch in

Louise's throat.

"You still question the existence of God?" Henri spoke as though wounded.

For a moment Nicole did not answer. When she spoke, her words were direct, chilling. It was as though a dark, cold shroud fell over the three who stood together. "If not His existence, at least I doubt that He can be trusted."

"Cannot trust God?" Henri sounded incredulous.

"Didn't you pray to Him all these years? Didn't I? It seems that He either did not care, or was powerless to be of any use."

A deep sorrow clouded Henri's eyes. "If you believe that, my daughter, then I have failed miserably as your father."

Louise blinked away the tears so as to see Nicole more clearly. She knew this person as well as she knew herself, and yet at this moment she wondered. There was such strength in those lovely features, and yet indecision as well. The girl struggled not with the heat or the voyage or the uncertainties of the future, it seemed, but rather with herself. Nicole forced herself to meet her father's gaze, but she could not completely hide her hesitancy.

Henri's voice regained its strength. "Always remember, my beloved one, you can never be where God is not. There is no place where you can outdistance Him. No dark corner where you can hide where He is not already there waiting for your arrival. No deep recess of your heart or soul that He does not know of. No secret that He does not share. And He does have *power*. To change, to keep, to do the impossible."

"He did not do the impossible for you," Nicole threw out.

"Ah, but He did. In all my circumstances He kept my heart from bitterness. He made my faith grow so I would cling to Him like the moss clings to the branch. For me, on my own, that would have been impossible. My soul would have withered and died. He did indeed work the impossible."

Louise and Henri looked at each other, then back to their daughter. Both parents took comfort in Nicole's inability to refute her father's statement. Louise took the first easy breath since they had arrived at the docks. Her daughter was leaving, yet despite her bitterness over the loss of Jean and the sudden realizations of her own heritage, Nicole was unable to utterly cast them aside or discount her heritage. Meager comfort in this moment, but somehow it seemed enough.

"I pray you might discover Him for

yourself," her husband went on, "for without Him, *nothing* of importance is possible. We can only fumble and stumble in darkness. But with Him there is light, even in the harshest of times."

Louise heard the rough call of stevedores and the clinking of iron and creaking of ropes. The dog barked again, straining against its tether. Louise felt as though her own life were being tossed adrift upon a restless sea. And yet, even here, she heard the truth of Henri's words. And in them she knew a glimmer of peace. Even now.

The peace granted Louise the power to see Nicole anew. What did she believe? At the moment, Louise realized, Nicole truly did not know. She had cast aside her childlike faith, but she had nothing to stand in its stead. Inside was anger and sorrow and bewilderment. Outside was heat and dust and confusion. Louise studied her daughter and saw a woman who wished to be free of restraints from the people she had known as her parents—yet at the same time she wished to cling to them. She was an adult, yet still a child. She wanted to find her own way at the same time she feared the darkness of the unknown future. She wished to cast aside all attachment to her French heritage, yet she wished to remain one of them for all time.

This newfound ability to see her daughter with fresh understanding gave Louise the strength to set aside her sadness. It would return, she knew, and the trail home would be awash in the sorrow of having lost yet another daughter. But for now she could offer this wonderful woman-child a smile and the words, "I love you, my daughter. And I trust God enough to see the future with hope."

Nicole seemed to be caught unawares by the words. "What, Mama?"

"I am certain you shall pass through your voyage safely, and from it you will come to know us better—your family here on earth, and your Father in heaven."

The appeal in Nicole's face burned with such intensity that tears formed in both women's eyes. Nicole whispered, "Oh, I hope so."

Increased activity on the dock drew their attention. It was time for Nicole to hoist her carpetbags and walk the gangplank that would separate her from all that she knew. Louise held her breath as Henri reached for them both.

"Let us pray," he said, and his voice seemed to boom across the expanse of wooden platform.

"Father, our dear child is leaving us today and our hearts are heavy with our grief. But you understand all about parting. Your own Son stepped from your side to make an earthly pilgrimage. His journey took Him to a cross. Our daughter has but to go to the land of her birth. Keep her safe. Make her faith to grow. May she find not just her parents but her heavenly Father to be *real*, and *there*. And when her pilgrimage is over, bring her safely back to us. To our home. To our love. In the name of your Son. Amen."

Chapter Twelve

Charles had never felt so trapped in his entire life. Not even the Atlantic crossing had left him feeling so helpless. At least there he had a ship's company at his beck and call. Here in Andrew's village he was not only unrecognized, he was unwelcome.

He had started off badly. Georgetown had but one inn, and Charles had criticized the innkeeper's only daughter for bringing him a breakfast platter of black tea and bread husks so hard he could scarcely bite through them. The innkeeper had heard Charles out, then coldly replied, "Feel free to get your own breakfast, for my family will serve you no longer." Nor had they. When he had complained a second time, the innkeeper told him straight out the only reason Charles did not find himself sleeping in the forest was because he was the pastor's brother, and a finer man God had never made—a pity the same could not be said for the reverend's kin. It was the last word anyone within the inn had spoken to him.

That had been five days ago.

Since then, Charles had taken his meals with his brother's family. When he walked the village lane he was met with cold stares and hostile faces. One word he heard most often muttered just within earshot—"arrogant."

Yet he had no choice but to stay in the village. Andrew had refused to further his search for Elspeth in any way, unless or until God directed their actions. When Charles had demanded to know how long that would take, Andrew had replied in his gentle but straightforward manner, "That too is in God's hands."

Charles remained utterly mortified at his brother's poverty. Certainly Charles had peasants who lived in far worse circumstances. But it was an affront to the Harrow name to live without a single item of furniture or clothing that could be considered fashionable. The village was a thriving market town and could well have afforded to support their pastor. But Andrew did not seem to expect it. He raised vegetables in his front garden, he kept two cows and two dozen laying hens, and he used a small shed attached to the back of their house as a leather shop. The fact that his brother spent every free hour making shoes and bridles insulted Charles's sensibilities.

And yet, and yet . . . after the shock of the dire straits of Andrew's family had worn off, new undercurrents had begun to unfold. Hints of a life that left Charles feeling unsettled and challenged.

As usual, Charles walked the lane soon after sunrise, leaving the inn before the other patrons rose. Georgetown sat on an elbow of land, with forest and steep hillsides to its back. To the west stretched the Bay of Fundy, so broad the other banks were seen only on the clearest afternoon. To the north opened Cobequid Bay. Trading vessels plying these waters called here in Georgetown, which was why there was an inn at all. Twice each week a market drew settlers from numerous outlying hamlets.

"Charles, good morning to you!" The old man, John Price, hobbled into view. "Grand morning, is it not?"

"Yes, I suppose so." He stared at Catherine's father. A stick figure, he seemed hollowed by age and illness. "How is your wound?"

"It pains me most mornings." The man's gentle smile did not seem the least bit disturbed by the acknowledgment. "Only thing I know to do is get out and walk."

"Shall I carry your burden?"

"Kind of you, son." He handed over the basket. "One of the neighbors offered us fresh-baked bread and ten still-warm eggs."

Charles overlooked the offense of being called "son" by such a decrepit elderly stranger. "I've noticed that you have found a warm place in the villagers' hearts."

"They have warm hearts for Andrew, you mean. They do indeed revere your brother."

"Yes, I've noticed that too." The fact rankled, but it could not be denied. Andrew's passage down a village street was enough to draw a smile and a greeting from even the most gloomy face. Charles had seen it happen.

"Andrew is without a doubt the worst leatherworker in Nova Scotia." John Price made the statement in a tone as jolly as the early spring birdsong. "But he never lacks for work. And he occasionally chides his customers for overpaying."

Unwilling to discuss his brother any longer, Charles asked, "Where did you pick up that wound of yours?"

"France. Fighting the king's war." Even this was said with the gentlest of smiles. "But that was in another lifetime, son. Before Catherine and Andrew led me to my knees and introduced me to our Lord."

There seemed no way to escape an uncomfortable conversation. Charles tried to head it off. "I find it rather curious to be addressed as anyone's son."

"Yes, I'm certain you do." This was good for a chuckle. "You may find it hard to believe, but I recognize myself in you—at least the man I once was."

Charles bit down hard on the sharp retort that rose hot in his mouth.

"Yes, I was a senior officer in the King's Own. Highly decorated—I imagine the medals and decorations are still around somewhere. After my battlefield wound I was appointed notary to the region around Fort Edward." John Price's gaze held Charles's without embarrassment or apology at the obvious inference. "Filled with my own importance and the power that came with my position, I was. And I turned into as cold and hard a man as you'll ever care to meet."

Charles found himself trapped by these turbulent emotions. On the one hand, he wanted to lash out and put this strange old man in his place, and right sharp. On the other, he felt tugged by something mysterious, as strange as this early spring sunlight, crisp and cold and warming all at the same time.

Before he could recover sufficiently to say anything at all, however, John Price stooped to open the gate to their little cottage, then turned to take the basket from Charles. "Thank you, son," he said. And the look from those twinkling eyes seemed to suggest that he knew exactly what was going through Charles's mind.

"Good morning, Grandfather." Anne's sweet voice sang the greeting through the open doorway. "Your water is warmed and ready."

Charles settled onto the bench outside the kitchen window. He listened to Anne assisting John Price, sharpening his straight-edged razor and laying out soap and a clean towel, all the while chatting and answering questions about the day ahead. Price's small pension saw to many of the Harrows' day-to-day needs—neither Andrew nor Catherine seemed to find any shame in admitting how much the pittance helped them. But

Anne's lovingkindness toward the old man went much further than just repaying his generosity. When Price's wound ached, Anne seemed to notice it even before the old man spoke and was always there to help him. She clearly adored the old gentleman. Charles shifted on the bench, uncomfortable in the knowledge that here was a bond Charles had never known in his entire life. And between two people who in truth were not even of the same blood.

Anne appeared in the doorway beside him. "You take your tea black, do you not?" Now that the truth was known, she treated him with kindly ease.

"Yes, thank you." He accepted the steaming mug, took a sip, and sighed through its steam.

Anne remained where she was. "This is very hard for you, isn't it? The waiting."

He looked up at her. "I fail to see why it should be such an enormous decision to permit me to search for my niece and offer her the Harrow legacy. Andrew may not care about it for himself, but he does seem to care about me. And about his daughter." He looked quickly to see if she was offended by the use of the term "daughter." But she stared back at him without flinching, her smile unwavering.

He expected her to repeat the arguments Andrew had set out. But instead Anne asked, "May I join you?"

Charles shifted along the bench. "Please. By all means."

"Thank you." She seated herself, then took a long moment to look about at the day. The light turned the dusty lane beyond their garden as white as the snow on the upper hillsides. "I do so love this time of year," she exulted. "The birds begin to sing again, life is returning to the earth, everywhere there is a sense of great expectancy."

Charles sipped his tea and said, "You astonish me. Your confidence, your demeanor, your sense of poise. I would never have expected to find such qualities in, well—"

"A village lass," she finished for him. If she found anything offensive in the comment, she did not show it. "I owe everything to my parents and my God."

"And this religion of yours. If you will forgive me for saying it, it seems so . . . so all-demanding."

"Oh, *I* forgive you, Uncle Charles." Another smile tugged at the corners of her mouth. He wondered if she used the title to tease him. But her thoughts seemed to be elsewhere as she continued, "But will God?

143

That is the question you have to ask yourself."

A second encounter of the morning was turning uncomfortable. Charles shifted on the bench, then said, "We have moved very far from the issue of my searching for Elspeth."

"Indeed we have." Anne folded her hands in her lap. "You may wonder why I became so distraught when you first put your proposal forth, thinking that I was Elspeth. It was not that I feared I would have to depart. I knew you were looking for blood kin, and I knew I was not the one for whom you searched. It was because I feared of what this . . . this probing would do to my mother and father. The wound of that awful time has never fully healed. I suppose such wounds never do. But their distress has eased. With God's help it has become bearable. Their Elspeth . . . they have never forgotten her. Even after all the years of searching, all the letters that were never answered. I know in their hearts they still long to know what has become of her." She hesitated for a moment while Charles shuffled his feet. "You said you seek to give her the Harrow legacy and its wealth."

Charles thought he heard an opening there and hastened to say, "Indeed I do. I

144

have tried likewise with Andrew. I would gladly provide him with a bequest enough to alleviate all this hardship and labor. But he refuses to even discuss it." He turned to face her. "Surely you would appreciate the opportunity for fine frocks. Imagine, your very own carriage with prancing horses, servants, a grand house, the chance to travel wherever you wish to go."

Yet again Anne did not respond as expected. "I would love to see my father be able to take his ease. He is beginning to suffer from back pains and joint ailments, especially in winter. He doesn't say anything, but I can see it becoming harder for him—the long hours in the cold shed, as well as long treks through the wilderness to visit an ailing parishioner."

He felt reproved by her response, the utter lack of interest in anything for herself. "Well, then."

Anne shook her head. "You are not offering to *give* to us, Uncle Charles. You have come to buy, to *barter*. You want something in exchange. You think that your payment is enough for us to accept the possible distress and disruption." Her gaze was as clear as the morning air. "We are at peace here. Yes, life is not easy. We worry about my grandfather, and Father labors enough hours for two men. It would be good to have time for rest, and to not have to work quite so hard." She smiled at him and finished with, "But most of all my father needs to know what is right, what is in God's plan in this situation."

His response was somehow robbed of force by her open honesty. "I merely seek to find Elspeth."

A call from her grandfather pulled Anne to her feet. "We are at peace. I think perhaps that was the reason why Father wanted you to stay here until he could pray and ask God what was to be done. He wants you to understand what we have. What we may be asked to give up." She turned to the doorway, saying simply, "God's peace is a gift my parents give thanks for every day."

The control and confidence Anne felt while speaking with her new uncle did not remain as constant as she would have wished. One moment she was unshakable in her faith, the next her emotions rolled and tossed her so she was left frightened and shaken.

She now sat staring out over the tranquil waters of Cobequid Bay. She was seated in her favorite place on the stump of a tree so large she and her grandfather had often used it as a table for a little picnic when she was younger. Anne knew without looking up that John Price was approaching, for his walk had a certain cadence to it, an uneven step that favored his old war wound. She kept her gaze turned seaward as he came over, stood above her for a time, and finally settled in beside her. They had been like this for as long as Anne could remember, friends so close that words often were not even required.

But today she needed to speak with someone, and she knew it could not be her mother. Even though the thoughts might distress her grandfather, she had to voice them. "I was thinking back to last autumn," she began. "Do you remember the big October storm?"

"I do indeed." John Price seemed to realize this would not be a short stay, for he settled himself more comfortably and put his walking stick down on the ground. "The first snowfall. Such winds as I thought they might lift me up and carry me off to England."

"I came out here that afternoon. Mother would not have let me if she had known. The sea was white as far as I could see, the waves tossed up and torn to pieces, as much froth in the air as snow." She squinted as she had that previous afternoon, only now the biting winds were all inside. "That's how I feel right now."

"Oh, my child." John Price laid his hand on her arm.

"What if Uncle Charles goes off and finds Elspeth?" Anne whispered, despair filling her heart. "What will happen to my own family? This family—the only one I have ever known. Will Mother and Father love me as they have? Will I become the *second* child in the family, or not be their child at all? If Elspeth comes back, will they make another exchange and send me to live with people I don't even know?" Part of her knew the answer, but another part wanted to hear it from another.

"Not now, not ever," her grandfather replied vehemently but kindly.

Anne turned and pressed him with, "How can you be so sure? What if you're wrong? What if . . . what if they don't *need* me anymore?"

John Price reached over and covered her hand with his own. They sat like this, her sorrowful questions met with that kind gaze Anne had known from earliest memory.

In the distance they heard the lowing of cattle and the clatter of cowbells. A thrush landed in the bush behind them, sending out a song clear as crystal chimes. Anne had a sudden image of long ago. She did not even know how old she was. The same soft loving face she looked at now was leaning over her bed. She had just finished her prayers, and her grandfather was tucking her in for the night. Anne remembered how she looked up into that soft gray gaze and decided that God must have eyes just like her grandfather's.

John Price finally said, "Anne, my girl, there is something I must tell you."

She looked into the much-loved face, at the grave expression, and nodded her question.

"Back before the Acadian expulsion, I did not know God." It was John Price's turn to look out over the sparkling blue waters. "Oh, I thought I did. But He was someone I was aware of only distantly. I read the Good Book only for what I could use to judge others. I was a man of rules and laws and judgment and war and revenge."

Anne smiled and shook her head. "You're telling me stories, Grandfather."

John Price neither smiled nor turned from his perusal of unseen distances. "I was a harsh father and a hard taskmaster. I lived for order and anger. And I confess that I did not take much notice of my first grandchild, the infant Elspeth."

Her smile slipped away. "I can't believe this. Not of you, Grandfather."

John Price's jaw muscles tightened. "I was pleased to have an heir to carry on the family heritage, but discontent that it had turned out to be a girl. There was nothing I could do about the infant being a girl, of course. So I decided to bide my time and let her grow up and perhaps then, one day, she would be of some use, some comfort to me. I paid her so little mind that I did not even know it was you and not Elspeth your mother carried with us to Halifax." Slowly he shook his head back and forth, obviously pained by the recollection. "Six days and nights I traveled with my own granddaughter, or so I thought, and I did not even know it was you. Did not care enough to see the infant who was there before me."

He sighed, and suddenly he looked old. Old and sad and defeated by all that was no more. He now turned to her, distress making his voice tremble. "Anne, I knew of the expulsion. I was one of the very few chosen to collect statistics on the region's French villages—how much land, how many cattle— all carefully recorded and readied for the seizures that followed."

"No," Anne whispered.

"I did not see them as people. I saw them

as the enemy. They were French, and the French had wounded me in battle. That was all I needed to know." He sighed, a broken rattling breath. "After it was over, after it was done and too late, I learned the truth. About you, and about myself. The Lord used my own actions and my own guilt to break me, to humble me before Him. Then He began the renewing, the rebuilding from the inside to become a servant of God."

He turned his gaze toward the sea and the sky's unbroken blue. "I shall carry my guilt with me to the grave. That and the fact that it is only God's loving grace, only the Lord's perfect forgiveness, only the Master's healing touch, that has changed me and brought me to where I am this day."

"Oh, Grandfather."

"In my private moments I long to have my *other* granddaughter restored to her parents, if only because I am responsible for wrenching them apart." He faced her again, his emotions clearly threatening to overpower him. "You are no longer a child, Anne. I have waited for just such a day as this to confess to you all that brought you to us. Confess my guilt and beg for your forgiveness."

Her own emotions poured out in sobs that nearly choked her. She flung herself into her grandfather's arms, and he held her tightly, stroked her hair, and said softly, "If God's gentle mercy can bind us in such a wondrous way, do you truly think your wonderful parents could be any less constant in their love? You are their blessed child, their daughter for life. Of this you can be certain."

The next day, the Sabbath morning, Catherine woke to feel as though the clouds had rolled in upon her internal world, the storm had suddenly broken. The instant Andrew opened his eyes, he must have felt it too, for his first words that Sunday were, "What's wrong?"

"Oh, Andrew, my husband, what if all my hopes are false?" She clutched at his nightshirt, seeking desperately for something to calm the turmoil. If only she could pull the coverlet of peace back over her terrified and wounded heart. "What if Charles goes and finds our little Elspeth, or what if he finds out—"

"Don't say it, please, I beg you." Andrew's gaze mirrored her anguish. "I can't bear to think it, not for an instant."

"I want my daughter so. And yet stirring

this all up threatens to destroy the peace and the life we've built here."

"I know what you are feeling, my love. I feel very much the same," Andrew confessed in a whisper.

"Charles is such a ruthless, uncaring, cold person." She waited for Andrew to defend his brother, but he said nothing, only looked over at her with eyes as tormented as her own heart. "I see in him so many threats against our family."

"It is so hard to hear you say these things," Andrew said slowly. "I have been leaning upon your calm confidence and faith in God."

"I wish . . ." She rolled away, no longer able to lie still, and sat upright on the edge of the bed. She looked over at her husband and said sorrowfully, "I don't know what I wish anymore." He reached for her hand, and the silent squeeze said that he understood.

Sabbath mornings were usually a time of quiet anticipation for Catherine, a culmination of the week while looking forward to seeing Andrew in the pulpit. But today there was none of this. Even Charles seemed affected, for he took his morning tea and retreated to the bench outside the window. When Anne, then John Price, entered the kitchen, Catherine watched her father and daughter exchange calm, loving glances. On any other day she would have questioned them about the secret they shared. But this morning Catherine had all she could do to prepare for church.

Andrew walked ahead of them, and Catherine watched him go through the motions of exchanging Sabbath greetings with the other villagers. His features looked strained along with his voice. Catherine tried to be interested in comments on the weather, on the first buds of spring appearing, on hopes that a late frost would not kill the nestling sprouts. But the questions, the endless doubts, the dilemma that trapped them, all whirled relentlessly through her mind.

Andrew's sermon seemed to be a struggle for him from beginning to end. His mental turmoil was clear to all, and worried glances were cast among those seated around Catherine. Charles had joined her in the pew, and she could feel as much as see his ramrod-erect figure and the arrogance with which he viewed the service and the congregation. Catherine wished he had never come, wished he would simply depart for England on the next ship. Leave them to sort out their lives and let the past settle back into comfortable memories and whispered, half-remembered dreams. And the waves of guilt pounded through her tortured soul.

She bowed her head, not so much in prayer as in defeat. *I cannot carry this any longer*, she prayed, and at the same time felt God was so distant it was more a conversation with herself than with her Lord. *Forgive me, Father. I don't know what to do. I don't know how to think. Every choice seems equally wrong. It is impossible, and it is tearing me apart. Please take this unspeakable burden from me.*

There was no room for concern about the rightness or wrongness of her feelings or even for a sense of correctness to her prayer. The words were simply formed from the impossible affliction of doubt.

Andrew seemed to stop in time to her prayer. She did not consciously recognize that he had halted in midflow, not at first. Catherine remained with her head bowed and clenched her hands into a tight ball in the center of her lap. *Help us. Please help us.*

Her head came up and eyes opened almost against her will. Andrew was gazing down at her. He seemed mildly surprised, halted in midsentence by some secret whisper.

Catherine felt a sigh escape her throat, and with it she seemed to expel all the distress, all the doubt, all the anguish. It was not something she did herself. The calm, the inner peace, arrived with such tenderness that she could only know it had come by the sudden absence of her sorrow. One moment she felt trapped in suffering, the next she was at rest in the hands of God. The moment was perfumed by an eternal presence, a gift from the invisible realm. And then she knew.

Andrew looked down at her and smiled. He understood. Of course he did. This was not a gift to her. This was an *answer*. One granted to them both.

Andrew's glance shifted, and she turned with him to look at his brother. Charles stared up at the pulpit with an expression of confusion. His brow was wrinkled, his eyes squinted, seeking to focus upon what he did not understand. Catherine did the thing that seemed right at that moment, which was to reach over and take his hand, the first time she had ever touched him. Startled, Charles looked at her, and she gave to him a smile drawn from the love and the peace that filled her heart—not her own smile at all, but God's gift, given first to her and now shared with Charles. They had their answer.

Chapter Thirteen

"Lord Charles, welcome, welcome." The owner of the largest bank in Halifax wore muttonchop sideburns and a smile as lopsided as his powdered wig. "What an honor it is, sir. An honor, yes indeed. No, please, take this seat, you'll find it more comfortable. A coffee, sir?"

"Thank you."

"A newly arrived vessel has brought fresh coffee beans straight from Curacao, the finest I've had in years." He turned to the door and said, "Coffee for two. Use the silver service."

Charles allowed himself to be ushered to the padded chair by the windows. "It is actually about a ship that I have come to see you."

"Then you have come to the right place, your lordship. No other house in all the colonies does as much trading business—"

Charles stopped the man's enthusiastic flow with his palm upraised. "Can you tell me which is the fastest ship in Nova Scotia?"

The man stared at him. "The fastest, Lord Charles?"

"Other than the military, of course." He had already spent a fruitless period at the Admiralty, seeking to borrow or rent or otherwise gain the use of one of their clippers. But with the rumors of troubles farther south, the officer in charge had the perfect excuse to refuse him, even the king's envoy. "I am not interested so much with its size, so long as it is able to carry me safely. My concern is speed."

"Speed, yes, of course." The banker clearly struggled to hold back his torrent of questions. "May I ask your destination?"

"Points south," Charles replied tersely. "I may require the vessel for some time. Perhaps the entire season. Rest assured I will pay well, and in gold."

The banker rose to his feet. "You will excuse me for a moment?"

"Certainly."

"My assistant will be in directly with coffee." The banker hastened from the room.

Charles stared at the bustling scene beyond the ornate bay windows, but in truth he saw little. He was too caught up in the conflicting images and emotions that struggled within his mind and heart. He *should* be impatient. He had a destination. He had a purpose. He was getting on with his business. And yet what he felt most of all was confusion.

The bank sat on the corner where Halifax's main street entered the harbor's market square. Traffic was heavy, and sheep and cattle and horses and chickens and children all added to the clamor of cracking whips and creaking wagons and hawking stall holders. But Charles's attention remained held by a different scene, one from the previous Sabbath afternoon.

The church service had been one of the most baffling experiences of his entire life. Andrew had stumbled over his sermon, and he seemed at several points to lose his place entirely.

And then, in the middle of the service, a change had come. Charles would have liked to attribute the change to Andrew alone. It would have been less mysterious and disconcerting. But, no, the change had come upon them all. One moment Andrew had been uncomfortable and distracted, and the next moment a calm had descended upon the entire gathering. Charles had felt almost overwhelmed by what he still could not fathom.

After church, Andrew had pulled him aside and asked if they might walk together. When Catherine approached and bestowed upon Charles a smile of warmth and cheer, it had wrenched his heart. No one had ever looked at him like that before. Neither of his wives, certainly. Not even his mother that he could recall.

Catherine had reached forward, spanning the impossible gap between them with a gentle hand on his arm, and said, "My husband speaks for both of us."

The confusion had only heightened then. He wanted to ask how she knew what Andrew was going to say. But she had already turned away, placing the same gentle hand upon her husband. And Charles had seen how her gaze had been returned by Andrew.

Charles could only stare in unbelieving wonder as Andrew also gave him a smile of love and acceptance. Charles could no longer deny the simple fact that his very presence was a threat to Andrew's family. Everything Anne had said to him earlier he had come to see as true. His quest for his own selfish ends could destroy everything they had carefully built and maintained for almost twenty years now.

Andrew accepted greetings from his congregation with gentle words and smiles, gradually drawing the two of them farther down the lane. When they were isolated by the trees and the twisting path, he had said, "I will help you in your quest."

Charles found himself rocked again, both by the statement and by the ease with which Andrew spoke. But he was not about to refuse his brother's offer, even though he was sure the price must be high. "In exchange for what?"

"I want nothing from you, brother. In truth, I am doing this for God, not for you." Andrew's smile held the confidence of one utterly at peace with his decision. "I no longer have any choice in the matter."

"I fail to see—"

"Yes, I would imagine that to be the case." But his smile did not waver. "Catherine and I spent years searching for Elspeth. If you find her now, it will not be because of anything you yourself do."

"Again, brother, I fail to understand your reasoning."

"Think on this, will you?" Andrew opened the gate to his home. Charles looked across the garden and saw Anne standing in the doorway, once more greeting him with a smile. "Perhaps you are here because of a much greater purpose than the one you suppose. Perhaps you have been selected as God's instrument to accomplish something we cannot even imagine." Andrew halted midway down the path and stared at Charles intently. "And perhaps your true quest is actually a search for something far greater than an heir, something far more lasting. Something eternal."

"Lord Charles, may I have the pleasure of introducing Captain Kedrick Dillon."

"M'lord."

"Captain." A handshake and an instant's inspection were enough to know the mettle of this officer. Charles had the experience in sizing up men that comes with wealth. He was also well aware of how things worked in the navy. The captain was lean and battle hard, in his late thirties, and had the direct gaze of one used to the endless vistas of the sea. "An honor to meet you, sir."

"The honor is mine." The officer gave the proper stiff bow of one trained not as a merchant shipper but rather by the Admiralty.

The banker bustled about. "Come, come, let us sit. I have ordered another pot of this excellent coffee, and then we'll follow that with a lunch in our dining salon. You will be able to join us, m'lord?"

"That depends upon the captain here." Charles resumed his seat by the window, took note of the younger man's involuntary gesture toward his side with his right hand. "I warrant you have recently left the navy."

The gaze turned keener. "How did you

know, sir?"

"As you seated yourself, you sought to adjust a sword you no longer wear."

The smile was tight, as measuring as the gaze. "There are few postings for captaincy these days. . . ."

"Unless, of course, one is born into a title," Charles finished for the officer.

The captain seemed to relax a trifle. "Just so, m'lord."

"I understand you now skipper a fast ship, sir."

"A swifter vessel you will not find in these waters. A clipper out of Southampton, the keel laid just five years past." The fire of pride shone in his eyes. "She is a sweet one, m'lord, holding steady at five degrees off the wind even in the belly of a gale."

Charles had spent the endless days of his recent crossing talking sea and ships with the naval captain and thus understood. "Which is vital if we are to head down the eastern coastline this time of year, is it not?"

"Indeed." The man's gaze held the grim wisdom of one who had seen his share of hardship and hard weather. "Where exactly were you intending to sail, m'lord?"

Andrew and he had discussed that very matter. After giving it considerable thought, Andrew's best estimate of where Charles might begin his search had been in New Orleans. Because of the current difficulties between France and England, letters sent to unknown authorities or to secondhand contacts with vague addresses were either not received or not responded to. Andrew had written for years and received nothing in reply. But he now explained to Charles that a decade earlier the Spanish had taken over control of the region from their French allies and had issued a decree inviting Acadians to come and settle. Over the past ten years, ships had arrived from all over the world—Africa, France, South America, the West Indies, and the American colonies—all containing Acadians desperate to find someplace they might call home. So it was in Louisiana that he would begin his search.

"To begin with—the colony of Louisiana. Do you know it?"

"I sailed there last year on my way to Mexico."

"Excellent." Charles had heard enough to make a decision. "Captain, I wish to employ your vessel."

"We are contracted to take on a shipment of timber, furs, and raw gold," the man replied cautiously.

"But you are free to accept new cargo and destinations?"

"My owners are Portsmouth and Boston traders, m'lord. They would be happy to consider any offer that promises additional profit."

"As your owners are so distant, I shall discuss my needs with you." Charles leaned forward. "I wish to hire your vessel for the entire season. It may not be required for so long, but I cannot take that chance. You will first take me to Louisiana, then perhaps call on other ports in the American colonies or the West Indies. You may trade as you see fit, so long as I have the authority to change destinations and departures. Eventually, you shall transport me back to England."

The officer measured him carefully, finally murmuring, "Most irregular."

"But profitable, I assure you." He turned to the banker. "I assume my paper is good?"

The plump financier nearly rubbed his hands in glee. "Most certainly, Lord Charles. Most certainly."

"Excellent. I wish to appoint you as my agent in these proceedings. Be shrewd, but be fair." Charles rose to his feet. "I shall take a turn around the town while you conclude these negotiations."

The captain rose cautiously to his feet. "This is rather sudden, is it not?"

"By necessity, Captain. I wish to depart

as swiftly as possible."

"Might I ask the nature of your quest?"

Charles hesitated, not through a reluctance to divulge his information, but rather because of the captain's final word. *Quest.* It reminded him once more of Andrew's words and how he might be searching for something else entirely. With an effort he pushed aside the reminder of his confusion and replied, "I seek Lady Elspeth, the future viscountess of Harrow Hall."

Chapter Fourteen

Charles walked the deck and listened to sounds that had become so familiar they seemed to form the song of his life. The wind was taught a man-made tune by the halyards and the masts and the sails. While the waves rose with crests decorated in white salty lace, the lookout shouted into the wind, the words sounding like a copy of the cawing gulls. The sailors' bare feet padded swiftly about the deck, compelled to labor by the officers' bellowed orders. Only Charles was silent, aloof, alone.

He stared westward, across the high seas with their wind-whipped froth. Somewhere beyond the horizon lay land. Two weeks and two days they had chased their way south, the days growing ever warmer. Though the land was never seen, it was always there, haunting his dreams and lacing the offshore breeze with hints of green and life that was alien out on the salty depths. He had taken to spending hours standing by the landward rail, feeling his troubled heart plucked and unstrung by the constant wind.

He had not yet achieved what he had left England to do, no, yet the time in Nova Scotia had gone far better than he could have ever expected. Instead of the battles and the shame and the bitter feuding Charles had been prepared to face, Andrew had granted him a family welcome. The memory stung his eyes still, the hugs and the hospitality and the openhearted reception. The Harrows had showered him with such a richness of affection that here and now, a thousand leagues south, he remained bound by it still.

A fierce blast of wind struck him, causing Charles to grab the nearest halyard. *Richness*. Such a strange way to describe a family caught in such poverty. And yet, despite Andrew's rejection of his own attempts to place them in a more comfortable situation, Andrew was rich in ways Charles had no words to describe.

His eyes flickered over waves painted a

scattering of blues and greens and golds by the clouds and sun, and he remembered the farewell. Andrew had insisted upon seeing him on board the ship. He and Catherine had come into Halifax along with Anne because she wanted to find a position with a doctor. During their journey to the town, she had explained her desire to help people, particularly mothers and children, with their medical needs. Georgetown had no one to turn to in times of illness and pain. She wanted to learn enough to treat the basic complaints. Through a Halifax pastor friend of her father, she had learned of a newly arrived doctor, a man of strong faith, who was in need of an assistant. Her parents wanted to meet him and see that Anne found a safe and appropriate place to reside.

Andrew alone had accompanied Charles on board the vessel. Charles noted Andrew's smile as he observed the officers' sharp salutes and his brother's response. When Charles had demanded what he found humorous, Andrew had replied, "You are far more comfortable with power than I could ever be."

Charles led his brother to the forecastle's relative isolation. "I have been waiting for a private moment to thank you properly, brother."

"You do not need to thank me."

"Ah, but I do." Charles reached into his coat pocket, his hand curling about the hefty purse. But for some reason he hesitated to bring it out. Everything in his experience told him it was the correct thing to do, to give his brother the gold. But Anne's remembered words seemed to rise with the noise of the harbor market, accusing him anew of not giving but merely buying. His unease left him stiffly formal. "I can only hope that I might be able to ease your burdens somewhat with this gift of—"

"Stop." Andrew reached forward and gripped his brother's hand through the fabric of his coat. "No. Please. Do not."

"I . . . I merely wish—"

"Don't even speak the words." Andrew's gaze seemed impossibly strong at that moment. "Just listen to what I am about to say. It is not that we don't need your money. We do. But I cannot accept it, and I would rather you not alter this moment by offering."

Reluctantly Charles withdrew his hand. "I fail to see how my largess would change anything."

"Listen, then, and I will try to explain." His brother's gaze seemed so clear as to look through to his soul. "Charles, my dear brother, I did not agree to help you for your own sake. I did it for God. There is only one thing I can accept from you at this point. One gift that will not distort God's peace and guidance, which Catherine and I have received."

Charles did not know why his brother's gaze left him feeling so naked. Nor was he certain that he wanted to know. "And that is?"

"That your quest be not just for Elspeth. That you seek God as well. And that your heart be honest when you find Him."

Charles did his best to hide how the words churned through his heart, his entire being. "I shall think upon what you say."

"I can ask for nothing more." Andrew had embraced him with such strength that Charles found it hard to draw a proper breath. "I love you, my brother," he heard in his ear. "May the Lord God bless your leaving, your quest, and your swift return."

Now as he balanced upon the wave-splashed deck, Charles felt as much as heard the wind's chant. *Your leaving, your quest, your swift return.* A burning rose from his chest to his eyes, and he was grateful for the privacy of that windswept planking. How could he, the eighth earl of Sutton, one of the richest men in all England, be brought low by the thought of his penniless clergyman brother? How could a man overlooked by the keepers of power and so destitute he worked leather with his own two hands leave Charles feeling utterly bereft? How could he think of his brother's clear-eyed gaze and yearn for things he did not even know how to express?

Chapter Fifteen

"Ah, your lordship, what a pleasure it is to welcome you into my home." The portly New Orleans dignitary wore a cloak of silvery blue, his accent heavy but the words correct. He bowed as only a Frenchman could, leaning over his cane and sweeping a frilly sleeve almost to the floor. Hundreds and hundreds of candles sparked and flickered from silver chandeliers and gilded wall candelabras. "I do so hope you enjoy our little fête."

"You are too kind, sir." Charles responded with a courtly bow of his own, aware that every eye in the manor's forecourt was upon him. "I was most gratified to receive your invitation."

"My wife is momentarily . . . ah, here she is." He turned and spoke in French to a woman heavily powdered in the fashion of the day. "May I have the pleasure of introducing the earl of Sutton." In English he continued, "My wife, Madame LaGrange."

Charles sought fragments from his long-unused French. "Your servant, my lady."

"Ah, the honored gentleman speaks our tongue." The woman's hair, piled in silver ringlets, caught the candles' light, along with the jewels about her neck and wrists and fingers.

"Not well, not any longer, I'm afraid, madame. Please forgive me. My studies were many years ago. And only twice in the past ten years have I had the opportunity to visit your fair land." The effort of finding those words left him feeling slightly stifled within his velvet longcoat and frilled shirt. Not to mention the evening's humid heat.

"Yes, Lord Charles did indeed visit France," his host for the evening explained, pacing his French no doubt for Charles's benefit. "Once as his king's emissary!"

"Hardly an emissary, sir." But the message was clearly understood. Someone with contacts to the French court had heard of Charles's arrival and no doubt instructed the trader to invite Charles in the hopes of determining what he was doing in Louisiana. "I was merely one of a very large number of guests hosted by His Majesty," Charles demurred.

"Oh, to be invited to the court of Versailles," the woman enthused coyly. "What was it like, m'sieur?"

"Most impressive." In truth, he had thought it rather outlandish. But the Harrow estate included holdings near Bordeaux that had been stripped away when the latest war had broken out. Charles had agreed to be part of the king's mission in the hopes of recovering some of his holdings. It had been a most difficult and fruitless month. The food in particular had been appalling. The royal banquet had contained nineteen different courses—one had been snails cooked in cream and wine and garlic, another consisting entirely of the tongues of small birds, yet another of peacocks stuffed with an oily fish. And upon the streets of Paris, Charles had seen poverty unlike anything at home, a beggary that had left him speechless. "Grand and glorious, madame. It was an honor to attend," he reported to her rapt attention.

"And now the English earl is here in New Orleans," the jolly trader announced to all who listened. The trader, according to the ship's captain, was one of the wealthiest men in New Orleans and a confidant to emissaries of both Spain and France. "No doubt to study our readiness for war!" And then laughed uproariously as if his words were merely in jest.

"In fact, I am only passing through." Charles spoke loudly enough to be heard above the din. "I seek a guide into the land of the Acadians."

This brought murmurs of astonishment. "You must be joking," the trader said in English.

One of the onlookers added scornfully, "They are uncouth and ill-bred, the consort of pirates and escaped slaves."

The trader waved his guest to silence, then continued to Charles, "M'lord, for a man of titles and wealth, even for a Frenchman to travel into Acadia would be suicide. For an *English* gentleman to do so—well . . ." The trader shrugged eloquently. "You cannot do this."

"But I must, m'sieur."

"Then you will die." The words were spoken with matter-of-fact regret. "The loathing they hold for the English is beyond belief."

"Where are your manners, Patrique?" his wife chided. "We have not even offered our guest refreshment."

"Of course, of course. Forgive me, m'lord." He waved the crowd through the ornate double-doors into the sparkling and candle-lit ballroom. "Let the festivities begin!"

The house was built in a strange mixture of Parisian grandeur and Louisianian necessity. The ballroom was high ceilinged and ringed by great double-doors. Each set of doors was curtained with a gauze so fine it invited in the night breeze, perfumed with the flowers that bloomed everywhere in the city, yet kept out the smallest mosquito. Charles had never seen such profusion of flora, nor such variety. Even the city streets were bordered with exotic bushes and blossom-laden vines.

The problem was the heat. Even now, three hours after sunset, Charles felt it difficult to draw in a breath of the hot and humid air. At midday it had been almost intolerable. The streets were empty of life for three hours, from noon to midafternoon, and then activity resumed when dusk purported to bring relief. And this was only early June. Charles could not fathom what this place would be like in August.

But the New Orleans society crowd did not seem to mind the heat. They laughed and danced and ate with a gusto unlike anything he had known in England. Or France, for that matter. The inhabitants of this charmed city seemed to have created a culture that was truly their own.

The men were attired in evening wear that resembled his in form alone. The cut was sharper, the material much lighter. When Charles asked about it, they proudly displayed a broadcloth woven not from wool, as was always the case in England, but rather from cotton. Their shirts were linen or silk and light as the evening breeze. The women wore gowns that appeared to be made from layers of chiffon, dyed a rainbow of colors and adorned with pearls and ribbons. They carried fans dipped in perfume that wafted aromas as sweet as the flower-scented air.

It was only after hours of chatter and eating and smiling and a dozen dances, two with the hostess, that Charles was able to draw his host to one side. "May I have a word in private?"

"I hope it is not about your journeying inland, Sir Charles. I would rather not be party to such a dangerous endeavor." But the trader led him into a side parlor, with the gilded mirrors and painted walls that Charles recalled from the manors around Paris. The trader offered him an inlaid box, half of which was full of hand-rolled cigars, the other half containing clay pipes and cut tobacco. "Do you wish to smoke?"

"Thank you, no."

The trader waved Charles into a seat, selected a cigar, and waited until it was lit and drawing well to say, "Whatever you seek to acquire from the Acadians, m'sieur, I can get it for you myself. Furs, wood, indigo—"

"I seek a man." Before the trader could continue, Charles held up his hand. "Please hear me out. He is an Acadian by the name of Henri Robichaud. He comes from the village of Minas on Cobequid Bay. He is married to a woman named Louise, or at least he was eighteen years ago."

The trader eyed him with a cautious merchant's gaze. "This village, Minas, it is in the northern colony of Acadia?"

"It was. In the region now called Nova Scotia. Yes." Charles pretended not to notice the change in expression that came with mention of the renamed province. "Henri Robichaud was formerly a clan leader. If he is alive, he might still be so today."

"*If* he is alive. You do not know this for a fact?"

"I know almost nothing. I am trying to pick up the pieces of a trail that has been lost for over eighteen years." Charles hesitated, then continued, "He may have a daughter."

Through the cloud of smoke came the question, "Her name?"

"I do not know. She was an infant at the time. She would be eighteen now."

"I see." Several puffs, then, "You seek a man who was expelled eighteen years ago from a province at the top of the continent. An expulsion in which almost half of the people perished, if the rumors are true."

"I realize it is a difficult task—"

"M'lord, *c'est impossible!*"

"—But I have no choice. I must seek this man." Charles let his genuine desperation seep into his voice. "I must."

The trader inspected his cigar, pursed his lips, and released a thin stream of smoke. "You must be willing to pay and pay dearly."

"I will offer a hundred gold sovereigns for the journey." Charles had spent the four weeks of his voyage south planning this. "Twenty now, eighty upon our return."

"That should be sufficient." Another puff, then, "And if this Monsieur Robichaud is found?"

"Then," Charles replied, "I intend to grant them both money and land."

The man rocked forward in astonishment. "I beg your pardon?"

"Everyone I speak with tells me the same things. The Acadians are still arriving here by the boatload. They are desperate for land they can call their own," Charles replied grimly. "I understand the Spanish grant them a small plot. And that there is more land available if one has means. I shall offer them enough for an entire village. Here or back in Nova Scotia. It is their choice."

"But, m'lord—"

Charles leaned forward and said with all the quiet force he could muster, "I must find this man. And his daughter. If they exist at all."

Chapter Sixteen

A morning mist rose from the bayou to greet the dawn. The rowers lifted and dipped their oars in a steady rhythm, the gentle creaking of the oarlocks echoing the birdsong in the air's stillness. They traveled a watery tunnel twenty paces wide and roofed by interlocking branches. Here and there sunlight lanced through the leaves, slender golden pillars that seemed to hold the bayou and the trees and the morning in proper place. Spanish moss hung from trunks and branches and along the banks. The motionless gray veils suggested to Charles that here, in this place, it was not just wind that was unable to reach through the verdant growth. Here not even time held much sway. Days and years and even centuries could come and go, and it all would remain untouched. In the distance a wild animal screamed shrilly, adding to the mysteriousness of this place and this world.

They had already been traveling for two hours in the early morning light. The guide had ordered them up and into the boats while the night was still black as the grave. His name was Albain, an Acadian who never spoke unless it was to order them about. There was something else to Albain, a dark shadow that had etched itself deeply into his eyes and his face. Had the New Orleans trader not insisted that the man was to be trusted, that he was the only man with any likelihood of getting Charles in and out alive, Charles would never have stepped into Albain's boat, much less traveled upriver with him.

Their company numbered ten and included two Spanish soldiers assigned to Charles by a nervous New Orleans mayor, fearful that his disappearance might spark an international incident. Besides Albain and himself, there were also two French mercenaries and four of the trader's most trusted servants. The ship's captain had wanted to send a bevy of his own men, but the trader had adamantly refused to include them; English soldiers, the trader had insisted, would never come out alive.

Charles had left his own clothes behind. He was dressed as the others, in dark long-coat and homespun shirt and sweat-stained hat. All the men save Charles carried arms. Charles had decided he should arrive with hands open and empty. It was the one time Albain had looked at him with anything that approached respect. As it was, their three skiffs sprouted a multitude of long-barreled rifles.

They held to small rivulets, never entering large bodies of water except in the dead of night. When Charles had asked about it, Albain had tersely replied that the best way to make sure nobody took his scalp was to not show it.

Up ahead their bayou joined with a larger river, one great enough to permit direct sunlight. Charles took an easy breath, glad to leave behind the suffocating tunnel, at least for a little while.

Albain muttered, "Be ready."

"What?" Charles looked about in alarm. "Why?"

Albain watched as the two mercenaries lifted their muskets and checked the triggers and the prime charges. "We have arrived."

Charles searched ahead. He saw nothing

but sun-dappled water, more forest, and Spanish moss. "Arrived where?"

Albain gestured with his paddle, motioning to the skiffs behind him to move closer to the side bank. "Plaquemine."

Charles's first impressions of this southern Acadian settlement were of woodsmoke and the sound of wailing. Long before he could see it, he could hear it and smell it. Bacon fat, woodsmoke, and voices drifted in the still air. Their three skiffs joined in behind nine larger vessels, all headed for the grassy embankment at the edge of a steep-sided bayou. Their own boat closed near enough that Charles could see most of the shipboard faces, immigrant Acadians who carried shadows so penetrating they seemed frozen in granite. He did not understand their words, but the emotions were clear. The immigrants were dismayed by their first sight of Plaquemine, the women in particular. Charles could well understand why. The settlement did not offer a welcoming first impression.

The village, large and haphazard, was built of wood and mud wattle as gray as

Spanish moss. Smoke from dozens of fires rose and drifted in the windless air, forming smudges above the rooftops and the high branches of the trees that had been left standing among the houses. Dogs and pigs and chickens clamored about the lanes along with the villagers.

No one paid their arrival much mind, suggesting that such overcrowded vessels as those ahead of them, or overarmed skiffs like their own, arrived here all too often.

Charles murmured, almost to himself, "What is this hamlet?"

"Plaquemine," Albain repeated. "The first Acadian settlement off the great Mississippi."

"This place is dreadful," Charles said, unable to hold back the feeling.

Albain seemed to find that amusing, at least enough for his eyes to squint in a smile that did not touch his mouth. "They say all the sorrow we have carried is brought and laid to rest in Plaquemine. Only then can we go ahead to a new future."

The village improved slightly upon closer inspection. Charles climbed a rickety landing platform and at Albain's direction moved to the shelter of a neighboring tree. An older man hurried over to inspect Albain and his motley band, dismissed them just as

183

swiftly, and turned to the people disembarking from the other boats. He ordered his three assistants forward to help the women and children. The platform was swiftly covered with tattered holdalls and salt-stained chests and bulky tarpaulins knotted around belongings. The villager began to speak in rapid French, clearly welcoming the forlorn group and pointing to where a pair of women tended a great black pot over a smoldering fire. Several of the older children moved over to the pot and were given wooden bowls and spoons. The villager kept speaking, pointing north, pointing west.

A piercing cry captured everyone's attention, and Charles turned with the others as a middle-aged woman stumbled across the village's central lane, her eyes wide in what could have been wonder or terror. She would have fallen directly into the cooking fire had one of the cooks not saved her. The woman probably did not even feel the arms that gripped her, for her entire being remained focused upon the landing platform.

A man standing by the boats shouted hoarsely in response. And another. They broke free of the gathering and raced up the bank. The woman shook off the arms holding her and lurched forward. The men ran to meet her, shouting, embracing, crying.

The cries were taken up by two women on the landing, who also ran to embrace the trio. They in turn were joined by half a dozen children, wailing and frightened by what they clearly did not understand. When the village woman saw the little ones, she broke free and dropped to her knees, holding her arms out to them. The men and women from the vessel gently urged the children forward, until all of the family were reunited upon the banks, holding one another and crying aloud.

A hand touched Charles's arm. Albain's eyes glittered darkly as he leaned forward and said, "This was true what you said about giving my people land?"

Shaken by the scene, Charles said, "Y-yes. Find Henri Robichaud and I will give these people money enough for a new village."

"Come," Albain said, turning away. "We must find a safe place to wait."

"Wait for what?" But Albain was already moving down the lane. The men closed in around Charles, scouting the village with warriors' caution.

Albain settled them at the back table of a squalid inn, then departed. The tavern's midday crowd was mostly male and all were armed. Their crew received more than a few glances, all of them malicious. The inn-keeper walked over and slapped down two pitchers and a stack of clay mugs, casting Charles a darkly vicious look before turning away.

One of the French mercenaries muttered something that Charles did not understand. He turned to the trader's senior man, a slight fellow with the look of a bookkeeper. "What did he say?"

The servant acted as the trader's inter-preter, and he spoke a precise English, though accented. He wiped his face with a handkerchief and replied, "The soldier, he says this place has the odor of a killing ground."

Charles leaned against the back wall, re-signed to the wait. He felt utterly powerless, friendless, nameless, bereft of all that shaped his world and his life. And for what? Because everything in his heritage had taught him that it was essential to have an heir. Someone to whom he could leave all his earthly pos-sessions. His land, his title, his wealth. And someone to carry on the Harrow bloodline.

Charles sat and watched smoke from the inn's cooking fire drift up to the raftered ceil-ing. Where was his land and his wealth now? What worth did his title have here? The inn's dank gloom reflected his own mental state.

For some reason the clear eyes of his brother seemed to pierce this dismal half-light. Charles thought of all Andrew had that he did not and found himself wondering what it would be like to pray.

Out of this same half-light appeared two figures, one their guide, Albain. The other man had a stocky build and looked solid as a fortress wall. The men about Charles stiffened, then relaxed at Albain's gesture. The man stood by the table and looked down at Charles for a long moment. His features were chiseled with the same deep sorrow lines as other Acadian faces Charles had seen. Yet his eyes held a deep glow that seemed unfazed either by the inn's gloom or the hostility surrounding them.

The man slid onto the bench directly opposite Charles and asked in a voice as soft and deep as his gaze, "Do you understand me?"

"If you speak slowly."

"How are you called?"

"Charles. Charles Harrow."

The man nodded. His raven hair was streaked with silver but thicker than a formal wig. Pulled straight back from his face, it framed his powerful features with age and wisdom. "I did not believe it when they told me. But I believe it now."

"What . . ." Then in a flash Charles understood. He looked up to Albain standing behind the stranger and said, "You knew where to find him all along."

"All Acadia knows Henri Robichaud," Albain replied. "All Cajuns know this name. The question was not where to find him. The question was if Henri Robichaud wished to be found."

Henri drew his attention back with the words, "I see your brother in you."

Charles gripped the table's edge. "You knew my brother?"

"We met but once. But, yes, I think it is true to say I know him. How is he?"

"Good. He is doing well."

"And his wife, Catherine?"

"She is fine."

"And . . ." Henri's eyes took on a deeper intensity. "The daughter?"

"Anne. She is fine."

"Tell me of her."

Charles shifted, not certain where the conversation was headed. The light suddenly dawned. Of course. Andrew and Catherine had this man's blood daughter. He understood now the expression on the face before him. He took a deep breath and leaned forward.

"She is not only well, m'sieur, she is a

lovely, gracious young woman. She has brought much joy to the home of my brother."

For one moment the man before him closed his eyes tightly, a shudder shaking his sturdy frame as his lips moved soundlessly. When he lifted his gaze, Charles noted that his deep-set eyes held tears that he could not totally hide. He said, "I thank you," with such deep feeling that Charles said, "Yes, I understand."

The two men exchanged a long look. Then Henri asked, "Is it true what Albain told us? That you offer land?"

The land. Charles bit down on his impatience. Henri was not the negotiator here—he was. *The land.* Though there was none of the desperation in Henri's question that he had seen outside, the intensity was the same. "Yes," he finally answered.

Albain looked down at the seated stranger. "Do you believe him?"

"This man I do not know," Henri said, cocking his head to one side. "But his brother I know. And his brother I would trust with my life."

Charles felt the words strike deep. Even here, in a circumstance so removed from his own that it might as well have been drawn from a different world entirely, even here his brother was known and revered. Not Charles with his wealth and his power and his titles. No. After eighteen years apart, with only one meeting to go on, still this man held Andrew close and called him a friend. "My brother is one of the finest men I have ever known," Charles grudgingly acknowledged.

His words seemed to have been the ones Henri was awaiting. With a tiny glimmer of a smile, he said, "I see a hint of her in you."

"Who is that?"

"My daughter." He rose to his feet. "Come. We go."

Chapter Seventeen

The group traveled all that day through sweltering heat. Even so, Charles took his turn at the oars, challenged by the silent, sturdy Frenchman to push himself more than was comfortable. He was not at ease with the silence of these Acadians, their sparing use of words or sounds of any kind. But he did not break it. The surroundings through which they traveled were too strange, too hot, too close.

The shock totally unarmed him when Charles had heard Henri's statement concerning Nicole. His heart had leaped within his chest when Henri had spoken of his daughter and the glimmer of likeness she bore to a Harrow. Charles had the immediate hope that she was someone who could easily bear the family likeness and carriage, the same regal manner. To find an heir was a great relief. To have one he could be proud of was an unexpected blessing.

Now, facing Henri's broad back, Charles carefully brought up the subject of the young woman, wanting to know more about her. Without turning around, Henri had replied, "Oh, she is not here. She has already left."

"Left?" Charles did not want to believe his ears. "What do you mean she has left? When will she return?"

Henri had sighed at that and shaken his head. "I do not know. It is a long journey— that I know all too well. We pray that with God's mercies it will go smoothly and swiftly."

"But where did she go?" insisted Charles. "To New Orleans?"

Henri had turned to face him then. The rhythm of his oar did not miss a beat as it swept in long strokes, disturbing only momentarily the calm surface of the deep, dark bayou waters. "New Orleans? No, no. She has left for Acadia."

The burly man had no idea how his news

smote Charles. For one moment he bowed his head in defeat. He had come so far, at such cost—and the girl was not here. Then the truth grasped his attention. She was heading for *Acadia*. With his swifter vessel he might still catch up to her there. Charles felt an urgency overtake his entire being. He must return to New Orleans and turn his ship northward again. He wanted to be on the scene if and when she found her parents.

But in spite of his desire to change course and continue his quest for the girl, something kept him silently rowing behind Henri deeper into the bayou. And of course Henri did not know of the full extent of his search, his ultimate goal in coming here. Or if he had guessed, he gave no sign.

In the hour after sunset they drew the canoes to a grassy embankment and made camp. They worked by torchlight, so weary they scarcely had the energy to gather firewood, much less talk. They ate a dinner of cornmeal baked on a stone, along with crawfish netted that afternoon and roasted over the fire. When the mosquitoes gathered like a swirling black cloud, Spanish moss was pulled from the trees and cast upon the fire. Charles followed the others' example and drew in close to the smoke. When he had finished eating, he lay down on the ground and drew an oily blanket about his head and shoulders. He had time for a single silent complaint about the smell and the sticky heat, then was asleep.

He was awakened by someone kicking his boot. Charles tossed back the blanket, rose, and stretched. A dawn mist had gathered and closed in about them. One of the men returned carrying three snakes, as long as he was tall. The fire was banked up high, the snakes were skinned and their meat skewered upon long branches, and Charles joined the others as they cooked and ate their breakfast.

As he was finishing, Albain pointed over to an opening in the mist and a passing alligator in the bayou. The guide and Henri exchanged quiet humor over Charles's and the Spanish soldiers' fearful fascination. The beast was eighteen feet long from spiny snout to the end of his swinging tail. Teeth as long as Charles's hand jutted from the long mouth, and the gator seemed to hold a hungry smile as he passed.

Charles really did not feel rested after the night on the ground. As they continued up the mist-clad bayou, he felt that he was becoming disembodied. The tunnel of moss-hung trees stretched on endlessly, like his quest. There was no end to his journey, no answer to his questions. None. He was doomed to travel for the rest of his life, without purpose, without meaning. Charles drank water from the gourd offered by the man in front of him, took his turn at the oars, endured the heat and the insects and the strange cries rising from the forest. He sweated and he rowed and he felt that all his life had been leading him to this moment.

The journey became a time of facing the utter hopelessness of his plight. Lonely and friendless and poor. He seemed to float outside his body, removed from all the trappings that had captured his attention and purpose all his life long. It was not merely that this journey had taken him away from all he owned. In truth, he had never possessed anything of value at all. He saw that now. The wealth and the responsibilities and the power had done little more than blind him to what he had carried within him. His heart had been as empty as the green tunnel through which he now traveled. He had lived a truly barren life.

A quiet murmur from his fellow travelers brought his attention back to the present. Charles focused with an effort and saw a mirage rise from the mists. White houses with tall roofs stood in orderly rows, surrounded by limewashed fences. A dog ran down the bank and barked, only to be silenced by Henri's quiet command. The banks were green and as well tended as the houses. Henri pointed, and they pulled into the well-built landing stage and halted.

Henri stepped lightly from the skiff, then halted the others with a single motion. He looked at Charles but spoke to them all. "You must wait here while I tell my wife and . . . wait here."

The stocky man then turned and vanished into the mist and the growing silver light of the morning.

Chapter Eighteen

All the way home Henri wrestled over the words to tell Louise. He tried one phrase, then another. None of them sounded right, none even the slightest bit adequate. How did one tell a mother that her daughter, lost for all these years, was as they had prayed, alive and well? How did you break a heart at the same time that you mended it?

At last he drew aside from the path and bent to his knees by the stump of a tree. Clutching his hands before him, he bowed his head and cried out his anguish and his joy. "God, I have such good news. Our prayers of many years have been answered—and I thank you." Tears began to stream down the creased face as the reality of the words sank deeper into the heart of the father. "And now I need to tell the news to Louise. The pain of loss will come again. She has just told the daughter she has known and loved good-bye, and now . . . now she must hear this. That her first daughter, the one she bore and fought to save, is still of this world . . . but not of our world. Help me to choose the right words, my Father. Give me wisdom, Lord. Prepare her heart for the news. Even now. Before I walk the path. Before I enter the stoop. Give her calm and quiet and peace so that she might receive this great news as heaven's blessing."

Henri remained silent for several more minutes, then he rose, wiped his cheeks on the sleeve of his shirt, took a deep breath, and proceeded on the path that led to home.

Louise was in the kitchen shaping the morning bread with sure and practiced hands. She looked up only briefly, then spoke with her eyes turned back to her work.

"You are back. I did not know when you would return. I have yet to make the porridge. I did not know what business of the clan had called you off on such sudden notice. You'd think they could let a man get his crops in before calling him down to Pla-quemine. Surely there is nothing so impor-tant that one should be dragged from his fields to—"

"It was important," said Henri, fighting for calmness when in truth his heart was pounding.

Louise did not even lift her eyes. "Ah, I suppose so. To men, all things to do with land and boats and nets and—"

"It was not of such common things."

Louise glanced over, then turned back to her kneading. "I am sorry to be late with your breakfast. Without Nicole's help . . ." She did not finish.

Henri remained silent. He still did not know where to start, and Louise had given him no opening. He studied his hands, then began to rub them together. He could feel the calluses. The roughness of the palms. He cleared his throat. But he did not speak, for Louise was speaking.

"I had the strangest dream last night."

He noticed the emotion in his wife's voice, as though she was musing yet deeply touched.

"Yes?" he responded.

"It was of Antoinette." Her voice broke on the name, and for a few moments she was not able to go on. Henri waited, willing himself not to hurry her.

"She was no longer a baby," Louise said softly. "I thought . . . I thought that strange. In the many dreams I have had of her, she has always been a child. The infant I left with Catherine. I always see her as I saw her last, bundled in her blanket, her face pinched and pale with pain." She stopped and shook her head again as though trying to make the pieces of the dream fall into some pattern that would make sense. "But not last night."

Henri noticed the brightness of her eyes, the unshed tears, before she turned back to the dough. Still he held his tongue.

"She was not a baby. She was grown. And her face . . . her face was no longer pinched. She looked so peaceful. I couldn't see her features clearly. There was a fog or a mist or something. But I sensed that she had a tender smile, as though she knew something she wished to tell me. She stood in the meadow and she . . . she reached out her hand to me. And then she was gone."

"Did it make you sad?" asked Henri, his voice husky. But even as he asked the question, he knew the answer. The tears that Louise struggled to hold back were not tears of distress. Her face was calm, her manner relaxed. She was simply sharing with the man she loved an experience that had touched her soul.

"No." Louise put the baking pan in the clay oven and turned to make the porridge. "Something about it put my heart at rest."

Henri cleared his throat again. "A man has come back with me. He is visiting our village."

"From Acadia?" she asked.

"Well . . . yes . . . but no," he tried to explain. "He comes from England."

He saw her eyes grow dark. Though the bitterness had been dealt with long ago, the mention of the English still brought pain.

"He was in Acadia on his way here. He . . . he has kin there." At the look in her eyes, he added, "He has brought some news."

Louise stood as a statue, pot and spoon in hand.

"He had spent time with his brother and wife." A deep breath, then, "His name is Charles Harrow."

His wife's face went deathly pale. He poised himself in case he should need to leap to her side. But Louise did not faint. She crossed to a kitchen chair and lowered herself slowly. Her eyes stared, unseeing. Her lips trembled as she worked at words that would not come. She put the bowl down but held the spoon limply in the hand that settled in her lap. Henri knew he had to quickly finish with the telling.

"He . . . he met our Antoinette."

"Antoinette." Just the name, but spoken with such depth of feeling. Such anguish of soul. But holding such thankfulness. Henri crossed to her quickly and took her in his arms. They clung to each other, their tears mingling, their bodies rocking in tune to the song in their hearts. It was many minutes before either of them could speak, but there was really no need. All that was necessary for the present had already been said.

Charles was ushered into the Robichaud home as though he were an angel in disguise. Louise had found her tongue and bustled about, seeking first his comfort and then plying him with questions. Over and over he had to tell them of Anne. How she looked, how she spoke, how she moved. Did she bear family resemblance? What color was her hair? Her eyes? Was she tall? Short? Dark or fair? Did she know of them? Charles answered them with courtesy and patience. He wished he had studied the girl more closely, but in most instances his memory served him well.

They were pleased to know that Catherine had taught their daughter her own French tongue. Louise, brushing at constant tears, exclaimed that it was so much like Catherine. The news that the girl was seeking to learn from a doctor so she might help those who were ill was particularly moving to her parents. When it came to their question of the girl's personal faith, Charles was at a loss as to how to describe what he had seen. He did not know the words. He'd never had the experience. So he told them of Anne's conversations concerning her deep trust in God. The news seemed to touch them most deeply, and they clung to each other's hands and dipped their heads in silent thankfulness.

Charles could only watch. If he had expected anger or hostility from this French family, he could not have been more in error. Even the sons of the home greeted him with respect. And the faith that he saw reflected in faces of people who had suffered dreadfully at the hands of others, at the hands of his fellow Englishmen, shook him to his very core. *How can people who have been harassed, plundered, nearly destroyed, look to God with so much open trust?*

Charles could only shake his head in wonderment. It was beyond his understanding.

Chapter Ninteen

The long lane connecting Halifax's harbor to the central square was a broad thoroughfare, lined on both sides by buildings of stone and timber. The effect this day was one of a funnel, directing the wind and the stinging rain straight into his face, but Andrew did not mind. The weather was in fact rather bracing, coming as it did after one of the mildest springs in memory. He welcomed the brisk salt air. He always enjoyed his visits in Halifax. He found the city an exhilarating and uplifting experience after weeks or months in his tiny village. If truth be known, his only concern this gray and blustery day was his daughter's mood.

Anne walked alongside him, her face hidden beneath the brim of her bonnet. But he had seen enough to know that her eyes were troubled, her expression guarded. For the life of him, Andrew could not understand why. Though her accommodations were spartan, her rooms were clean and located in a fine Christian home. The landlady seemed genuinely taken with his daughter, and she had even gone so far as to say that

Anne had become one of the family.

The young doctor she worked for was equally impressive, a tall Welshman with the fine red hair and freckled complexion of his heritage. He was a clear-eyed, intelligent young man, and from the three visits Andrew had made to Halifax since Anne's arrival here six weeks earlier, he had gathered the impression that Dr. Cyril Mann knew the Scriptures and lived their creed.

Yet something clearly was now troubling Anne. She did not respond beyond a few murmured acknowledgments to his comments about her mother or events in the village. She had concluded her errands with a minimum of words, barely returning the market woman's warm greetings. Andrew could not help but appreciate the fact that Anne was being warmly accepted by these townsfolk. But today she seemed guarded and withdrawn.

Andrew checked his pocket watch. It was approaching midday, and he had planned to depart for Georgetown that afternoon. But with the distraction Anne was showing, perhaps he should postpone his return one more day. Catherine would worry, but certainly they would both worry more if this immediate concern was left unanswered. Andrew slid the watch back into his vest pocket and cast a tentative glance over his daughter's bonnet. Anne was a child no longer. He had observed the way the patients in Dr. Mann's outer chamber treated her, showing her similar respect as they did the doctor. He had watched the way Anne had responded, with warmth and concern and a special love for the ailing children. Andrew's heart had swelled with pride over her manner and her genuine gift of compassion. Yes, his little Anne was a child no longer.

They crossed the final street and walked down the covered plank sidewalk to the building where Anne worked. The wood bore new gilded letters announcing that this was the office of Dr. Cyril Mann, trained in the arts of medicine at London and Edinburgh. A small placard included the information that the office was closed over the noon hour from twelve o'clock until two. Anne used her own key to open the door, then stepped aside for her father to enter first. Andrew watched as she closed and locked the door behind them. She put down her basket on the bench by the window, calling out, "Dr. Mann?"

When there was no answer, Anne briskly turned from him and walked to the back room, calling once more.

When she returned, it was to announce,

"He is not back. Good. Father, please sit down."

"Anne—"

"Sit down, Father. Please. There is something I must tell you."

Her agitated and rather formal tone only increased his unease. But Andrew felt he had no choice except to do as she said. Indeed, she was a child no longer.

Anne stood before him, her arms crossed and hands clutching her elbows. She started to speak, then released her hold on her arms to untie her bonnet. She lifted the hat and shook her head, allowing her hair to spill down over the back of her dress. It was a gesture Andrew knew so well, one he had seen her make a myriad of times. Only today it seemed to forebode change and mystery both.

She looked down at him, her hands clenching and unclenching at her side. "Father, I wish to ask you your impressions of the doctor." Her words came in a practiced rush, as if she had carefully planned each one.

"Well, I—"

"Please. I must know what you think, Father."

"He seems to be a fine man," Andrew replied quietly. "I do not know him well, but my impression is of a good Christian and a caring, skilled doctor."

"He is that and more. He . . . I . . ." She seemed to struggle to find breath.

Andrew nodded. He could see where this was heading. He found himself wanting to smile and weep at the same time. But he forced his emotions back with a noisy swallow.

"I know this is very sudden," she hurried on. "I know we have not known each other even two months. But we have been working together every day, and we have had opportunities to talk at length—about our families, about our interests, about faith." Anne stopped suddenly and carefully searched Andrew's face. She then said, "Cyril and I have come to love each other."

Andrew observed the tension in his daughter's face and knew she had spent sleepless hours preparing what she would tell him. He held himself very still, granting her the time to say this at her own pace. But in truth his eyes were burning slightly, and he wanted nothing more than to take out his watch and turn back the dial. Just a few more hours. Another day or two to cherish her as the beloved daughter who had been a light to his and Catherine's life. Another week of knowing her as theirs and theirs alone. But he said nothing and made no motion except to blink very hard. Time stood still for no one. Not even a father who wished to weep bittersweet tears for a daughter who was a child no more.

"I have seen the way he is at work and at prayer. And he is a man who lives his faith." Her words were as shaky as her breath. But she pressed on, "I . . . I love him dearly, and I know that time will only strengthen these feelings. Cyril has asked for my hand in marriage, Father. I know he should be the one to say this, but I wanted to speak with you first and tell you that he is a good man."

"I believe you," Andrew murmured.

"He is a fine and caring . . ." She paused. "You do?"

"Yes." Andrew forced down another swallow. "As I said, I do not know your good doctor very well. But I know you. And I know that you would take great care in whom you allowed to capture your heart."

Her legs seemed to give way, and she sank onto the bench beside him. "Then you don't object?"

"To your marrying? No." He hesitated, then confessed, "Well, perhaps a little bit."

"But Father, he is—"

"Oh, it is not because of him. It is because of you."

Anne's mouth opened, but it took a long moment for her to form the word, "Me?"

"You are so precious to Catherine and me, I find it hard to think of you ever growing up and away from us."

One moment she was a carefully composed young woman, the next her face seemed awash in tears. She flung herself into Andrew's arms and wept quietly. Andrew held his daughter close and traced her soft hair with one hand. She whispered to his shoulder, "Oh, Father, I was so afraid you would object."

"I cannot." Oh, to hold his child like this for years and years and years. But the time of holding her as his little girl had already passed. He could not mourn the loss but must look to the promises of the future. He cleared his throat and spoke and was amazed that his voice was strong and even. "I shall bless you and give you up. And if you like, upon the day you two choose, I shall wed you before God and pray that He bless your union with a daughter as fine as you."

Chapter Twenty

In the seven weeks Nicole had been gone from home, less than half the distance to Acadia had been traveled. She gripped her hands together in frustration.

The ship they had boarded at the mouth of the Mississippi was the largest she had ever seen. Now she realized it was merely a coastal vessel, one made to sail into shallow waters and take on produce from hamlets that could not afford a true harbor. The problem was that such barques kept to no set schedule, halting at every village with goods to transport. Towns hailed the barque by flying a signal flag from a tall pole—or in some of the smallest settlements the flag was hung from a rooftop or a tree. It seemed to Nicole that they had stopped at every hamlet along the entire eastern shoreline.

Seven weeks after their departure, they were only as far as Charleston. In desperation, Guy had ordered them off the boat. His intention had been to arrive in Acadia before winter, see the place for himself, and either return together or send Nicole back while ships were still able to navigate the northern port. At this rate, he declared, they might not arrive in Acadia at all this season. Nicole had been heartily relieved to see the last of that cramped little vessel.

Not that being on land proved much better. They had been in the port for three days, all seven of their group crammed into one room of a harborside inn. There were many problems. None of them spoke more than a smattering of English. Returning to Charleston had brought up all the bad memories from Nicole's half-forgotten childhood in the area. Many of the locals still viewed the Acadians with grave suspicion. The same was true for many of the arriving ships' captains and crews. From dawn to dusk Guy and Pascal scoured the waterfront, and still they could not find a ship willing to take them north.

Guy was now off buying food for the family. He had taken over the task from Nicole because she became so enraged with the market folk when they refused to sell her anything. Besides, the prices they charged for meager fruit and day-old bread were outrageous. She was certain they were cheating the family because they were Acadians. But she had no way of knowing for sure, since she spoke almost no English. All she could be certain of was that the carefully hoarded store of silver coins was steadily dwindling.

Nicole sat on the stone seawall and made a lunch from two wizened apples and a wedge of hard cheese. On any other day the view would have enthralled her. The weather was balmy, the breeze perfumed with sea salt and spices carried by a nearby ship recently arrived from some faraway land. Tall masts rose from a dozen ships and more, and the quayside was crowded with a rainbow of people. But today she was tired and she was worried. Guy's youngest child had cried most of the night, and the blanket on which she had lain, with the middle cousin tucked to one side, had not offered much cushion from the hard plank floor. Her eyelids felt gritty from lack of sleep. If only they could find a ship—

Her eye was caught by a man stepping down from a carriage. He was dressed in clothes so fine and new they seemed to sparkle in the midday sun. His tricorner hat was lined with black velvet ribbon, his cuffs were laced, and his coat buttons shone like new silver coins. All the quayside paused to watch as two servants scrambled down from the carriage roof, both burdened by great sacks of fresh produce. The man carried nothing heavier than a silver-tipped cane.

On sudden impulse, Nicole found herself hurrying over to him. "Pardon me, m'sieur. Do you speak French?"

One of the sailors growled at her in what

was probably English, but she did not understand. Nor did she care. Her mother would have been horrified to think that Nicole had approached a strange man by herself. She did not care about that either. Heart pounding, all she could think, could hope, was that here stood a man in a powdered wig and clothes worth a king's ransom. A man of culture and education who might perhaps speak her language.

He waved the seaman back and replied in French with an English accent, "I speak a little. But you must talk slowly."

With her hopes racing ahead so, it was difficult to hold her impatience. But Nicole forced herself to form the words carefully. "My family and I search for a vessel to carry us north."

One of the seamen shifted his load and spoke up. The man waved him to silence and said, "Where north?"

"To Acadia, m'sieur. The city of Halifax."

He closed the distance between them with such speed that Nicole was hard pressed not to bolt. He studied her face with an intensity that frightened her. But all he said was, "You are Acadian?"

Nicole hesitated. She had been taught from an early age to value the truth more highly than silver. But she had also heard all her life how the British hated the Acadian people. So she finally answered, "French, m'sieur. We are French. From the province of Louisiana."

His face showed great disappointment. "And your name?"

Again she paused, knowing full well that Acadian names were as distinct as their heritage. But the second slur of the truth came more easily. "I travel with the family of my uncle, Monsieur Guy."

"I see." It was strange to interpret how the news affected him. The creases about his eyes and mouth deepened. "Well, it was too much to hope for, I suppose."

"M'sieur?"

"Nothing. You say you are traveling to Acadia?"

"Yes. We have relatives there. We wish to acquire land for farming."

"Land, land. Everyone is wanting land," he muttered. "How did you come to be here?"

"We traveled by coastal barque from New Orleans. It has taken us nearly two months to come this far." She could not keep the entreaty from her voice. "We must arrive before the autumn storms. Please, m'sieur, can you help us?"

The man inspected her searchingly. Then he slapped the cane on the side of his trousers. "Very well. Yes. I can offer you berths. How many are you?"

"Seven, m'sieur." She could scarcely believe her good fortune. She rushed on, "But three of them are very small, and we can all stay together in one cabin. Or on deck, we don't mind at all. We will take up no space, none."

"Slowly. You must speak more slowly."

Nicole took as great a breath as her pounding heart would allow and repeated what she had said.

The man waved her words away. "You can discuss that with the captain. He wishes to depart with the tide. How long will you be?"

"A few minutes only!" She reached for his sleeve, stopped herself in time. "Oh, m'sieur, a thousand, thousand thanks! I will go and fetch the family."

"Yes, and hurry."

"Of course, m'sieur!" She was already racing away. "I will fly!"

Chapter Twenty-one

Charles paced the ship's foredeck and tried to ignore the stifling heat. Confined to twelve paces east, twelve west, back and forth, his enclosure circumscribed by blue as far as he could see. The sun beat upon the ship and the sea like a hammer striking an anvil. The sails hung from the masts like forlorn flags. Every hour Captain Dillon sent the crew aloft to douse the canvas with water so as to catch the slightest bit of wind. Even so, the ship lay motionless, trapped in a prison of unbounded heat and sun and water.

The captain had rigged a sail for cover amidships for the sailors and passengers. But the shade offered little comfort, for there was no breeze to disperse the sun's fierce power. There had been none for three days. And every day the crew's muttering had grown stronger.

Charles was surprised the captain did not see fit to silence his men. Captain Kedrick Dillon was a taciturn fellow, as were many of his kind. He was also a strict disciplinarian, maintaining a taut and generally harmonious ship without use of the myriad of punishments available to a master at sea. He had said nothing when Charles had requested that berths be granted to the stranded French family—after all, Charles had paid well for the ship's exclusive use. And one look at the young lady's vibrant beauty had been enough for Captain Dillon to order a place where the family could be isolated from his men. So that morning, when the decks had been hollystoned and washed, and the crew then had gathered in tight clusters and cast dark glances about the ship, Charles had been surprised that the captain had not shouted at them to disperse and get about their business.

Instead, Captain Dillon gathered with his officers, who also spent much time muttering among themselves. They climbed the crow's nest and searched the endless blue expanse with telescopes. They inspected the mercury barometer, and they examined the almanacs. They cursed the vagaries of nature as the captain's face grew ever more creased with stern worry. And with each passing hour, the heat grew more suffocating still.

The captain approached Charles and said, "M'lord, with this heat I think we'd be better off serving our noon repast on deck. Perhaps you'd care to join my officers and myself."

"As you wish." Charles watched as

sweating seamen set up plank tables astride sea chests and hauled benches up from be-lowdecks. They served a cold meal of mutton and hardtack and cheese and small green apples in a bowl of water to keep them fresh. The mutterings did not diminish with the meal, however. As the captain approached the table, one of the seamen was pushed forward by his mates. Charles watched as he knuckled his forehead and said, "Beggin' your pardon, sir. But we was wondering if p'rhaps we shouldn't lower the boats."

"I appreciate your concern, Malthus. But there is nowhere to row." The captain's words halted all activity about the decks. Again, however, he did not reprimand the crew as Charles expected. Instead, he pitched his voice louder and said, "A few of you have sailed these waters with me. As you know, the coastline here is as treacherous as any around the world. Barrier islands are fronted by sandbars and shoals that shift with every storm." His features turned hard, his voice stern. "I appreciate your concern for this ship," he repeated, "but I will not have my orders questioned again. Is that clear?" When the men did not respond, he barked as loudly as one of his cannons, "*Is that clear?*"

"Aye, aye, sir," came the chorused response.

"Very good. Bosun, pipe the men to their meal."

When the officers were seated and the meal joined, Charles ventured, "I hope you will forgive my forthrightness, but I am not certain exactly what just happened here."

"The men are worried about being overcome by a blow. They wanted to man the longboats and attempt to tow the ship into a safe harbor," the captain replied tersely. "Simmons, pass the hardtack, if you please."

"A blow," Charles said and pushed his plate aside. "Not again."

Dillon's gaze raised from his plate. "You've seen an Atlantic storm?"

"On the way from England." Charles could barely repress a shudder at the memory. "A dozen times and more I thought I was done for."

"Yes, the Atlantic is a treacherous lass, full of fire and brimstone when it suits her." Despite the grim words, Dillon ate with good appetite. "We're early in the season for a nor'easter, but this heat is uncommon close. And three days is long enough for trouble to brew out somewhere in deeper waters."

One of the junior officers ventured, "Begging your pardon, sir. But if we were to row in while it's still calm, wouldn't that be safe?"

"It would if we made it in time." He addressed his lieutenant. "Simmons, how far would you say we are from the coast?"

"I make it fifty miles, sir, give or take five for the jut of the islands, maybe even ten."

"You see? Between us, Simmons and I have made this journey a dozen times, more, and neither he nor I can even say for a certainty where landfall lies." The captain gave his head a grim shake. "The worst thing we could do is try for landfall, make it halfway, and lose the sea room we have now. Believe me, sir, you do not ever want to meet a barrier island in a storm. They lie low in the water, so low you can't make them out from the wave's peak."

"Like warm-water icebergs, they are," Lieutenant Simmons muttered. "Storms make them all but disappear. You're on them before you know it. First warning you have is when they rip out your keel."

"We are safer where we are," the captain agreed. "And hope—"

All talk ceased; all movement on deck suddenly was as if turned to stone. The sail rigged for shade ballooned up, almost lazy in its motion. Charles then lifted his head with the others but could feel no wind. Even so, the sail puffed once more and this time flapped down.

The officers rose as one man, leaping to the starboard railing. They stood tensely searching the horizon with telescopes and shaded eyes. Charles stared with them, yet saw nothing save the same relentless heat and sun and blue.

Even so, the captain snapped, "Have the sails rigged for storm. And cut down these awnings."

"Aye, sir."

Captain Dillon turned a hawk's eye toward Charles. "M'lord, I understand you speak a bit of the heathen tongue."

"Some, yes. But what—"

"Please tell our passengers they soon had best get below." The captain's eye moved from his telescope to add dire warning to his quiet tone. "And tell them it might do good to pray."

Chapter Twenty-two

Pray. The word echoed through the hot air like a challenge flung directly at Charles. He returned from speaking with the French family to observe the entire crew gathered along the eastward railing. A thin dark line appeared, so low it seemed to be wed to the sea and not the sky.

"You there!" The captain's roar spurred the men to instant action. "Batten down the hatches! Simmons!"

"Aye, sir!"

"Place your three best men on the wheel. With the first breath of wind in the sails, steer north by northeast. And set the storm anchors!"

"North by northeast it is, sir!"

That swift exchange was sufficient time for the horizon to be transformed. No longer was the storm a mere distant stain. Now thunderclouds were banked like a wave above the sea. The wall streaming toward them was a thousand hues of gray.

"Sir Charles! If you insist upon remaining on deck, I must require you to bind yourself to the lifeline."

Charles raised his hands and allowed a seaman to knot a rope about his waist, and then watched as the line's other end was attached to a longer rope attached to the center mast. He tested the rope, looked back to the horizon, and gasped aloud.

In the space of a half dozen breaths, the menacing clouds had raced so close as to now dominate their world. Where their ship lay becalmed, all was heat and windless waiting. Yet just a few leagues away, the thunderhead was a solid wall stretching from the sea's face to the highest heavens. Charles briefly recalled a painting he had once seen of a storm at sea. The artist had depicted approaching chariots of lightning bolts, drawn by steeds of wind and fire. He now understood the imagery.

The clouds were hanging so low to the water that he could no longer see beneath them. Blasted by occasional flickers of lightning, the storm raced toward them with the low rumble of distant thunder.

Charles turned and cast a glance aloft. All was furious activity now as sailors lashed the sails into tight quarter moons, just enough remaining to grant them steerage. He watched the last of the crew fly down the halyards to the deck, landing lightly as sparrows. His eye was then caught by the young Frenchwoman. She stood by the last opening below decks, watching the storm with the same sense of fearful fascination that he felt himself.

She chose that moment to turn and look up at him. Charles found himself giving a small wave and smile in reply. He liked her spirit. There was fear in those lovely young features, most certainly. No one but a fool would not be frightened at a time like this.

But the fear did not possess her, did not dominate her. She remained strong and steadfast, enough so that she could offer him her own smile in reply before vanishing belowdecks. Charles found himself regretting that the captain's shipboard discipline had not offered opportunity for him to know her better.

The first breath of wind caught the canvas and turned him back to sea. A mere featherweight, the swift puff lifted his coat and breathed the first measure of coolness he had known in days. He could no longer see the top of the clouds. They reached from just above the masthead to the very firmament, and they seemed close enough to touch.

The first breath of wind was utilized to steer the ship about, heading it directly into the face of the approaching fury. Charles understood this maneuver from his Atlantic crossing. Storms of this magnitude had to be met head-on.

Pray. The captain's charge came back to echo through the reaches of his mind, in time to the thunder that now rolled and roared almost continuously. He felt as though his entire life could well be captured in the symbolism of this day. He had lived for years in the calmness of wealth and power and position. Then suddenly, without warning, he realized the distant dark on the horizon meant jeopardy for his future and his legacy. Now he was beset by a storm so powerful it defied his imagination. Every last vestige of control of his life was suddenly whipped from his grasp. He felt as helpless as a child. And there was only one answer, one clarion call above it all. *Pray.*

Pray. The storm shrieked and wailed about them, so loud the youngest child's squalling could not be heard. The only word that fully formed in Nicole's mind was the Englishman's suggestion that they turn to God—which Guy and his family did with fervor. All huddled together in one corner, bracing against one another, sheltering the littlest ones with their bodies, and bedding down as best they could. They were praying aloud, but even seated directly alongside, Nicole could not hear the words. But she could see the fervency on their faces and the fear. Of course they prayed.

Yet she could not. It seemed such a simple gesture, to turn to the God of her father and mother and ask for help in this time of defenseless need. Was it only pride that kept her from joining the others? She could not seem to form a single complete thought, not even enough to ask the question, much less respond. All she felt was stubborn anger—at her weakness, at her fear, at her desire. Yes, she could not deny that she *wanted* to pray. So why not do so?

The ship rolled and crashed against the waves with maddening violence. It rode up high peaks, then slid down and down troughs so deep Nicole felt her stomach rise in her throat. At the bottom they struck what felt like solid walls, hammering everyone about with a force made worse because it seemed to be so careless, so random. The two middle children had become copiously ill and were now groaning and crying for it all to stop. She could not hear the words, but she knew what they were saying, for it was what she wanted as well.

A great roaring wave crashed into the boat, sending it sliding up and up and up, then pitching it down to slide again into the next trough, this one deeper and longer than the others, so deep Nicole thought she would lose control of her stomach also. Then they struck bottom with such force a great torrent of water poured in through the hatch, drenching them all. The water was so cold it made her gasp, but she also realized it at least cleaned the hold of the smell of fear and sickness.

She was tired, she was bruised from being knocked about, and now she was wet to the bone. She found herself thinking of the rich Englishman and the way he had spoken to them. He had seemed weary with what was to come, as though he had experienced such a storm before. Nicole found that hard to believe. How could anyone survive such a tempest and return to sea again?

Another rising peak, pushing them toward the back wall. Up and up they rose, then poised at the top, the wind shrieking so loud it seemed to tear at the wood with claws of air and rain, and the death-defying slide down the other side. Nicole gripped her little cousin beside her and tried to form the words to God. But they did not come. She was too honest for her own good, or so it seemed at that moment. She was terrified that this day might be her last, and yet there was no one to whom she might turn. No one she could believe in. Though all the arguments she had used against the existence of a God who cared enough to act on her behalf seemed to have been swept overboard in the storm, they did not leave her able to turn to the Lord. She felt an empty cavern at the center of her being. One so vacant and barren it felt as though the storm could blow directly through her, touching nothing in its passage.

Thunder boomed from all sides like a thousand voices shouting inside her terrified head and her empty heart. The storm mocked her when she could do nothing but hold to the wet and shivering bodies nearest her.

At the storm's height, an earsplitting crack shuddered through the vessel. The sound seemed too loud to be a mere fracturing of wood; it was as if the ship itself was splitting.

"All hands on deck!" Those were the first words shouted above the sea's roar since the storm had struck. Perhaps they could be heard because the shouts came from the bosun, the lieutenant, and the captain, almost within the same breath. "All hands on deck!"

The ship's mizzenmast had broken in the gale. The sailors and the officers grabbed hatchets and machetes and swords and hacked with all their strength at the ropes.

Charles himself was tossed a bone-handled knife by a seaman whose face he never saw, and he too joined in the frantic effort to saw every rope that connected the mast to the ship. Thankfully, the mast did not give way all at once. It fractured a head's height above the main deck and hung there, tilted at an angle. They raced to release the ropes before the mast whirled overboard in the wind, taking with it whatever was still attached.

Charles could not say why he had remained on deck. Without conscious thought, he had grasped at the railings as the wind tore at him with such force it had literally ripped away his coat, leaving him in shirt sleeves and drenched. Twice he had been saved from being washed overboard by the line about his middle. His flesh was burned raw and aching from the salty spray and from the rope's hold, yet still he did not go below. Every wave that rose before the ship seemed directed straight at him. Somehow he felt he had to stand and face whatever fate was sending his way.

The mast cracked further, and the men redoubled their efforts. A single remaining line would be enough to turn the mast into an anchor, tilting the boat to leeward until the roiling sea washed in and sunk them. A third crack, a fourth, and Charles released his death's grip of the rail to use both hands for sawing frantically at the next line. Men shouted and cursed and chopped with all the energy they had left. The mast gave a final ripping sound and careened overboard. Ropes flew like hemp snakes, lashing out as they followed the mast into the depths of the sea.

The men stood, chests heaving as they watched the last of the ropes disappear. As though finally convinced the ship would not give in to its fury, the wind shrieked a further delirious note and began to die. Charles could scarcely believe it was happening, and yet with each swooping rise upon the next wave, less wind lashed at them. The sea remained demented, but in the space of a quarter hour the wind eased to such a point that the captain sent sailors aloft to stretch out more sail. This meant they could steer around the worst of the seas. The trio of storm anchors were hauled up, some crew were directed to work the pumps, and the ship began to make way just as the first ray of sun lanced through the clouds.

Charles was mesmerized by the sight. Out of the terrifying darkness and desolation, a pillar of hope seemed to pierce into his very being. Though the storm continued to roll and shake the ship, though the sea remained blanketed in froth, still there was this sign that it would be over soon. He felt a powerful connection to that ray of sun, felt it with such intensity that he craned against the rail and searched the storm-flecked horizon, seeking the source.

"Give God the glory, sir!" The captain walked the tossing deck as easily as he would a village street. "We have survived another one, and you have shown yourself a good hand in a bad time!"

"It was nothing," Charles muttered, wishing the captain would go away and leave him to search for the message he feared would be lost to him.

"Quite the contrary!" Now that the storm was passing, the captain was full of cheer. "Rare is it that a landsman can act properly when the sea beasts roar." The captain nodded his approval. "It is a pleasure to sail with you, m'lord."

"Thank you," Charles murmured, but not merely to the captain. No. There before him, dancing about on waves still rising as high as their remaining two masts, he saw the answer. The message was clear. There would be more storms in his life, more times when human power and earthly possessions were stripped away. The challenge was not how to avoid them, for they would come. Oh yes. They would come. The question was, how would he use them? What would he learn? When the fury passed and he was in control once more, what lesson would he take from the encounter?

Charles turned from the rail, satisfied that for once in his life he had managed to ask himself the right question. He did not fully know the answer yet, but for the moment, the asking was enough.

Nicole handed the little girl, still weak and whimpering with passing fear, up to Guy. Then she climbed the ladder herself and stepped into a world transformed. The air and the sea and the ship itself seemed to shine. The light was impossibly bright, the sea and sky so beautiful it brought tears to her eyes. She staggered to the rail and took great draughts of the sweet air. The storm was passed, the world was sane once more. And she was alive. It was the sweetest breath she had ever drawn. She was alive.

And yet, and yet. As she opened her eyes, she found herself still hearing an echoing refrain. But the call to prayer was no longer shouted. It was whispered as soft as a distant gull's cry, almost lost upon the gentle wind.

Yes, she still wished she could pray. Thanksgiving welled up within her. But another part of her mind wanted to push it all aside, push the desire to pray down deep with the fear that was now passing. She had survived, and now she was free to go on with her life. *Her* life.

Even so, the whispered refrain called to her, and the empty feeling at the center of her being softly vibrated to the voice that only her heart could hear. Even so.

Chapter Twenty-three

Nicole walked over the cobblestones from the market back to the mission. A restless wind tossed her hair, and though she was still weary and bruised from the storm and the passage, she felt her heart responding with gusts as impatient as the wind. But to what, to whom? She no longer knew where this journey was taking her. To Acadia, yes, but what about this inner journey?

Nine days after the storm had blown itself to sun-tossed shreds, the ship had limped into Boston Harbor. The captain had informed them of the unplanned halt, to no one's surprise. A shattered stump had been all that remained of the mizzenmast, and four men were required to work the pumps every watch to keep the ship from foundering. The vessel's home port was as good a place as any to lay over for supplies and repairs. Besides which, the crew had been desperate to see their loved ones again.

The captain explained the layover this way: "My lady is not mortally wounded. But she is ailing and needs laying to and refitting."

Guy had listened to the wealthy Englishman's translation, then said in speech slow enough for Charles to understand, "Please tell the captain we are ever in his debt for saving us."

"It was my duty, sir, nothing more," was the message Captain Dillon had sent in return. He had halted further thanks by telling the travelers, "There is a seaman's mission run by the local pastorate. You'll find lodging there. And I'll pass word along the quayside that you're honorable folk seeking passage north."

Nicole had found herself studying the wealthy Englishman, the titled gentleman whose name she did not know other than "Lord Charles." He looked as tired and battered as all the others, yet there was something new in his gaze. Nicole had listened as much to the man's voice as she had to the discussion, and wondered if it was the life-threatening experience itself that had marked him so. In the end she decided not, as the man did not seem afraid so much as uncertain. It was a sentiment and a confusion she could well understand. As they had broken away from the discussion, Nicole found herself asking, "What will you do, m'sieur?"

He had examined her with a frankness that matched her own. "I have holdings, a new land grant, in the eastern portion of this colony. I am considering a trip out to inspect them."

She had nodded, feeling the eyes of the others watching. "Your haste to arrive in Halifax has lessened?" she asked, lowering her voice.

His gaze had remained on her face, and he gave a brief smile. "To be perfectly honest, mademoiselle, I am no longer certain of what I seek."

"I understand," she had murmured. "All too well."

———— ✤ ————

Nicole turned into the side alley that brought her to the mission entrance. She almost collided with an elderly man, the one person she had come to know by name. "Oh, your pardon, Monsieur Collins."

"What a lovely way to brighten up a morning," he exclaimed, doffing his black hat with the sharp corners and the hard round crown. "You are well this glorious day, I trust?"

The Reverend Collins served as both an overseer of the mission and a teacher at the seminary. It was in fact the seminary and the attached church that financed the waterfront mission. Many of the quayside inns were also bawdy houses, and all served strong drink. Many years back the seminary had seen a need for housing visiting seamen and families in an atmosphere of wholesome Christian principles and offering the Samaritan's hospitality. Those who were able to pay did so. All others were housed and fed for two weeks during the summer traveling season. In the winter those who wished to stay and work were made welcome. All this Nicole had learned from Reverend Collins, the only member of the seminary faculty who spoke French. He did so with a mishmash of accents, for the man had lived in Normandy as a child, back before relations between the French and English had become strained, and then served as a missionary in the province of Quebec. As professor of New Testament, he spoke German as well, and read Greek and Latin and a little Hebrew. Over his years of ministry he had added to this a smattering of several American Indian tongues. Nicole had observed how others within the seminary community, both students and faculty alike, treated the professor with deference and warmth. Yet he held no airs whatsoever, as though his knowledge and his intelligence were of little importance.

What mattered most to Nicole was the light in his eyes, a gentle flame that seemed to reach below what she was able to see herself and soothe the torment that had remained long after the outer storm had passed. Nicole hesitated, then replied, "I am rested, thank you."

"Ah, well, that is good, is it not? We all must find a safe harbor, a place to recover from life's tempests." He displayed an untidy gray beard, one long enough to tickle the upper buttons of his black coat. He seemed as unaware of his appearance as he was of his talents. "And how are the rest of your family?"

"The young one rested better last night,

and the children are eating well."

"Yes, I have noticed how the two boys seem to be losing their pallor." He smiled as two students passed them, both doffing hats and bowing low to their instructor. "Such a pity that you had to endure that frightful storm."

"It was most wretched, m'sieur." Nicole found it surprising, both that he was willing to stand and speak with her as though she mattered, and that she wished to remain as well. "Have you ever been to sea yourself?"

"Not since my youth, and only then with great trepidation. I even made the trek from Quebec overland, and that was back when there was not even a trail to follow." He chuckled and patted the broadcloth covering his ample belly. "I fear my constitution does not agree with the sea. I have been known to grow queasy just standing on the dock and watching the waves roll in."

Nicole tried to return his smile but was unable to keep her mouth from trembling. Pastor Collins must have noticed instantly, because his face creased with deep concern and he said, "My dear! Have I distressed you in some way?"

"No, no, nothing like that." But his concern made it even harder for her to maintain control. Nicole tried to laugh, but the sound was made false by the catch in her throat. "I am tired, nothing more."

"Of course you are. Here, let me take your basket." Ignoring her protests, he plucked the basket with its parcels from her hands. "It is so difficult to be the strength upon which others seek to draw, is it not?"

"I am hardly that, m'sieur."

"You will permit me to differ, mademoiselle. Your fortitude is evident to all here. You are a strong one, a pillar against which all of your family leans."

The matter-of-fact but gentle way he expressed himself left Nicole blinking back a hot flood of tears. "I fear I have misled you. They are not my immediate family at all. Guy Belleveau is my uncle, my mother's brother."

"If you mingle your affairs with them, they are kin," Pastor Collins replied firmly, pushing open the mission's front door. "If you take their cares upon your heart, they are family and more."

Instead of handing the basket back, he opened the door that connected the mission to the seminary. "Why do you not join me in our central hall for a moment? It is bound to be quiet this time of day."

For reasons she could not understand, Nicole followed him, grateful for the opportunity to share a few minutes more with this warm-eyed pastor. "You are too kind, m'sieur."

"Not at all. I am a lonely old gentleman who is charmed by your beauty and your strength. As are we all." He led her down a long connecting passage of stone and narrow windows, through another door and into the communal kitchen. He set her basket on the counter, then led her through a final door and into the dining hall. Two girls at the far end were setting the tables for supper. He selected a table by the window, waiting until she was seated to lower himself into the seat across from her. "Now then. Tell me what is in your heart."

The simple words held such a potent invitation, yet Nicole's proud nature was sorely tempted to refuse. It would have been so easy to deny there was anything at all. If she said there was nothing, he would not press. A single glance at that seamed and bearded face was enough to show that he was not a man who probed where he was not welcome. But she also knew that here was a man who did not judge, did not condemn, who would not distort what was already so confusing. The warmth in his features and his gaze seemed to draw from her the torment she had carried since the storm. And even long before that. "I am so confused," she began slowly.

"Ah." Nothing more. A single nod, a leaning back, a waiting. Ready for whatever it was she wished to say.

"But there is so much to tell, so many tangles, I do not know. . ."

"Of course, of course." Another nod. Slower this time, taking in all his upper body. "So many of life's greatest woes are such because they do not come alone. They attack with gathered force, do they not?"

"Yes," she sighed.

"Tell me not in order, not in place. Tell me only what you wish. And at your own pace. I am in no hurry."

Nicole found herself thinking back to the journey down the bayou. The day she had refused Jean Dupree's request for marriage. And all the confusion seemed to leap up into her being once more, all the torment that had seemed to commence with that day. As she spoke, she found herself filled with the images of her home. The bayou waters sparkled green and soft and warm. The scents of home wafted through the stone hall. Baking bread and steaming crawfish and spices and the rich warm earth of planting. Her father's voice seemed to reach across the distance and speak to her, as though he had been waiting for just such a moment to tell her that they missed her and loved her and . . .

Nicole could not help but lower her head to the table and sob. A gentle hand patted her arm, then the back of her head. But nothing was said. Nothing except the one hand, letting her know more than words that she was not alone. She gathered herself as best she could, raised up and stared through the window as Pastor Collins rose and went to the basin in the opposite corner. The scene outside was washed with distortion by the leaded glass. Exactly the same as the feelings within her heart.

"Here you are, my dear."

"Thank you." She accepted the damp cloth and wiped her face and pressed hard against her eyes. "You must think me such a fool."

"I think nothing of the sort. Those who are expected to be strong sometimes find themselves unable to be weak. Even when it would be better for their own health and well-being."

Nicole found it uncanny how he seemed to know exactly what to say. She was able to set her shame aside with the cloth, take a deep breath, and confess, "I feel torn by so many different desires."

"Yes," he murmured, the single word an

invitation to continue.

"I want to go on to Acadia. I need to. But I miss my family." She realized she had broken down before even explaining why it was she wished to travel on. But at the moment, his understanding this was less important than her need to shape her confusion into words. Not for Pastor Collins, but for herself. "I have always wanted to travel. I have never felt fully at home in Louisiana." A sudden thought struck her, one that rose unbidden. She tested it by forming it into words. "Perhaps that is why I have not married, because I did not want to be tied to one place and one way of life."

She waited, almost expecting this older man of the church to tell her that this was a woman's place. Yet Pastor Collins said nothing at all, merely watched and waited.

Which allowed another thought to rise from the shadows of her own heart. "I think perhaps I was too scarred by what happened when I was young. I was just a few months old when the British expulsion began. My earliest memories are of living in places that were not our own. We traveled, we worked, we saved, we traveled on. Always looking for a land and a home of our own. Now my parents are happy in Louisiana. They are settled. My brothers as well."

"But not you," Pastor Collins murmured.

"I am and I am not. I want to stay and I want to go. I love my Louisiana home, and yet I still feel the call of my younger years, and all the journeying. Always that feeling that the . . . the place of rest is just ahead . . . somewhere." She felt a new freedom with this examining of herself. "And all the mystery of what lies beyond the road's next turning. I want this—and I don't."

The older man seemed pleased by her response. "So much of life is like that, is it not? Pulling us so hard in two opposite directions."

"Yes." She felt so relieved by his words, not just that he took her seriously, but that he was able to understand her meaning. "Yes, it does."

"So hard to know which direction to take. So hard to make harmony of it all. Or of ourselves." He cocked his head to one side, his gray eyes twinkling. "Do you feel as though this confusion reflects a conflict at the very center of yourself?"

His question seemed to peel back the layers of her heart. Nicole whispered, "Yes."

"Oh, so do I, my dear. So do I. Often. Sometimes a conflict is there at the deepest point of my existence. So many *outside* problems seem to reflect this *inside* uncertainty—at times an anguish. And do you know what I have found?"

The simple truth of his quiet words delved with knifelike precision. Nicole wanted and yet did not want to hear what he had to say. But she nodded for him to continue.

"It seems to me that the friction and the discord spring from my very humanness. Do you ever feel that?"

She nodded once more, almost against her own will. She wanted him to stop and yet willed him to continue. The mirror he had suddenly lifted and held before her face hurt to look into. Yet it was so brilliantly clear that she could not turn away.

"Oh, so do I," he went on. "The apostle Paul declared there was something he bore, an illness, a pain—we don't know exactly what it was—that forced him to turn to God. Day in and day out, he had to seek God because it was only with His presence that Paul could bear his burden. Do you see what this confession makes of this thorn in his flesh?"

"A gift," she whispered, surprised that she spoke at all.

"There! I knew you were a brilliant lass. A gift! Is that not a wonder? Who else but God could take such a thorn as the conflict that stirs in my mind and heart and turn it into what keeps me *closest* to Him? It is only through God that I can choose the right path. Only through God that I can hold to peace. Only through God that I can see what is eternally right, and what is merely smoke rising from the fires of my sinfulness." He smiled with such joy, as though he was sharing with her the labors of his lifetime. And perhaps, she realized, he was.

Pastor Collins continued, "And how is that possible? How can I achieve this transformation from confusion to calm? There is only one way I have found. And that is by choosing correctly at the very outset. By turning to God.

"Every time the doubts arise, every time I am unable to decide, every time I feel the choices are too hard to make, I must wait upon my Lord. I must fall to my knees and confess that though I am strong in some ways, I am weak in so many others. And I need Him as much where I think I am strong as where I know I am weak. It is only through His strength and His wisdom that I can see my way clear."

———— ❧ ————

For much of that day, Nicole found herself moving through the mission in dread of her next contact with the pastor. Though his words had been kind, they had also been deeply personal. It was not that he had delved where she did not wish, she finally decided, so much as that he had quietly urged *her* to do so. She was left feeling uncomfortably vulnerable. Nicole remained so quiet and removed that both Guy and Emilie asked if she was coming down with a fever.

But when Pastor Collins came searching for her, he came at such a rapid pace she had no time to duck away. He drew her to one side of the bustling commons room and announced, "I have located a ship traveling north. One with berth space for all of you."

The confusion she had known that morning returned in full measure. "I suppose I should go speak with the others," she answered slowly.

"That is precisely why I wanted to speak with you first," he countered. "Perhaps it would be a good idea to settle the decision in your own mind before telling your family."

His meaning was clear. The invitation she had found so appealing and yet also frightening was again there in his gentle features. She sighed, "I wish I knew what to do."

"Have you prayed about this?" When

she hesitated, he answered his own question with, "You find it difficult to separate a confusion over your faith from the confusion as to your journey, is that so?"

"Yes," she sighed, relieved that he would not condemn her for this lack as well.

"Then I shall pray for you until you are able to do so yourself," he replied, as though it was the simplest thing in the world. "Perhaps it would help me if I knew why you were traveling north."

Again Nicole paused, then responded with, "My uncle received a letter . . . no, that is not it, not it at all. That is his reason. Not mine."

He did not seem the least put out by her ambiguity, or her need once more to halt and struggle to make sense of her thoughts. Finally she decided it was not just that he deserved the truth, she wanted to tell him. "In truth, sir, my birth parents are English."

His reaction was astonishing. The clergyman's features paled, and a deep tremor shook his portly frame. "I beg your pardon?"

"English." She took no satisfaction in his bewilderment. "It is the truth, m'sieur, though I speak almost none of your tongue. I did not know of this until only a few weeks ago. It is a fact. My English mother offered to take an ailing French baby to an English doctor, and I was left with the French family. The plan was that it would be only for a few days. But during that time the English"—her voice faltered on the word—"drove the French from Acadia. . . ." She drifted to a stop and watched in alarm as the pastor reached up with one tense hand and began massaging his chest above his heart.

"Would you happen—do you know the name of the village where you were born?" he asked in obvious agitation.

"Even that is a part of the confusion," she confessed, finding that though this good man was distressed, still she found comfort in speaking with him. "I had always thought it was a village called Minas. That was the place my French parents spoke of all my life."

"Minas," he repeated, the word almost a moan. "Minas."

"All the tales of my childhood, all the comfort we found in the hardest of times, came from the stories they told of Acadia and our village of Minas." She took a shaky breath. "But I learned this very spring when I was told of my true heritage that I was born in the neighboring English settlement of Fort Edward."

A second hand reached up to grip his heart. "And your English parents . . . do you know their names?"

"Yes." She was watching him curiously now, wondering at the man's sudden affliction. Surely he was not offended that she was in fact English—as he was himself. "A-Andrew and Catherine Harrow."

"Oh, dear Lord," he moaned and reached toward her with a shaky hand. "Dear, sweet Lord above."

"What's the matter?" she cried as she felt the tremors of his hand through his grip on her arm. Shivers of uncertainty and wonder ran over her own frame.

"My dear child, come over here and sit down." But he was the one who leaned upon her now for support, walking unsteadily over to a side table, all eyes in the room following their uncertain progress as she helped him settle on the bench.

Once he was seated, Nicole asked, "Can I get you something? A glass of—"

"Sit, please, child, sit, I am fine. It is consternation, nothing more." He examined her with a new frankness. "Yes, I see the resemblance. How remarkable. Perhaps I noticed it before on a deeper level. But, yes, now I can see it for certain."

"M'sieur, you are beginning to frighten me."

"Fear not, my dear sweet child." But his

eyes were clouded by tears as he laid one trembling hand over her own. "For this day we stand in the presence of God's holy power, a God who sees the end from the beginning."

"I don't . . . you are not—"

"You are so much like your mother," he said, smiling and trembling now together. "So much. I can see her—"

Nicole pulled her hand from his grasp. She gripped one hand with the other to stop their trembling. "What are you saying?"

"Your mother . . . and your father both," he said through trembling lips and eyes full of tears. "My dear, Andrew and Catherine Harrow were here."

She would have risen if her legs could have supported her. Her hands went to her lips. She could only stare at him.

"Here. The both of them. Your father came to study for the ministry, then returned to Acadia. Such a heart for God, your parents have. One heart, I said, and so I meant, for truly they lived and breathed within a holy union that could only have come through the Lord's blessing." He blinked, and one tear released to spill over the seamed features. "I remember one night, full of storms and snows and cold, and how they told me of the child that was theirs. Anne is her name. Yes, Anne. And how they had gained her by losing another."

"My parents," Nicole whispered.

"I remember, I remember . . ." Pastor Collins lifted one trembling hand to his beard, tugged it hard, as though seeking to hold his voice and features steady. "Your name . . . it was Elspeth, is that not correct?"

"Nicole?" Guy walked over and looked from one face to the other. "Is something wrong?"

When Nicole did not answer, Pastor Collins replied for them both, "No, no, only that your family has both the means and the reason to travel north, m'sieur." Pastor Collins gathered himself with great effort and pushed to his feet. He looked down to where Nicole remained seated, stunned into immobility. "I shall miss you, my dear. And I urge you to count this day as a gift from the Lord."

Chapter Twenty-four

Anne slipped from the wagon seat, looked up at her fiancé, and wished there were some way to express what she was feeling. "Take care, my love."

Cyril Mann held the reins with the unease of someone not born to the trail. But he had been the one who had offered to take the place of the ailing Georgetown teamster, saying there was no need for them to hire another since he had to return to Halifax anyway. And besides that, it was time he learned to handle a team. In so doing, he had further cemented his place within this village that took a man's measure by his ability to be a good neighbor.

Cyril looked forward, saw the leader was still adjusting the first wagon's harness, then smiled at Anne. "I will be the most careful teamster this trail has ever known."

She could see he was excited about the journey. She was glad that he was so pleased about learning this new skill. It was a part of him that she loved. And yet she could not help but feel a pang over his eagerness for the new adventure when it meant separation from her. Anne bit her lip, then said, "I will count the days until I can join you in Halifax."

"And I the hours."

Anne reached for his hand, ignoring the chuckles and jests from the watching bystanders. Cyril pulled his hat from his head and used it to shield his quick kiss. The laughter that surrounded them was friendly.

Anne searched his face as he returned his

hat to his head. He had eyes the color she had always imagined of an English sky, a delicate china blue, and flecked with little golden sparks she liked to think only she could see. "My heart travels with you," she said for only him to hear.

A call rose from the front wagon. Cyril straightened in his seat as a whip cracked. He took a firmer grip on the reins and gave her a smile that warmed her heart. "Then I shall have to leave my own here with you. Good-bye, my love."

Anne stood and waved until the wagons followed the trail around the curve of the first bend, then slowly turned back toward her village. The two had come for a July visit with her parents, a time for them to get to know their son-in-law-to-be a bit better. She knew it was right for her to stay a few days longer with her family, and yet she missed him terribly.

Though it was only ten weeks since she had left her home and village for Halifax, Anne walked the trail leading back into Georgetown with wonder. She knew it as well as she knew her own face, yet she saw it as for the first time. Not because she had forgotten, no, but rather because she now viewed everything from a new perspective.

She took her time, drinking in the sights

and sounds and smells. Birds chuckled and chattered, lifting her melancholy over saying good-bye to Cyril. Trees swaying overhead etched quick messages of welcome upon the clouds and the sky. Wild flowers shivered and beckoned. She filled her hands with blossoms and found herself thinking of her mother's tale of other wild flowers, ones gathered in a meadow above the village of Minas. As she entered her own familiar village, Anne was struck by the sudden idea that it might be nice to go back to the meadow, just the two of them, and see the place as adults. Where her two mothers had become friends and her own destiny was set into place.

When she pushed through the little gate and walked down the path to their front door, it was to the sound of weeping. She hurried through the doorway, entered the front parlor, and discovered her mother collapsed in the chair by the unlit fire. Catherine's face was bowed over her knees, and she sobbed so hard her entire frame shook.

"Mother!" Anne dropped the flowers and rushed over to kneel by the chair. "Mother dearest, what is wrong?" Had something terrible happened? Her father—?

"Oh my." Catherine struggled to sit upright. "You weren't supposed to find me like this."

"Why on earth not?" Her voice rose from the strain of forcing out the words. "Tell me what is the matter!"

"No one was supposed . . . I thought I was alone for a while." Catherine wiped her face with the edge of her apron. "I'm just being a silly old woman."

"You're not silly and you're not old. Please tell me what's wrong, Mother!"

"This is so much harder than I ever imagined," Catherine sighed, staring at the cold hearth. "So very, very hard."

Anne gripped her mother's hand with fear. Her voice did not sound like her own. "What is?"

"Waiting for word about Charles's search for Elspeth." A sob escaped her obvious attempt to control her emotions. "His journey has left me with so many unanswered questions."

"I think I understand," Anne murmured, relieved that it was not something much worse. "I'm so sorry, Momma."

"I feel so selfish. I wish I could set all the uncertainty aside and simply be happy for you and this fine man you've brought into our home."

Anne found it hard not to cry herself. "I'm so glad that you and Father love him too."

"Oh, my dear sweet child." Catherine smiled through her tears. "He is everything I have prayed you would find in a man, and more besides. I truly feel this is a match ordained of God."

Anne could only manage a whisper, "Thank you, Momma."

"Which only makes my worrying worse. Because I am not only robbing myself of the chance of being happy with you, I am not honoring God. With His hand upon your coming union, I should be praising Him. But I can't help but think of Charles and his quest—and my other child."

A tear escaped and traced a warm trail down Anne's cheek. Her *other* child. Anne felt there was such a gift to her in these words. Her hands drew Catherine's arm over close enough for her to rest her forehead there.

Catherine murmured, "I am fearful of every answer. As though some questions were just not meant to be asked." She paused. "As though I was mistaken to believe I was strong enough to hold on to His peace. As though I should have never . . ." Catherine shook her head and did not finish.

Anne forced herself to lift her face and search her own heart for an answer, something that might ease her mother's distress. "I have been afraid as well."

"You?" Catherine drew her gaze from the empty hearth. "Why?"

"Many reasons, all of them selfish." She did not want to say anything more, not now, not confess her own fears of becoming the second daughter. The love and the grace that filled this home, even now in a time of such uncertainty and remembered sorrow, left her feeling as though the words themselves did not belong, much less the feelings.

But Catherine said, "Tell me, Anne. Please."

"I was so afraid you and Papa would not love me as much."

"Oh, Anne. My precious child."

"I know it sounds silly. But I was worried that if Elspeth came home, things would not be the same." Anne felt her mother's free hand trace its way over her hair and down her neck and back. A touch she had known all her life, given new meaning by the strength of this confession.

"But what I feared the very most was that I . . . might be asked to go."

"Go where?" asked Catherine, her tone aghast.

"To . . . to my other family. Oh, Momma, I know it's wrong to be so frightened of those who are my own flesh and blood. I love them, yet I do not *know* them. They are total strangers to me. If I had to leave you and Papa and Grandpa Price—"

"Shh," said Catherine, drawing her close. "You are about to make your own home. You and your doctor. You need never worry again about where home will be."

Though her own heart had already made peace with her worries, the words brought further comfort to Anne. "I found the strength through God to set those fears aside. To be at peace. To trust that I would always know a place in this home, even though I may have another also. I have felt that you will always remain my family, that I will always be loved by you and Papa."

"Of course, my daughter. Of course you will." The hand continued to stroke her hair, until Catherine finally said, "I have never felt more proud of you than I am at this moment."

Anne stared at her mother's tear-stained face, saw with a woman's awakened awareness the strength and the weakness, the sorrow and the joy, the love and the price of loving, with a heart opened by God. "Why, Momma?"

"Because of that peace you speak of. Because of the woman you have become."

Catherine's smile through her tears touched the deepest place in Anne's heart. "Would you pray with me now, and ask God to grant me the same strength and inner peace He has given to you?"

Hands clasped, mother and daughter bowed their heads.

Chapter Twenty-five

Ten days after his ship had limped into Boston Harbor, Charles returned from points west where he had inspected his newest land grant. The journey had proven more arduous than expected, with signs everywhere of coming tension between England and the colonists. The evening of his arrival back in Boston he was fêted by the finest of the city's society. Everywhere he found himself surrounded by worrying talk and rumors of uprisings and conflict. Charles endured the social whirl and the political intrigue as best he could. In the days following, he endured the swirl of parties and socials and political discussions and overlong dinners, while demanding daily updates on the ship's repairs and urging the captain to more speed.

On the fifth afternoon of his return,

Charles had excused himself from attending yet another gathering of the powerful, this one to discuss the rising number of colonists who wished to secede from England. Instead, he made his way on foot along a series of cobblestone ways. Three times he had to stop and ask directions, and on each occasion he wished he had dressed in his seaman's garb before setting off. His finery drew looks and muttered comments, something that had never bothered him before but now left him wishing he could simply return to his quarters on Beacon Hill and forget the whole business. But a sense of obligation and the tuggings of a confused heart pushed him forward.

By the time he arrived at the alleyway by the quayside, Charles was in a dark mood indeed. He halted before a man sweeping the broad landing and humming what might have been a hymn. The stocky gray-bearded man wore a vicar's black coat and starched collar, as well as an odd black hat with a bowl-shaped crown and stiff peaked edges. Charles searched the stone wall to either side, but the copper plaque was in the shadows and he could not read the address.

"Yes, can I help you?" was the friendly query.

Charles drew in a breath. "I seek the

seminary."

"Then your search is ended." The man seemed neither surprised nor perplexed at the question from the well-dressed Englishman. "Welcome, friend. How—"

The elderly man stopped abruptly and squinted against the brightness of the sun. His own face paled as he leaned suddenly on his broom for support.

Charles reached forward. "Are you all right, sir?"

"No . . . I . . . you . . ." The man swallowed and stared into Charles's face. "Forgive me, I thought for a moment I was seeing, well, the ghost of an old friend."

Charles found himself shaken. He knew that the man spoke of Andrew. Even here, even now, his brother's imprint remained. "Actually, sir, I might be the ghost's brother." He managed a small smile. "My name is Charles Harrow. I am—"

"Andrew's brother!" The man flung the broom aside and stepped forward with a broad smile and outstretched hand. "Miracles do indeed fill my life, sir. You are most welcome!"

———— ✿ ————

"Andrew was a good student. Not the best, no. It would not be truthful to suggest he was a particularly gifted man when it came to books and study. But he worked, oh my goodness, how that man worked."

Reverend Collins puttered around a cluttered chamber, one apparently shared by several members of the seminary's faculty. It was a large room, high ceilinged and flanked by a pair of vast sunlit windows. Four broad tables were spaced about its length, each surrounded by books and tomes and papers. Charles watched as his new acquaintance lifted a whistling kettle from the fire, filled a teapot, and asked, "How do you take your tea, sir?"

"Black is fine, thank you." Charles accepted his cup. "It's really not necessary that you go to all this trouble, Reverend."

"Nonsense. It's not every day that I have such joy brought to me through my afternoon chores." The bearded gentleman chuckled as he eased himself down in a high-backed chair opposite Charles. "Although such miracles do seem to be coming more often these days."

"I'm not sure I understand, sir."

The old man had the ability to show enormous good humor with the mere lifting of an eyebrow. He smiled at something only he could see, took a sip from his cup, then turned to stare out the window. Finally he said, "You must forgive me, Charles. It is all right if I call you that, I hope."

"Most certainly, sir." Charles had not told the gentleman of his quest, of his wealth, or his earldom. And apparently Andrew had not even mentioned the fact that he had a brother. Charles decided that seemed fitting, to have been dismissed so completely from his brother's life that Andrew did not even speak of his existence to a friend. "I am honored."

"And I am Samuel. Samuel Collins." For some reason, this admission caused the vicar to emit another chuckle. He leaned over his ample belly. "How is Andrew?"

"He is fine, sir. Actually, he is better than that." Charles swallowed another sip of tea, then added, "The villagers of Georgetown seem to feel the man is a saint."

"Ah, then he has continued to grow in faith. I am glad, sir. So glad. And Catherine?"

"She is a worthy wife for my brother." Never had his own lacks and losses bit as deeply as then, not even when left standing morose and solitary by his second wife's grave. "A lovely woman in every sense of the word."

"Yes, Catherine is truly a gift from God." His gray eyes blinked. "And their young child, Anne is her name, is that not so?"

"The name is correct, sir. But a child no longer. She is eighteen and as beautiful—" Charles was about to say how she resembled her mother. But then there was the question of *which* mother, and this left him thinking that in truth the young lady resembled both. "She is as beautiful as she is poised."

"I am so glad. So very glad. You add great joy to an old man's day." Another sip, and the cup was set aside. "So tell me, Charles, what has brought you to our door this fine afternoon?"

Charles found himself retreating behind his cup. He started to tell the man about Nicole, but then there was the issue of who he was. Which could only result in confessing the dismal way he had treated his own brother. No. Yet when Charles pushed all that aside, he found himself confronting a second set of facts. Deeper ones and newer both, truths that were only now taking a coherent form.

Charles lifted his gaze and inspected the man across from him. Pastor Collins seemed more than merely a gentle, likable man. Much more indeed. Those kind gray eyes held a light that resembled the illumination within Andrew's own gaze. The glow signaled an inner contentment that Charles previously had considered more fitting to myths and childhood fables. Yet here it was, the same peace he had found in his brother, and in Henri and Louise Robichaud. A strength and a security that seemed able to withstand life's harshest winds. A light that was in truth not of this world at all.

Samuel Collins seemed most willing to wait him out. No doubt his teacher's patience combined with a pastor's ability to accept whatever moment the visitor chose to shape. Charles took an easy breath, knowing with certainty that here was a man he could trust. "Truth be known, sir, the reason that set me on my voyage is no longer the reason I journey on. At least, no longer the only purpose."

"Ah." The vicar laced his fingers across his belly, seemingly content to remain there indefinitely.

Charles took another breath and began with the storm. It was as good a place as any, though images of watery tunnels of lush greenery, and the warm, fragrant closeness of bayou country intruded into the telling from time to time. He could not describe it all, not if he were to sit and speak for days and weeks. For as he continued with his tale, explaining how he found himself confronted not by the tempest so much as with his own inner turmoil, other images continued to crowd up close. As though part of his mind sat and told the story and remembered the ship and the storm, and another part entirely sat and recalled even earlier days. The absence of childhood love. The sterile quality of his wealthy upbringing. The political intrigue in court. Two marriages for yet more property and position, rather than for love. The journey across the Atlantic. Finding Andrew. Facing himself.

Charles realized he had stopped talking. Guiltily he straightened in his chair and said, "Forgive me, sir, my mind must have wandered off, causing me to ramble—"

"Think nothing of it," the vicar replied. "I was just telling another young seeker the other day how life's greatest problems are often such because they are tied to so much else."

"So much," Charles agreed solemnly. "So very much."

"You were saying how the storm had forced you to confront your own inner state."

"My own inner emptiness," Charles confirmed, marveling at the ease he felt in speaking thus to a near stranger. Known only to him by a brother he hardly knew at all. "My own inner void."

And there he stopped. There was nothing else to say. Whatever experience he chose to speak of, whatever journey he brought to mind, it would all return to this simple confession. Yes, he saw that now. Here was the center of his quest, this one and the one before and the one that had started when he had been born.

The vicar seemed to gather himself, as though poised to launch into reaches Charles felt were lost to him forever.

Then he smiled, the vicar did, and the light in his eyes gathered and strengthened. "In the Gospel of Matthew, Jesus speaks of the need for each of us to take control. Not of our lives, no. That is a myth that men of power and wealth pretend to, that they control their lives and their destinies. But in truth, none of us can claim such control. It is a lie, a veil of falsehood those with power pretend to believe, and in doing so, hide themselves from the deeper truths."

Charles found he could not help but murmur, "The rudest surprise of this long and harrowing season is just how little control I do have."

"There, you see? Honest perception *requires* us to admit this. But as we accept our lack of control over *life,* we find we do have control over our *choices.*"

Charles leaned forward, drawn by an unfamiliar sensation within the deepest core of his being. It felt like a hunger of his very soul. "I'm not sure I understand."

"Everything that is here on earth will wear away. What we place so much importance upon—all of this will soon disappear. Yet we cling to it all. We seek to increase our possessions. We hunger for more, always more. And because our desperation is so great, we fail to see that this in itself is a choice. And the result of this choice is a life lived to a tragic litany. Over and over, day after day, year after year, we chant, *Just this one thing more.* First I will have that, then I will be content. Then I will be happy." Solemnly the vicar shook his head. "But this chant is a lie, my friend. Oh yes. A calamitous and deadly lie."

Charles found himself not nodding so much as rocking in his seat. A fraction of a movement, back and forth. Rocked upon his very foundation by the truths he now absorbed. "What is one to do?"

"There is only one answer to that, my brother. Just one. If there had been any other way for this lost and forlorn world to gain entry to the eternal, God would *never* have permitted us to nail His Son to a tree." Samuel Collins closed the distance between them, leaning forward until his brilliant gray eyes and softly powerful voice filled Charles's vision. "The truth is, life is just a preface for what is to come. And there is *one* way to enter the kingdom. *One* way to gain salvation. *One* choice that you and all of us must make."

The eyes bore into Charles's gaze with a force so powerful that his quiet words rang like a great bell. Though the vicar spoke softly, Charles felt the words sinking deeply into his mind.

"That choice is to serve the one true God. With all that you have. With all that you are."

Chapter Twenty-six

Nicole ever paced the windswept deck, feeling as trapped as she ever had in all her life. Rain fell in cold and misty curtains. The wind was so light the droplets drifted as much up and sideways as down. Like all the family, she wore several layers of clothing and still could never feel warm. She quickly had learned that the worst thing she could do was remain seated, for then the chill seeped into her very bones. No, it was far better to meet the weather and the cold head-on and walk and work and endure.

Here it was the beginning of August, and Nicole was as cold as she could ever remember. No, that was not exactly true. Once before, in the dim recesses of her childhood memories, she had known such cold. It had been the winter of her mother's grave illness, when Nicole had been forced to jump straight from youthful play to looking after a house. She recalled standing in the doorway of their Carolina hovel and watching white flakes falling from the sky, far too gentle for something so piercingly cold. Here upon the gray ocean reaches north of Boston, the cold seemed a wet and endless chill that burrowed deep and remained. Even her dreams had become laced with storms and grayness and cold winds.

Her pacings took her back to where Emilie stood at the opposite rail, cradling and cooing to the fretting baby. "Here, let me take her for a time."

"Oh, you are an angel." Emilie's features had started to take on the pinched quality of deep exhaustion. She was not sleeping well. None of them were. "She's started dripping the yellow fluid again from her nose. Look, it's even in her eyes."

"It's just a fever, nothing more." Nicole took the child and turned swiftly away so Emilie could not see her own worry and concern. She rocked the child as she crossed to the boat's opposite side, in truth scarcely hearing the whimpering. Her exhausted mind remained trapped by the gray world and the beckoning memories. Oily waves rose and fell and finally melted into the unseen horizon. The wind began to blow more strongly, pressing her ever onward toward a goal she could no longer clearly identify. As though once she arrived at the destination she had set for herself, still the journey would go on, still her search would continue.

Nicole found herself remembering her departure from the seminary and the reverend's final words. He had clasped her hand with both of his with such warmth and fervor that it seemed to Nicole as though he were actually embracing her. "I wish you a good and joyful journey."

She had tried to laugh, the unease from her earlier confession still surrounding her. "No voyage upon the sea can be called joyful, m'sieur. And all of them are too long. In truth, I feel as though the voyage is already endless."

"Not endless, and not without purpose," Pastor Collins had responded in his quiet and gentle manner. "When you find yourself growing impatient, remember that God's timing is not our own. There is a reason for His delay. Find that reason, and your own journey will grow shorter, even if the time remains long."

"I . . . I am not sure I understand," she stammered, once again shaken by the sheer mystery of this man's wisdom, his deep care.

"There is a lesson here for you, my dear. It is not my lesson, so you must discover it for yourself." The smile broke free then, showing a confidence in her ability to find out what was there before her. "You must seek the answer by seeking God. In that you will find the reason for all life, and all life's journeys."

Nicole had departed for the ship and the next stage of her journey, reflecting not only upon the man's words. As she mounted the gangplank she had been struck by the fact that these messages had come from an Englishman, one of the race she had spent her entire life loathing. The race to which she now belonged.

Nicole drew the child in close to her

chest, seeking to draw comfort from the little body. Not only did she feel as though the answer was hidden, she felt she was unworthy to even search. She was homeless, rootless, without haven or purpose, drifting upon an endless gray sea.

With the ease that came from sorrow and exhaustion, Nicole found herself drifting away on a second ocean—that of memories. This time the image seemed clearer than the surrounding gray vista. It was a vision from their time upon the road. Another time when the journey had seemed endless. Nicole rocked the baby and wondered how she had ever forgotten how measureless that trek had seemed. She stood there upon the rocking deck and gave herself over to the wash of remembrances.

The clan's trek from Carolina to Louisiana had taken almost a year, for they had stopped three times to work and earn enough money to keep going. The journey had scarred her middle brother the hardest, and even two years after they had arrived and founded their village and begun building their homes, still he awoke the family with his nightmares. When asked by her father about these, the boy had cried that he could still remember the day they had passed through a village in Georgia that had greeted them with stones, calling them scum and gypsies and thieves. Perhaps that's all they were, the boy wept. Welcomed nowhere, never to know a home of their own.

Henri had been silent for a long time that day, his silence drawing Nicole from the cooking fire to where she could see them clearly. Finally Henri had stood and walked over to the nearest tree and pulled down a great fistful of Spanish moss. He had come back over and seated himself by his son and said, "Do you see this? It is trash, is it not? It grows everywhere, covering this good tree and so many others throughout this land. We pay it no attention whatsoever. And yet even this has purpose. Many purposes. We burn it to make the smoke to keep away the insects. We mix it with mud to make the mortar to build our houses. We knot it into ropes to bind our boats to the shore."

Henri had shaken the gray lichen and said, "If the Lord our God can take something so common as this and give it such meaning, such a *vital purpose*, just stop and think what He must have in store for you, my son. What *grand* purposes. What *glorious* meanings."

Nicole paced the deck, reflecting upon her father's love and strength and words. She wondered what purpose God might have for her own life.

Perhaps it was a sudden jolt from a passing wave, perhaps a blast of wind. Whatever the reason, it seemed as though a hand reached down from the gray sky above and touched her very soul. The words appeared in her mind, fully formed and as clear as if they had been shouted in her face. *Ask God.*

So simple, yet so challenging. It meant bowing her head and acknowledging that God did indeed exist. Not only that, it meant accepting that she *needed* Him. That she could not find her way on her own. That the Lord knew more than she did, had answers she could not find by herself. It meant learning to trust Him. Completely.

Nicole wiped her face, clearing away more than just the rain. She noted that Guy had moved over close to his wife and was holding her. By the way their heads were bent, almost touching, she knew they were praying. They were doing much of that recently, as though finding in this simple gesture the only source of strength that mattered in this cold and mysterious world. Hesitantly she walked toward them. They would not mind if she joined them. No, surely not.

Chapter Twenty-seven

The gray sky had descended until the sea was the color of slate and utterly without motion. Even the ship's sails were gray, hanging limp and empty of wind. Every rope, every surface, every mast and sail and hat and cloak dripped rain.

Charles had been trapped on board the ship within this stormless rain for two days. Two days of knowing his goal moved further and further from his reach. Charles's present impatience, two days of constant frustration and alarm, was precipitated by what he had learned in his second meeting with the vicar.

Charles closed his eyes to the fog and the shadowy day, recalling his second visit with Pastor Collins. The day after that first encounter, Charles had received word that the ship was ready to sail. He had returned to the seminary to thank the old man and say farewell. The professor had held on to his hand for a very long time and then finally added, "Would it be proper of me to ask what is the purpose of your journey?"

Charles had found himself tempted to respond simply that he was returning to his brother's village. Yet the closeness he had felt to the old man during his first visit and the power of the reverend's words remained with him still. "It is all rather complicated," he said tentatively.

"Ah." Again there was the patient nodding, the quiet invitation to continue.

So Charles had told him briefly what lay behind his quest. As he spoke, the reverend's eyes grew rounder and wider. Finally Charles could not help but declare, "You seem surprised, sir."

"Indeed, surprised is the correct word. Amazed, in fact." He tugged upon his beard, then sighed, "My new friend, you must prepare yourself for what I am about to tell you."

"I beg your pardon?"

"Since your first visit I have wondered if I should tell you about a previous 'chance encounter' that related directly to your brother Andrew. But what you have told me now indicates that it also relates directly to you." Pastor Collins' chest swelled with a great breath, then he announced, "She was here."

"Who?"

"Nicole. She was here."

The realization of what the pastor was telling him had struck Charles with the force of a lightning bolt. He leaped to his feet, toppling his chair over with a clatter. "You're not saying that you have seen Nicole—Andrew and Catherine's daughter—"

"In this very mission," Samuel Collins affirmed.

"It can't be!" His mouth worked in time to his panting chest.

"Elspeth was her name originally, yes? Strange that I would recall this after all these years." Samuel Collins rose to his feet, moved around Charles, lifted the chair, and set it back in place. "Please, sit down."

But Charles was no longer listening. His thoughts had tumbled forward, confused and mocking, over and over in his mind. His niece. Here. So close. Yet so far. He had been right in the city, holed up in a dismal inn, marking time till the ship was ready by accepting social engagements in which he had no interest whatsoever. "She has left, you say?"

"Just two days ago. She is truly a lovely girl. Andrew and Catherine will be so thankful to have her home again. Imagine. After all these years. A miracle. That's what it is. A miracle." He had smiled at the memory. "She stayed with us over a week, she and her uncle's family. They all arrived on a vessel that had lost its mast in a storm." Pastor Collins cocked his head to one side. "Why, Charles, you've gone pale as a ghost."

In a voice so hoarse he scarcely recognized it as his own, Charles groaned out, "She said she was French."

Samuel Collins registered surprise of his own. "You mean to tell me you have *met* her?"

Charles's legs finally gave way, and the chair kept him from sprawling on the floor. "That was my vessel. We were all together for three weeks. I never . . ."

"She did not say who she was?"

"Not a word." Charles struggled to make sense of it all. "You are certain we are speaking of the same young lady? Tall, willowy yet strong—"

"Hair the color of autumn's foliage, eyes like a sunlit summer meadow. An independent lass who radiates strength and determination." The smile flickered upon the pastor's lips. "I shall miss her. She had a seeker's heart and a teacher's mind. Such a combination. She reminds me of her father."

Charles's mind reeled from what he had heard. He had missed his niece by a hair. Had unknowingly shared a ship with her for days. What incredible irony. Was God playing tricks on him? Was He mocking the venture that to Charles was so important? Or did He have something far more important ahead than simply allowing Charles to find an heir?

He realized the pastor was watching and waiting. The only response Charles could think of was, "Sir, I am at a loss."

"Not altogether a bad thing," Samuel Collins murmured, then spoke as though he were able to read Charles's thoughts. "Sometimes the greatest challenge to finding the right answer is learning to ask the correct question. Do you understand what I am saying?"

"I . . . I am not . . . yes, perhaps."

"Good. So what you might want to ask yourself is, Why would God bring you together and yet keep you apart?" The pastor's gaze seemed to reach across the distance separating them, illuminating the deepest recesses of Charles's heart. "Could it be that the Lord has something else in mind for you than your earthly goals? And if so, what do you need to do to discover His purpose?"

Somewhere overhead the chapel bell rang, and the vicar moved forward. "I fear I must go before they come looking for me. A meeting." He offered Charles his hand. "Know you shall journey onward with my prayers in attendance."

Charles accepted the hand and the clear smile and the illuminated gaze, yet could not find any words to say in reply.

The vicar had seemed pleased with his

reaction. "I wish you well, sir. And success with *all* your quests."

As Charles stood upon the rain-washed deck, he envisioned the vessel carrying Elspeth catching the wind and flying away to places he could never find. It did not help to know she was headed for Halifax and her family. What if she became lost upon the way? What if her ship went down with all hands? What if she became ill, or ran afoul of brigands, or . . . Charles resisted the urge to beat his fists on the rail and roar out his frustration.

All that time, through that awful storm, the journey, the forced docking in Boston, Elspeth had been with him. He could not believe it when the vicar had told him, and could not believe it still. Even if it were true, still it was impossible. What strange fate had placed them so close together and yet held them apart? Why was he, the eighth earl of Sutton, made a mockery before men, before God?

Charles stared sightlessly over the sea. His hat gathered the mist and dripped rain like a triangular funnel. He watched the front peak drip steadily, knowing within his heart that all of his strivings and all of his battles and all his acrid hunger had done nothing, nothing at all, save bring him to the point where he was forced to admit his own helplessness. Trapped within a storm that refused to blow, blinded by mist so thick he could not even see the ship's other side, much less his destination. Lost from the world and all that had mattered so much, left with no choice but to accept that alone he was nothing and going nowhere at all.

Yes, what reason did God have *not* to mock him?

Charles had been touched by the vicar in a strange and stirring way, but he had not yet sought out the Scripture as he had then promised himself. There was, deep within his being, a hesitancy. A pride that could not allow him to acknowledge the need of a God. But he could not escape the truth he was seeing presented in the lives, in the words, of people he had recently encountered.

He recalled the struggle his brother Andrew had known that day in the pulpit, and the moment of transformation he had beheld. It had emphasized his own empty lack. All of that had been repeated anew within the vicar's high-ceilinged chambers. If the journey had taught Charles anything, it was how to be honest with himself.

So why? Why was he holding back? What had he to lose, he who was becoming more and more conscious of his own inner emptiness, his powerlessness? What might he gain if he could only let go?

Charles stood at the railing, stared at the enveloping mist, and knew exactly what the answer was. He was still insisting upon doing it on his own, accomplishing his goals by sheer force of will.

He gripped the railing with both hands and lowered his head until the hat's front corner poured a stream of water upon his wrists. He closed his eyes and struggled through the inner storm of thoughts and emotions to find words, just a few, that might be directed beyond himself. *Help me, Lord God.* He stopped then, as though drawn up short by a soundless whisper. Then he went on, and this time the words seemed to come easier and more clearly. *Help me to know you. Help me to understand who I am and why you should want to draw me near. Help me to know what you want me to do.*

He raised his head and opened his eyes. It was not much, as prayers went. But it would have to do. He turned from the railing, feeling only a sense of confusion over why he had refused for so long to do something that had come so easily, at least once he had started.

Chilled and drenched, Charles walked toward the stairway leading to his quarters. He would need to change before joining the captain for dinner. As he reached the steps, it seemed to him that a faint hand reached under his hat and stroked his cheek. He stopped and turned back. From somewhere in the locked quarters of his mind, there sprang up a vague memory of his mother singing to him a nursery rhyme about the touch of an angel's wing.

He smiled to himself. And at that moment, a call rose from the seaman upon the masthead, "Ho, the wind!"

Chapter Twenty-eight

The morning mist lifted from Halifax Bay like a shroud removed by unseen hands. The city of Halifax glowed in the dawn light. Birds sang from full-leafed branches, and flowers bloomed in window boxes of newly built dwellings. Nicole could have enjoyed it had she been of another mind. But she could only halfheartedly appreciate that the day was not rainy, the cold was not paralyzing her limbs. In fact, the overhead sun shone down with an intensity that made her wish she could throw back her black bonnet and let in the rays. With summer sun, her dark tresses always lightened to a soft reddish golden color. Secretly Nicole liked the auburn highlights. She thought the lighter, warmer shade lent more flash to the green of her eyes. But perhaps she felt that way because that is what Jean, in some long-ago days that no longer belonged to her, had told her.

She knew she should be thankful that they were at last in Halifax. And she was—of a sort. But Halifax was certainly no Eden. And even though she had stepped ashore, her body insisted on the rhythm of the sea, making her feel light-headed and tipsy even with the solid boards of the town sidewalk beneath her feet.

Nor had the people welcomed them or treated them with anything but muted hostility. Nicole could see it on their faces, hear it in their voices, sense it in the stiffness of their bodies whenever she tried to converse.

That the family knew little English was definitely a burden. Guy spoke a few words that had been learned in business transactions. Nicole knew a few more that could be used in the market. Please. Thank you. A good day to you. Excuse me, please. What is your name? How much the cost? But these few phrases did little to appease the English, who looked at her with suspicion and often dislike. That the area was now reopened to returning Acadians did not matter to the port city's inhabitants. It was clear that they'd had no say in the matter—if they had, the Acadians would be kept in the lands to which they had been dispersed.

Though Nicole would have liked nothing better than to stay in the ramshackle room her uncle Guy had finally found for the family, she had no choice but to journey forth. In her walks about the city to find food, she had seen a sign with an emblem that she understood. The building housed a doctor, and a doctor was what they needed.

They had all been ill. All but Guy. And he was now out tramping the streets looking for any kind of work that he and Pascal might do to earn a wage. They were almost to the end of their limited resources. Emilie was sick in bed with her youngest cuddled up against her. The other child remained ill and was of course too young to be sent out alone to seek medical aid. So the task befell Nicole, who had sufficiently recovered herself to make the short journey.

Though she was still exhausted from the sea journey and illness, the child beside her needed medicine. With the boy in one hand, she clutched in the other the small coins Guy had given her tied in the corner of a clean cloth.

There was fear in her heart—not so much fear for their safety as fear that she might fail. That she, with her faltering English, would not be able to explain their need.

Young Michel whimpered, and Nicole pressed him closer against the skirts of her long summer coat.

"It's not far now," she tried to console him. "Just around the next corner."

When she pushed open the door of the small room that served as the doctor's surgery, her first impression was of orderliness and cleanliness that reminded her of her Louisiana home. After their months of crowded quarters and total chaos, she felt restored to see such scrubbed charm.

The child must have felt it, too, for he reached out small hands as though to catch it by the handfuls and draw it to himself.

The room already held quite a few patients. Every chair was taken and their occupants all turned toward her at the sound of the door. As she stood hesitantly, her hand on Michel's shoulder, a middle-aged man nodded in her direction and rose from his seat. Embarrassed yet thankful, Nicole crossed to it, accepting it with a smile and a returned nod. She dared not express her thanks in words, for she knew the moment she opened her mouth to speak, the atmosphere of the room would change. She reached down and drew the fevered child up onto her lap, holding him close for her comfort as much as his.

Someone entered the room from a back door. Nicole's attention was immediately drawn to the young woman. She was petite to the point of seeming to be fragile. But her demeanor was one of calm self-assurance. She lifted dark eyes to a child nearby and smiled as she spoke. Nicole could not understand the words, but she caught the meaning. They were words of comfort. Of compassion.

It was a long, tiring wait. The child grew impatient and restless. Finally, in feverish exhaustion, he fell asleep in her arms. How could one so tiny be so heavy in sleep? One by one the chairs were emptied, only to be occupied by new patients. The young woman, her starched white cap bobbing with her words, called out names and blessed their owners with smiles as she led them through the door at the back of the room. They returned later, some carrying small vials clasped with both hands.

Michel awoke and fussed again. Nicole knew that by now he was hungry as well as sick. There was nothing she could do except to try to soothe him and patiently wait their turn. At last the smile turned their way and the young woman nodded. Nicole placed Michel on his own feet and led him forward.

Nicole was confused and afraid. What should she say? Her limited English seemed so paltry in the face of Michel's great need. Her eyes must have shown her uncertainty, for the smile turned to concern.

Again the woman spoke—and again Nicole was unable to discern the meaning of the words. Her chin lifted slightly and her shoulders straightened. She decided that she must, for the sake of the small child, take matters into her own hands. "Michel," she said, pointing to the child. "Med-i-cine."

The young nurse pointed at Nicole. "Your name?"

This Nicole did understand. But how should she answer? Her life had been totally turned upside down because of the attempt to find English medical aid for a French baby. If she gave her French name now, would they be turned away? Would the child who clung to her with a feverish hand be denied the help he needed?

She stammered, "Elspeth. Elspeth Harrow."

A shock rippled through the slim figure. *It is happening*, grieved Nicole. *The doctor will not see me now. An English name does little when spoken by a French tongue.*

Then a further strange thing occurred. The warmth returned to the brown eyes before her. Even so, the delicate face seemed to be fighting for renewed control. She saw the young woman swallow, her head dipped down. "Pardon me," she said in a choked whisper, and she was gone before Nicole could even respond.

Nicole was about to turn and leave the building when resolve straightened her shoulders once more. With a flash of determination her eyes swept the room of people waiting to be treated. It was not fair. She would not leave. She would stay and demand the medicine that Michel needed.

She marched back toward the seat she had just vacated, the child herded before her by her firm hand on his shoulder. She would not be pushed out into the street without what she had come for. She would not.

Had Doctor Mann not been with a patient, Anne would have burst in and flung herself into his arms. As it was she could only take herself to the small closet that held the medical supplies and bury her face in trembling hands. Sobs shook her small frame. She wasn't sure at the moment why she was crying. But the emotion sweeping through her being, wave after uncontrollable wave, could not be denied.

It couldn't be. Yet who else in the whole wide world would bear the name of Elspeth Harrow? The young woman was telling the truth. She could see it in her eyes. This . . . this was her sister. Yet not her sister. Someone whose life was strangely intertwined with her own. Someone she did not know, yet shared an intimacy that denied explaining. This was the baby turned woman, the person she should have been.

It was all so confusing, so shattering to mind and soul. Here was the individual who had taken her place. Who had been shaped by the world that should have been hers. A woman whose place *she* had taken, molded in a life and manner that were not really her own, by parents who did not belong to her . . . and yet did. For the first time in her life, Anne felt cut adrift. Just who was she? Who was the woman who had given *her* own name, the one announced at the baptismal font those many years ago?

Pray, came a silent voice. *Pray*. Anne leaned her head against the shelf of linens. As she prayed the sobs began to lessen, the shoulders lost their tremble. She blew her nose, her composure gradually returning. She must get back to the waiting room. There were people there who needed her. The sick were waiting. Elspeth Harrow was waiting. . . .

She wiped her cheeks and eyes. "God help me," she whispered and braced herself to return to her work. She longed to speak to the young woman—alone. To share with her just who she was, but she knew in her heart that now was not the time for such a disclosure. To attempt such a thing would surely cause a scene. *Like Joseph*, the little voice whispered, and suddenly Anne understood the Genesis story. No wonder Joseph had drawn apart to weep at the sight of his estranged brothers. No wonder.

The young woman with the child was still there when she pushed her way back through the door. Anne breathed a sigh of relief. She crossed to her desk and took her seat, "Elspeth Harrow," she said calmly but clearly.

With a sigh, Nicole stepped forward.

They were to be seen after all.

"We need a little information before the doctor sees you," a calm voice spoke as the smile was lifted again.

Nicole could only stand and stare. The woman before her was speaking in softly accented French.

Chapter Twenty-nine

That evening, Anne found it almost impossible not to weep. After a day filled with patients, she still had not been able to tell Cyril about the extraordinary visitor to their office that day. Now they were busy whitewashing the front rooms of what was to become their home. Their *home*.

Earlier that same week Cyril had found the place, walking back from seeing a patient. He had made inquiries and discovered it had been built for a young merchant and his family. The merchant had been sent to the southern colonies, and the house had never been lived in. The merchant company was eager to have someone take it from their books. Three nights earlier, Cyril had walked Anne around the place, concerned that she might not like it with its large empty rooms and the unfinished walls and unvarnished floors. Anne had scarcely been able to believe it might actually be hers, a home of their own, one never lived in, one she could finish just as she herself wished. And yet now, as she and her husband-to-be coated the parlor's walls with limewash and two other women from the church scoured the back rooms, she was forced to wipe away tears just so she could see where she laid her brush.

"You might as well tell me," Cyril finally said from across the room.

She tried for a brightness she did not feel. "Tell you what?"

He rose from his crouch in the corner and crossed the floor. He gripped her wrist and steered her brush back into the bucket. Anne protested, "But we have so much to do! And our friends—"

"I will tell you a secret, my dear," he said, gently lifting her and leading her out the front door. "We will be working on this house until our dying day. It is the way of loving a place, always wanting to do more."

One of the women glanced down the hallway and waved them on with, "You two have worked hard all day—get yourselves a bit of rest," then returned to her work. They were there both to help make the house into a home and to be Anne's chaperone—not that anyone worried over Dr. Cyril Mann's actions, no, but rather because proper decorum required that the couple not be alone in such circumstances before the wedding. Cyril settled her down on the front stoop, walked back inside, and returned with their lantern. The refined whale oil cast a light more white than yellow, a clear brilliance that made his features glow softly. He eased himself down beside her and said, "Now, my little lady, tell the doctor where it hurts."

She breathed in the fragrances of summer flowers and fresh-cut lumber and lime. She turned her head to look into the face of her beloved, and she saw the freckled features of a boyish young man whose intelligence and goodness drew her like a light. A man who loved her dearly, who loved his Lord even more, who had asked her to be his wife, a man to fulfill her lifelong dreams. She sat upon the top step, lowered her face into her hands, and wept so hard she could scarcely draw breath.

Dr. Mann might have looked boyish, but he had a doctor's wisdom with people and troubles. Patiently he sat beside her and stroked the space between her shoulder blades. When the worst of her sobs had subsided, he gently asked, "You're not having second thoughts about us, are you?"

"What?" Anne raised her tear-streaked face.

"I know things have been moving swiftly." He looked unnaturally somber, the uncertainty biting deep. "We could wait a while longer if you—"

"Oh no, don't say it, don't even think such a thing!" She clasped his hand with both of hers, the tears making her grip wet and loose. "It's not you. It's not, I promise. It has nothing to do with us."

He took a breath. "Then you must tell me so we can face this together."

Her chin quivered, but she held on to control. "I fear there is nothing anyone can do."

"Then tell me so we can weep together."

"Oh," Anne leaned her forehead against his shoulder and found there the strength to say, "Elspeth came into the surgery today."

She felt the shock race through his form. "Elspeth? Andrew and Catherine's child?"

"That lovely auburn-haired French-woman with the consumptive child."

"Of course. She was indeed lovely. But her child was not consumptive, dear. Merely weakened by a lingering chest ailment."

"It also was not her child." Anne wiped her cheek with her hand, then moved to see him better. "Think back. Did she not remind you of Mother?"

He thought a moment. "There was a little resemblance, yes, I can see it now that you mention it."

"More than a little, Cyril. Much more. She looked like a younger version of Momma."

"My love," he cautioned, "surely you can't begin to make such a crucial decision based on a resemblance, no matter how—"

"She told me her name."

"—strong. . . ." He drew up short. "I beg your pardon?"

"When I asked her name, she said Elspeth Harrow. She speaks almost no English and yet she gave this name." The tears returned. "She was bringing the child of her uncle, who was looking for work and whose wife was too weak from the voyage and illness to bring the child herself. They have just arrived from Louisiana. I learned that much. Louisiana was where Papa sent Charles to look for her. And here she is."

Cyril's mouth worked once, twice, and finally he managed, "Elspeth . . ."

"She is *here*. She walked in from the street and told me her name. She has no idea who I am. I said nothing. I have been praying for my sister all my life, and she walks in the door. . . ." Anne had to stop and fight for control. Finally she managed enough of a breath to continue, "At first I could say nothing. I had to go in the back room and weep. When I came back out I still could not tell her who I am."

"She doesn't know—"

"Nothing. Only that the doctor in Halifax has an assistant with very red eyes and very bad French." She struggled to see him through her tearful gaze. "What about Momma? This will—should I rush to tell her so that she will not be caught by surprise as I was? I couldn't have anticipated how emotional the sudden meeting made me. What will it do to her? Her child. Her lost child. And Papa. Do we just wait for Elspeth to arrive on their doorstep? Oh, Cyril, what do I do? And what about Elspeth? She . . . she looked . . . troubled. But brave. How will she respond when she learns who I am? Elspeth is to return with the child, so I will see her again."

She thought he might tell her how time and patience would heal most wounds, how many worries seemed far worse in the night than they did the next morning. She had heard him use these kinds of words often enough with frightened mothers of sick infants. And yet he said nothing, only rubbed his chin and murmured, "Yes, yes, I do see. . . . I'm not at all certain I would have known what to say at such a time."

She turned to him again.

"You have waited all your life for this moment," he said, his eyes looking into hers. "And you thought it would never come. When it did, without fanfare or preparation, you would not be expected to know immediately what to say, what to do." He took her hand. "I would say God's hand was laid strong and sure upon this meeting."

Her chest seemed suddenly released from bands of tension. She found both the tears and the need to weep had vanished. "What should I do, Cyril?"

"If this is God's act, as it surely must be, then God should be the one to lead you forward." He spoke with the confidence of one who lived in daily contact with his Maker. "When she comes again, I should ask her to pray with you. If she agrees, listen carefully for His voice."

With the morning came a rain from the sea, cold and far too harsh for August. Nicole sheltered the child as best she could as she hurried across the slick cobblestones.

Salt-laden wind blew the scent of sea through the covered walkways and a bitter chill besides. Nicole moved as fast as she could along the crowded streets, struggling against the feeling that her inner storms had followed her ashore, intent upon battering her forever. At least on land she was no longer confined to pacing from rail to rail. At least here she could plan for reaching her goal.

A horse cried in shrill protest against the rain and the mud and its wagon's heavy weight, and the driver cursed at her as she and Michel barely escaped being run down. By the time she arrived at the doctor's abode, her dress was wet and stained with mud almost to her knees.

As Nicole scrambled for the doctor's door handle, to her surprise it was opened from within, and she faced the same bright-eyed young lady she had met the day before.

Nicole stiffened and put her arm protectively around Michel. She knew what was coming, that the townspeople's hostility would cause the doctor to refuse to treat the child again. Nicole set her face against what was to come.

But the woman greeted Nicole with a smile so genuine it seemed like the sun itself on this cold and rainy day. *"Bonjour!"* she said as she drew them inside. "I've warmed a towel for you on the stove. Undo your bonnet and dry your face and hair. Please call me Anne."

"*Merci.*" Surprise turned Nicole's hands clumsy, and she fumbled with the bow at her chin. "I must look frightful."

"Not at all. You look like someone who has walked through a summer rain. How is Michel this morning?"

"Better, thank you."

"Oh, I'm so glad. And the mother?"

"She slept better last night, now that she knows Michel is being taken care of." The young lady's cheerfulness and evident concern gave Nicole the courage to say honestly, "I was afraid . . . when you were here at the door, I thought, well . . ."

"Yes?"

"That you—that the doctor did not wish to treat the French."

"You thought that?" For some reason, the young lady's chin quivered. "Why, nothing could be further—we treat all people here."

"The doctor seems very kind," Nicole agreed.

"I'm so sorry I gave you a wrong impression." The young woman's eyes looked troubled. "I know I was abrupt yesterday. I ran into the back and left you standing there at the desk with everyone staring at you. I'm sorry." Her eyes were overbright now. "Come, the doctor is waiting. And while he sees to the child, I would like to have a private word with you."

"Yes, all right," Nicole said doubtfully, wondering if it was appropriate to leave someone else's child alone with a stranger, even if he was a doctor with very kind eyes. But before she could draw up a protest, the young lady led her through the waiting room and straight into the doctor's inner office. When she turned again, Nicole could not help but notice the tear trickling down her cheek. But she smiled at Nicole and said merely, "I'll tell the doctor you're here."

The doctor's surgery was as plain as the outer chamber, with a long table by the window and several plaques on the whitewashed walls. Before she could do much more than cast a quick glance around, however, the door reopened to admit the doctor. "Good morning, Miss Harrow," he said in English, and then continued through Anne, "I understand the child is doing better."

"He seems to be feeling much better. He even ate a bit of porridge this morning. I think . . ."

Nicole halted because Anne was not

translating, and she and the doctor were exchanging a private look.

Baffled by it all, Nicole saw Dr. Mann turn back to her, and his eyes held a gentle intensity that brought to mind the pastor in Boston. But when he spoke it was to Anne, and she did not translate. Instead, she gave Nicole another quivering smile and said, "Perhaps we could have that private word now."

Nicole's mind swirled with questions as she followed Anne farther down the narrow hall. They entered what were clearly the doctor's private quarters. In a small kitchen, Anne pulled out a chair by the table, indicating that Nicole should sit. "Would you like a cup of tea?"

"Y-yes, all right, thank you. But what—"

"Dr. Mann and I are to be wed in six weeks' time," she said, lifting a cast-iron kettle from its place by the fire and pouring water into a pot. She set a wicker tray with two cups and a small pitcher of milk. She carried the tray over and set it on the table, then pulled the napkin off a small plate to reveal fresh-baked pastries. Nicole realized that the tray had been prepared ahead of time. "Will you have one? I made them this morning."

"Thank you, I . . ." Nicole's hand was

stopped in midair by the sudden thought, *The child.* Something had to be wrong with the little one, something so serious—

"Little Michel will be fine," Anne said, clearly understanding the shock and fear on Nicole's features. "You mustn't worry. Dr. Mann is the finest doctor I have ever met." She gave a shy smile. "Well, I have not met that many doctors. But I have heard other doctors speak of his skill, and I know him to have a good heart. Your little cousin is going to be fine."

Nicole accepted a pastry out of courtesy and nibbled at one edge. When Anne poured her cup and set it in front of her, Nicole placed the biscuit on the saucer and waited with hands grasped tightly in her lap.

Anne settled herself across from Nicole and took a breath that seemed to go on forever. She looked up and gave a very shaky smile. Nicole was unable to stifle a tremor that passed through her body. What on earth was the matter?

Anne said in a voice scarcely above a whisper, "I was wondering if you would please pray with me."

"I . . . pardon me?"

"Pray. To God, our Father."

The mild tone held the same power as the pastor in Boston, a strength that needed neither volume nor argument to carry the message straight to Nicole's heart. Was God her Father? She had been praying with Guy and Emilie each morning and night since that day upon the boat. Sometimes she felt herself searching for an answering harmony within her heart; other times she did it because it was quickly becoming habit. But did she believe in God?

Nicole focused upon the young woman's intense gaze, and for some reason she found herself thinking of her own mother. Louise had that same expression sometimes, the furrows across her forehead forming a series of V's that framed the dark eyes and accented the sweep of her brows. Come to think of it, there was much of her mother in this young woman's face—the high cheekbones, the fragility balanced with strength. Maybe it was just her desire to find a little something familiar in this strange and cold land. Perhaps it was the ability of this woman to express such love and deep emotion in her gaze and her voice. But the fact remained, here was a touch of comfort, a hint of home.

Nicole took a breath of her own and confessed, "If truth be known, mademoiselle, I am not sure of this myself. But if I am a believer, then I am a rather uncertain one."

For some reason, the response brought

tears to Anne's eyes and a quaver to her voice as she said, "If I had gone through everything that you have, I wonder if I would be able to hold to faith in God at all."

Nicole cocked her head at the strange words. "How can you know of my life?"

"All the people here, at least those who are willing to listen beyond their own small needs, have heard tales of the Acadians. And my parents have searched . . ."

Again she watched the young woman approach the brink of weeping, only to draw back with great effort. "Again I ask, would you pray with me?"

"Yes, if you wish." It was only after she bowed her head that Nicole realized the young woman had said *Acadian*. She tried to recall if she had actually claimed that for herself the day before. She was fairly certain she had said nothing except her English name. But why . . . Further questions were cut off by the sound of this unusual young woman beginning to pray.

"Our Father who art in heaven, we give thanks for this day." She drew a ragged breath. "So long, our Lord. So long. And now, please let us hear your voice. We thank you for your mystery and your majesty, dear God. Please let us hear your voice."

Nicole was both challenged and comforted by the way this woman spoke—how she gathered herself so comfortably to the invisible that she asked not just for comfort but also to hear the impossible. Nicole realized Anne had stopped speaking, and she found herself wanting to pray. To speak aloud. The impossibility of this act—to sit with an Englishwoman, her enemy of all her life, and pray words that had escaped her for years and years—was so great a mystery she could not help but smile. What did it matter, all the things of this world? If she was speaking with God, if God did indeed exist, what did it matter? So she took a breath and said the words that formed all by themselves.

"God, I really do not know you. I don't think I ever have. But if you exist, then I need to know you for myself. I can't ask to hear your voice. I don't deserve this now and probably never will. But if you are real, then I am ready." She stopped, astounded at the simple clarity of those final words. Because they did indeed hold the truth of the moment. After all the struggle and the journeying and the hardship, it was true. So true, in fact, they had to be spoken a second time. "If you are real, then I am ready."

She opened her eyes and found the dark-haired young woman was weeping so hard she could do nothing but reach across the table with open hands. Nicole grasped them in her own. They sat there, Nicole content for the moment to abide in the strangeness of this young woman's tears and her own calmed heart. So many mysteries. So much she did not know. And yet, for the here and now, it was enough to have a sense of having talked to God and having been heard. At least part of the challenge that Pastor Collins had set before her had been answered. The journey was not just about finding her earthly home and English parents. She had been on her way toward this moment, she knew now, when she could set her own strength aside, accept that it was not enough and probably never had been. And admit to the unseen God that if He was indeed real, she was truly ready. With all her heart. Ready to receive.

Anne drew herself up and released one hand to wipe her eyes. "I have prayed for this moment all my life long. And now that it has come, I can hardly bring myself to speak."

Nicole waited with an inner calm she knew was not her own. A great burden had been lifted, and though she did not understand, still she was content to sit and wait. Answers would come.

"Elspeth . . ." Anne broke down once more, shaking her head and obviously struggling hard for poise. Finally she managed to say, "You are home."

Yes, it was true. These were the words that matched the feeling that now filled her heart. Was this God's voice? For the moment it was enough to suppose that she was hearing more than the words—she was hearing also the unspoken. Though she couldn't understand the strange words of this woman who sat across from her, clutching her hand in her own, she easily identified with the feeling. She was indeed home.

Anne straightened in her chair and released Nicole's hand. Her own hands brought out a white linen hankie to wipe her eyes and cheeks. To Nicole's surprise, she reached into her skirt pocket and withdrew a second clean linen and laid it on the table without comment.

The slight shoulders seemed to straighten and the dark eyes held an even warmer glow.

"Forgive me," Anne began. "In the next few minutes you may conclude that I am meddling. Please . . . please bear with me. I have reason—" She broke off long enough to draw a deep breath, then continued, "I . . . I have knowledge that you might find surprising. I . . . I know your parents."

Nicole could only stare. Certainly the

young woman could not be speaking of Henri and Louise Robichaud—which meant only one thing. She spoke of Andrew and Catherine Harrow. Nicole swallowed. Her tongue refused to form a word.

"I also know your story."

"You know. . . ?"

"About your illness as an infant. And . . . the exchange." Again Anne had to fight for control.

"But how. . . ?"

"We—your parents—have been searching for you for years. Have tried every means . . ." Whatever Anne saw upon Nicole's face brought her up short. It was a moment before she continued. "None of their letters were ever answered."

"Are they . . . are they still living?" asked Nicole in a choked voice. And suddenly she knew that it mattered. That she cared. It was a shocking revelation. One that came from deep within. She could feel the tears forming along with the thought. She reached for the handkerchief.

The young woman managed a trembling smile. "They are alive. Very much so. They will fall on their knees in thanks to God when they learn that you are home."

"Are they here?"

"No," she replied with a shake of her

head that made her starched covering crackle. "They are at their home, some distance from here."

Nicole was still attempting to clear the cobwebs of confusion, trying to comprehend. A frown furrowed her smooth brow. Her green eyes darkened with all of the unasked questions. But she was getting close. She could scarcely believe she had met someone who actually knew her parents. Knew their precise location. How had it come about? Did God really work so mysteriously? So quickly?

"But I don't understand," she managed. "How do you know all this?"

The young woman lifted her own white hankie to her eyes and took a deep breath. "I am Anne," she said softly. "I am also Antoinette Robichaud."

Nicole felt the air leave her lungs. She stared, trying to take it in, to understand what she had just heard. Yes. Yes, she could see it was so. It was Louise's daughter who sat before her. It was Antoinette whose tears spilled down her cheeks unashamedly. With a sob that caught in her throat, Nicole reached across and Anne took her hands in both of her own. They leaned toward each other, and their tears mingled on the table between them.

Chapter Thirty

Though she had never done it before, Anne had heard it was possible to make the journey between Halifax and Georgetown in a day and a half. Given strong horses and no awkward carts, such a speedy trip could be made. But she never had the money or the inclination to hasten so, until now. This day, however, the reason shouted from every hillside. It echoed amidst the birdsong and the sunlight. Even the gentle summer wind carried refrains about her haste. She who had been lost was now found. Her sister was coming home.

Cyril rode with the two women on horses loaned by a grateful patient. They were accompanied by one of the owner's servants, a trail hand used to guarding convoys on rough-hewn frontier paths. The two men gave them space and privacy, but even so Anne found it almost impossible to talk with Nicole. All the things she wanted to say, all the emotions and dreams gathered together and caught in her throat.

Nicole was equally withdrawn, but whether for the same reasons Anne did not know and was afraid to ask. Earlier that day, the only time she had spoken more than a few words, she had asked that they not call her Elspeth. Her name, she had said, was Nicole. Things were confusing enough without being forced to respond to a name she had heard for the first time only a few months earlier.

The young Frenchwoman's silence contributed to a general lack of conversation among the four travelers. Even that night, when they halted at a popular resting place where a stream formed a freshwater pool, they gathered about a fire and spoke little. They ate with the hunger of a long trail ride, said their prayers, and slid into their bedrolls.

Yet as Anne lay and listened to the fire crackle, she found she could not sleep, not without asking at least one question. She rolled over to find Nicole's shadowed eyes regarding her. Even so, she had to struggle to force the whisper around all that remained unspoken and crammed about her heart. "May I ask you about Louise and Henri?" she said, and found just speaking those names was difficult around the lump in her throat. "What are they like?"

The only signal from Nicole that she found her own response difficult was in how she rolled away from Anne and stared up at the night sky. The heavens were awash in silver, the moonlit clouds like froth upon a dark sea. In the starlight and the glow from the dimming fire, Nicole's features looked strong, full of all that remained unspoken.

Finally Nicole said, "Everything good about me, everything worthy, is just a faint shadow of who my parents are."

There was such quiet comfort in those words they seemed to ease Anne's way into slumber. Everything else could wait, now that she had received this one assurance. She closed her eyes to the night and the mysteries of life, and was on the verge of sleep when she heard Nicole whisper, "And Catherine and Andrew, how are they?"

"They are among God's chosen," Anne replied, so sleepy now she could not even open her eyes. "You will see for yourself tomorrow."

When Anne awoke just before dawn, she discovered that Nicole's bedroll was already empty. She scouted the figures stirring on the other side of the broad campsite but did not see Nicole. She rose, pulled on her boots and bonnet, and hurried off.

She found Nicole standing by the side of the trail, separated from the campsite by a gradual curve that took travelers around a steep hillside. Nicole turned at the sound of her approach, then went back to staring over the eastern hills. Anne walked near, and in the soft morning light she saw upon Nicole's features similar emotions she felt within her own heart. She turned and stared out over the hills, for the moment content with the silence and the gathering light.

The hills held the morning mist, the air was full of flowers and summertime scents. Birds surrounded them with a chorus to the coming sunrise. The light strengthened, the cloudless sky opened to depths of gentle blue. And then the sun appeared.

The sun's glow rose above a distant hill and rested there, a crown to the day and the world. The mist was transformed to a sea of shimmering gold dotted with islands of bronze and green. Anne stood and watched until the sunlight grew so strong she could stare no longer. Her heart was full, and she turned to Nicole at the same time Nicole also faced her. They shared brief smiles, then Nicole said, "This is a strange place. It seems cold and hard and unfriendly one moment, and so beautiful the next."

There was much truth in the words. Anne responded with a treasured memory, carefully selecting each French phrase. "When I was little, my mother tried to make the time when she and Louise exchanged babies live for me. She told me about the trip to Halifax when I was very sick and they had to get me to a doctor. She said one morning she awoke and was so afraid because she didn't feel she could find God anywhere. The mist hung heavier that morning than it does now, but that is what made me think of it. Suddenly, she said, the mist cleared, and the sky was blue and she could see for miles and miles, almost as though she could see to the ends of the earth. To the end of time and the end of worry and the end of stress and strain, that is how she used to tell me. As though she could see right to the gates of heaven. And in that moment, even though she was frightened and she missed her baby . . ." Anne found it necessary to turn away and bite her lip. She did not want to let all the emotions get in the way of this day or this opening up to each other. "Even though she missed her baby terribly, she knew the morning was a gift from God, and she had done the right thing," she finished.

There was a long moment, then Nicole said softly, "The right thing."

Anne turned to stare at her and said just as softly, "It was very difficult, wasn't it? Everything you and your family—my family—had to endure."

"So difficult it pains me to stand here and remember," Nicole murmured.

Anne reached over and took her hand. "I

owe you my life."

Nicole spun toward Anne. "What?"

"The doctor in Halifax those many years ago said I would never fully recover, and he was correct." Anne held the hand loosely but firmly and met the open gaze with her own. "The only reason I am alive and preparing to wed this wonderful man is because of everything that happened. All that you have suffered was in my stead—I would not have survived it." She stopped there, not wanting to lessen the moment by saying her thanks with mere words.

Nicole studied her features one by one, silent and pensive. Anne felt the pressure of the day and the coming reunion surge up within her, until the words seemed formed of themselves. "God's hand is upon this journey," Anne declared with quiet certainty.

As far as Andrew was concerned, that Saturday was as fine a day as ever had been created.

After lunch he sat on the bench outside the kitchen window. There was work waiting for him. There was always work. But he had already decided he was done with work for that week. Everything could wait until Monday. Or even Tuesday. Andrew leaned his back against the house's front wall and drank in the afternoon's sunlight and warmth. Bees drifted lazily in the still air, their wings humming contentedly. Catherine worked at the table on the window's other side. He could hear her softly singing a hymn, one he decided then and there to include in the Sabbath service.

A neighbor passed by their garden gate, calling afternoon greetings, and chiding him gently for sloth. Andrew chuckled his agreement and stretched out his legs.

He might have drifted off to sleep; he was not sure. The sun seemed to have shifted its place in the sky, and now Catherine was singing a different hymn. He debated about whether he should bother to rise and go inside for a genuine nap. But the sun felt wonderful, and the day was so fine. Yes, so very fine.

In all the days left to him on earth, he would recall it as the moment of gathering— as though all the memories and all the time and all the yesterdays lost and gone forever had returned in a single instant.

He squinted through the bright sunlight beyond the garden gate. No, not one form. Two of them. Standing and looking in to where he sat upon his little bench, his back against the home, surrounded by Catherine's rosebushes and blooming wisteria and birdsong. Andrew sat up straighter, not certain whether he had become trapped in his own afternoon dream. For it seemed as though Anne had suddenly appeared at their gate, but she was not scheduled to return for another two weeks. And she was standing with another young woman, a bit taller than Anne, who seemed familiar, yet remained a mystery because of the sunlight and his dreamy state.

Andrew squinted against the light and the mystery and felt his heart rate surge. It seemed to him that he was staring back through the years, back to a time of memories and fragrant dreams. On this perfect summer afternoon, he was granted the impossible gift of seeing Catherine as she was on the day of their marriage, her shimmering youth and vibrancy. The vision was so powerful he actually heard the village bells peal in celebration. But no, no, it was not the wedding bells he heard, but the bells of their very own chapel, chiming as they did every Saturday afternoon. And this was not an image of the past. No. It was a real person, one who was standing beside his own beloved Anne.

Andrew struggled to find the strength to stand up. His hands moved across the surface of his bench but could not find purchase to push himself erect. And he saw that familiar but unfamiliar face there beside his Anne's shed tears. He wanted to say, "Don't cry, all is well, all is truly well." But he could not speak. And suddenly he could not see her at all, for his own tears poured out from a heart filled to overflowing. Yet he was not certain of the reason, for his mind seemed unable to form a single coherent thought. He was crying and could not tell why.

Then from the open window behind him came a gasp and a sound like an infant's first cry. There was the crash of broken glass, and a second cry, this one more piercing than the first and coming from the doorway. Andrew turned, and there upon his wife's face he found the answer his mind seemed unable to form for itself. He turned back to the figure cloaked in the afternoon light, and though he could not shape the word, could not name the name, he knew. He knew. With the realization he wondered why he had not known it immediately. Catherine had. He could tell that by the wrenching exclamation of joy, the steps that flew down the pathway.

He finally found the strength to stand, then watched as Anne stepped back. She had been welcomed home by open arms many times, but this was not her moment. This moment belonged to her mother and Elspeth.

Andrew struggled to keep his balance. The whole experience had sent his head to spinning. This day that in his mind he had been sure would never come, but in his heart had yearned for, had arrived. Unexpected. Shockingly. He had dreamed about a day like this, some waking and some sleeping. But always there were first hints, leads, follow-ups, and finally distant contact. Never, never this sudden appearance of their first-born at the gate. He staggered down the path after his wife.

As Catherine reached the gate, the young woman seemed to hold back, uncertain, hesitant, but at the last possible moment she moved forward, her own arms lifting to welcome the embrace.

By the time Andrew reached them they were locked in each other's arms, swaying gently back and forth. He could hear Catherine's broken sobs. "My daughter. My little baby." All the sorrow and loss and pain of the many years seemed to be captured in those few words.

Andrew could only wait his turn. Anne moved toward him and he took her in his arms. He noticed through his own tears that she, too, was weeping. "It's a miracle. A miracle," he whispered in his daughter's ear, and she nodded her assent. He had no idea how long it would be until Catherine relinquished their daughter so that he might welcome her also. But he would wait. He'd gladly wait.

Chapter Thirty-one

After the embrace, the tears, the laughter, and the tears again, the mother and daughter realized the bittersweet reality; they had found each other, but they were total strangers. Their worlds, their lives, their speech and dress and manners and customs—everything about the two was a contrast. Nicole found it confusing and difficult. Despite Catherine's brave and quiet smile, Nicole believed this mother of hers was finding it difficult as well.

"We cannot expect the years to vanish like smoke. Your life has been much different than ours," Catherine commented one evening. Her years of teaching French to Anne were standing her in good stead, she had explained to Nicole. As they sat by the fire, each with needlework occupying her hands, Catherine continued, "Though we too have faced lean years, we have not faced your sort of trials. I thank God that Henri and Louise have kept the faith and raised you to know that God is the one to whom we turn in time of need. I have prayed for you—every day of your life."

Though the words disturbed her, Nicole loved the sound of the voice. There was a comfort in sitting with Catherine in this small cottage while wind rushed about the sturdy outer walls. Anne had left the very next day, drawn back to her work and her Cyril. Evenings such as these, Andrew and John Price had taken to visiting parishioners, granting mother and daughter an opportunity to be alone together.

Nicole felt herself studying Catherine as from a great distance, connected and yet utterly apart. Struggling to sort through the tumult in her mind and heart.

"Would you try to paint for me a picture of your village in Louisiana?" Catherine asked. "I'd love to try to walk with you through one of your days. To follow you about and sense and feel and see your world. I have missed that, the *knowing*."

Nicole tried to do just that, but she knew her words were inadequate. Never would Catherine understand the feel of village dust upon sun-browned feet as she raced toward a father coming home from his fishing. Never could she know the musty smell of the bayou or see the murky pools that lay dark and dank beneath the overhang of Spanish moss. Never would she understand the depths of what it meant to struggle for years to arrive at a place they could claim as their own—today and tomorrow and every day that followed.

Though Catherine's interest did not wane, Nicole soon realized that the telling was causing more homesickness than she could bear. Her voice trailed off, then fell silent. Catherine did not press her further.

And there was so much of Catherine's world that Nicole would never know or understand. Why was it necessary to put the lace cloth, just so, on the tea tray? Why must one always put the kettle on to boil at precisely ten to four? Why did one add starch to a kitchen apron? *Not* stitch a bright border to the hem of a skirt? Put both butter *and* jam on a piece of bread? As day followed day, Nicole knew that she and Catherine both had become more and more conscious of the differences of their two worlds.

Yet they were making the attempt to close the rift that time and circumstance had hollowed between them. As they sat in the comfort of the evening blaze, silent now, hands working adroitly, Nicole chose to look for the similarities, not the differences, and noted with some satisfaction that their hands were shaped alike. Moved alike. Louise's hands were broader. More direct and solid in their approach to a task.

"Anne will be home this Sabbath," Catherine cut through her thoughts with a sigh. "I cherish each of her visits."

Nicole lifted her head.

"Soon she will be caring for a home of her own and the visits will be fewer. . . ." She paused and looked at Nicole. "I had wondered—have thought that it would be—I mean, would you be interested in visiting the meadow?"

She had Nicole's complete attention. "Could we?"

"It's not so far. I'd like to. Just the three of us."

Nicole smiled. It would be hard to wait.

His Excellency the Viscount Charles, eighth earl of Sutton, adviser to His Royal Highness King George III, former member of the royal embassy to the court of His Majesty King Louis XIV of France, holder of the

Royal Garter, royal magistrate for the counties of Devon and Somerset, rode wearily down the Fundy Trail. Instead of the gilded carriage and eight black Arabian stallions that normally transported him, he rode upon the scruffiest nag it was ever his displeasure to approach, much less mount.

Instead of advisers from the court of Saint James, for company he traveled with a group of itinerant carters taking a load of barrels into apple country. He had forsaken his dress of frills and silver buttons and peacock feathers and velvet; instead, he wore what the carters wore—breeches of buckskin, a white shirt tied shut at the neck, simple trail boots, a slouch hat, and a long woolen coat thrown open to let in the midday warmth.

Earlier that morning, the trail from Halifax had meandered inland, and now the sea was lost to all but his nostrils. All around him pines and hardwoods rose to towering heights, higher than the steeple of St. Paul's. Instead of pealing church bells and choir, he listened to a sea breeze hum through the branches and birds sing a constant refrain to a summer too slow in coming, too swift in passing.

His sense of bafflement was not caused by his state or his companions. These he had chosen himself. While the governor of Halifax had been away on official business, the city had been seized by a frenzy of work unlike anything Charles had ever known in England's balmier climes. Here, he learned, people worked while the weather permitted. August and September were the most important months for preparing shipments of furs and hardwoods and minerals and produce. Everyone involved in trade of any sort, and this seemed to be almost everyone in Halifax, worked day and night and day. Even now, when the world was blooming a thousand different hues and the forests and fields were alight with green and gold, winter was only a hairsbreadth away.

But Charles had not required the company of his peers for this jaunt inland, nor had he wanted an official escort back to Georgetown. Instead, he had gone to his banker and requested the company of trustworthy, trail-ready folk. The banker had taken in Charles's simple seagoing attire, and the easy manner now set between the ship's captain and Charles, and said simply, "You have had a good journey."

Charles started to object, to say he had not completed his quest. But in truth he was no longer sure exactly what his chief objective was to be. So all he said was, "I am here because of Captain Dillon's skill and that of his crew."

"Lord Charles has proved himself to be a solid gentleman in the storm's crush," Captain Kedrick Dillon replied. "And, if I may be so bold as to add, a worthy mate to have at one's side when the tides of time go against you."

"I am deeply honored," Charles said, inclining his head.

The banker looked from one man to the other and repeated, "A good voyage indeed."

The banker lost no time in finding Charles a company of teamsters headed inland. Being a market town, Georgetown was a common enough stop, and no question was made of Charles's desire to surround himself with protection against the uncertainties of the trail. Finding a horse was another matter entirely; no steed of worth or beauty could be had for any amount of gold. Charles had waved the banker's apology aside and accepted the nag as simply another part of the journey's mystery.

Now that the trail had curved back inland, the forest fell away in the graceful swiftness that was possible only in the highlands. A vista was revealed, one that reached toward an infinity of greens and blues. In the far distance, slender columns of smoke drifted upward. Charles squinted and thought he could make out the man-made needle of a church spire.

He prodded his horse and rode forward to the lead teamster's wagon. "Good sir, is that Georgetown up ahead?"

The driver paused to spurt a brown stream of tobacco juice over the wagon's side. He shifted the chaw from tongue to cheek and replied, "I ain't your good sir, but you've pegged the town right enough. We should be there by midafternoon, unless we throw another wheel."

"Then I shall bid you a pleasant journey onward and ride ahead alone."

"All right, matey." The teamster waved his whip handle in farewell. "Stick to the main trail and you can't go wrong."

Charles hid his smile at the offhand parting by lifting his hat. He spurred his horse, and the two moved down the trail at a commendable pace.

He did not know what he was going to say once he arrived at his brother's house. Did not even know why he was hurrying so. But after a voyage of six months and one week, after crossing from England to Halifax, after journeying up and down the eastern coastline, after storms and frustrations and journeys into the mysteries and trage-dies of life, he was finally coming to the end of the trail.

The closer he drew, the faster he urged his steed. The nag seemed to have caught the sense of destination, for it showed a greater turn of speed than Charles would have thought possible for such an ungainly beast. Hooves the size of plates drummed down the dusty trail. The swayed back rocked like a ship in heavy seas. Charles lowered his head almost to the rangy hide to keep from being knocked off by low branches. He gripped the reins with one hand and the mane with his other, and his heart raced in anticipation.

The outlying houses swept by in a flash. He made the turning at the church and up the narrow way. There was the familiar cot-tage and the fenced-in vegetable garden. Charles pulled hard on the reins. The horse halted with a snort and a stomping of its front hooves, as though regretting that its chase had come to an end. Charles slipped from its back, patting the neck in deep grat-itude before looping the reins around the fence and opening the front gate.

His brother appeared in the doorway, clearly not surprised to see him. Andrew of-fered the same gentle smile and clear-eyed welcome as before, then moved forward to grip Charles in a fierce embrace. Only this time Charles was able to respond in kind, holding his brother close and tight, finding here in this moment an achievement of its own. He closed his eyes to the trail and the journey and the hardship, and gave himself over to the simple realization that here indeed was a homecoming.

"Charles, welcome, welcome, we have missed you so."

"And I you, brother. And I you." Charles released Andrew, pushed back a step, and said, "Elspeth, has she—"

"You know?"

Charles nodded. "Fancy that, will you. I've chased halfway to the other end of beyond, and all the time she was on her way here." He stopped to shake his head. "Well, I can't claim to have brought back your daughter. I've no credit on that score."

"She has arrived, and that is by far what is most important," Andrew responded. "How God brought her home is another matter entirely. We just thank Him that He did." He paused, his hand resting on his brother's dust-covered arm. "She goes by the name of Nicole now, but I suppose you already know that." Andrew's smile was tinged with regret. "She is not here. She has gone off with Catherine and Anne for a few days."

Charles found the immediate disappointment tempered now by an even
stronger sense of peace. As though somehow
the goal he had sought was no longer the
treasure he was after. He could not explain
it better than that, not even to himself. For
the moment it was enough to simply say,
"Brother, I owe you a lifetime of apologies."

Andrew's gaze turned keen and more
light-filled than was usual. He clasped his
brother's shoulders with one strong arm and
led him inside. "Come. We must find you
something to wash down the trail's dust. Will
you take cider?"

Charles pulled off his hat and tossed it to
the bench by the window, then passed
through the doorway and entered the simple
country cottage. With the comfort he found
from his brother's arm laid upon his shoulders, it seemed to Charles that he was entering into the finest palace upon the face of the
earth. "I should think a mug of cider would
taste like the nectar of heaven itself."

The telling of the journey's events took
them through the afternoon. Charles

watched the shadows pace time's passage across the wooden floor, and knew that even as he described the places and the people, from Louisiana bayous to the seminary in Boston, he still had not divulged the most significant encounter. Finally, as Andrew rose to prepare them some supper, Charles admitted to his brother, "You were right in what you said."

Andrew looked up from where he was cutting strips of side meat. "I beg your pardon?"

"You predicted that the journey would be in search of more than just your daughter. You were right." Charles halted, searching for the proper words. He could feel his mouth opening and closing, grasping for appropriate definitions. "These have been the hardest times of my entire life."

"From what you have described," Andrew replied, "I can well believe it."

Charles looked over and added, "And the best."

Andrew stood with knife in hand, the lowering sun illuminating him from behind.

Charles stared at the light as much as at his brother. "I found myself desiring what you had, and feeling poverty-stricken in the process."

Andrew waited through a long moment

before quietly asking, "And did you find it?"

"I . . . I believe so."

"God has spoken to your heart?"

"He is trying." Charles worked at a smile. "The stone of my heart is hard for Him to crack, I fear."

Andrew solemnly shook his head. "Not for God. If He works slowly, it is only out of compassion and gentleness."

Once again Charles had the sense of being rocked by truth. "I prayed. On the ship. Not during the storm but in the calm. I was pleased with that, how I did not fall to my knees when the ship was in the most peril. I waited until the quiet, when I could look at myself clearly, and come to God out of a need that was within me, rather than because of a need forced upon me from without."

Andrew set down his knife, wiped his hands on a towel, and moved around the kitchen table. "I understand."

"I do not say this out of pride. I think it was God's hand at work in this, rather than my own choice." He had the sense of realizing things as he spoke them, as though the clarity came through Andrew's listening and not from his own power of speech. "If it had been a storm from without, once it had passed I could return to relying on my own strength. But in the quiet, I was forced to see how poor my life has been, how devoid of love and peace."

"Charles . . ." Andrew turned away and stared at the light and the fading day. When he turned back, it was to walk over and take the seat beside his brother. "Could we pray together now?"

"I would be honored." But he found a barrier there, something that needed to be said before he could bow his head in peace. "Andrew, brother, I went in search of your Elspeth for my own selfish reasons. There was no concern for you or your family, none whatsoever. My only desire was to find her so that I could take her from you once more. It was wrong—and I ask your forgiveness."

Andrew reached over and gripped his arm. "Because of your words, brother, if she so chooses, I am now willing to let her go."

Chapter Thirty-two

Nicole stopped in the middle of the trail to look back at Catherine. In unspoken agreement, she and Anne had shortened their strides to accommodate the older woman.

"It's just up ahead, through that stand of

trees," Catherine panted lightly. "I didn't remember that the climb was so steep."

But when Anne stepped forward to swing back the branch blocking their entry, Catherine halted her by saying, "I think perhaps I need just a minute." She stood still and shut her eyes, breathing deeply.

Nicole watched as Anne walked over and took Catherine's hand. *She understands her better than I*, thought Nicole. *She knows what Catherine is thinking. Feeling. Now if it were Mama . . .*

The thought that had formulated into those words in her mind left her shaken. Since coming to Acadia she had been trying so hard, so very hard, to make Catherine into her mother. To make it feel right. To push aside the past, the circumstances, the loss, and the pain. But she could not do that by denying her other parent. She knew that now. For as long as she lived, deep in her very soul, she would think of Louise as her mother.

Catherine was opening her eyes, managing a trembling smile. "I'm ready now," she said, but her voice was still shaky.

Anne did not release Catherine's hand as she reached out again to push aside the tree limb. Catherine took a deep breath and passed through. Nicole silently followed.

They took only a few steps, just enough to enter the meadow. Catherine reached for Nicole's hand and the three stood, fingers interlocked, looking out at the scene before them.

"It has not changed," murmured Catherine in a soft voice. "I was so afraid it would be different. That the spell of this place would be gone."

Nicole let her eyes drift over the expanse of meadow grasses and small shrubs. Fall flowers carpeted the ground before her in lavish abandon. Tall trees bordered the enclosure except for the side open to the bay below. One lone fishing boat bobbed far away on the stillness of the afternoon waters. Overhead birds darted and called and dipped and rejoiced, one song mingling with another. Nicole held her breath, drinking in this moment.

"It was right over there that I first saw Louise. I remember it so vividly. I can even see the colors of her dress. So rich and vibrant. I almost envied her. I had to wear such drab things. And her eyes—I will never forget those eyes. Every now and then I catch the same expression in yours, Anne."

It was a shared moment that felt to Nicole as if she had waited for it all her life.

"And look—berries. We both used to fill

our baskets." Catherine laughed. "Or our mouths," she added. "We caught each other more than once with berry-stained lips."

Catherine led them farther into the meadow.

"And over here," she said, still holding the hands of the two daughters, "here is where Louise was picking the meadow flowers when we first met. I was by that little scrub bush. We were gathering wedding bouquets—though at first we did not know we were both at the same joyful task."

Nicole closed her eyes and pictured a very young Louise, arms filled with flowers, a smile playing about her lips.

"And the log. I'm almost afraid to look for the log. It's been such a long time. I fear that time and storms and insects may have reduced it to a pile of decay. But it was right over there—by that tall spruce."

The two girls pulled her forward.

"It is *still* there." Catherine's little cry was one of sheer ecstasy. "Look—it has hardly changed over the years. Oh my." The tears were falling now. She released the hands and moved forward, stroking the worn timber. "Oh my," she said again. "The stories this old log could tell. We'd sit here and we'd talk and share and she'd tease me about my poor French and help me with the pronunciation.

We read the Scriptures here—hour after hour. I got in trouble over that. One old village woman was bound to tattle. It got your father in deep trouble too. I was sorry about that. That was the beginning of the end to Andrew's military career."

Nicole watched as Catherine's eyes clouded and then cast aside the somber thoughts as she might a worn porch rug. "And this little hole—right here. Here is where we used to leave our messages for each other." Catherine moved forward and put her hand into a hidden hollow of the log. "Oh, it makes me feel so close to Louise."

Anne reached to pluck a flower that nodded beside her skirts. She drew it to her breast and clasped it with both hands. Her eyes were misty, and suddenly Nicole realized that here, in this meadow, the girl was meeting the mother she had never known. Without thinking about it, Nicole slipped an arm about the waist of the slender form. Her thoughts pictured two other young women sharing life, sharing fears, sharing dreams.

"And it was right here that we both cradled our babies, gave you one last kiss, and then exchanged our bundles. We didn't know . . ." Her voice caught and she paused for a long moment. "How could we have known that it would not be for the few short days we had expected?"

Catherine was weeping now, and both daughters moved to her to offer their comfort. "Oh, if only Louise could be here," she managed to say through her tears. "If only she could share this moment with us."

"Momma—can we pray?" asked Anne with trembling voice.

For answer Catherine nodded and drew them both to the old log. They sat together, their skirts overlapping, their hands intertwined as tightly as their thoughts and feelings and prayers. It was Anne who began, and Nicole was surprised at the control of her voice.

"Our Father, the One who has formed us and loves us and directs our paths, thank you for this special time in this hallowed place. Thank you for the blessings you have given. Thank you for love in abundance. We have been blessed. Not cheated. Blessed. Be with Mother Louise. At this very moment, Lord, may she feel our love. And should it please you, Lord, may the day come when we can all be united together. Bound by blood and spirit. By love and joy. By common faith. For you are good—and you are faithful, and we love you for who you are and for what you have done. Amen."

Catherine's prayer followed, and though

her voice faltered many times, she expressed many of the same thoughts in different words. When she had said amen, it seemed more than natural for Nicole to offer up a simple prayer of her own. Suddenly her tensions of trying to fit into a world she did not know, of feeling lonely for the ones she had left behind, or trying to sort through the people in her life and what her feelings should be toward them, all slipped away. Her mother Louise had been right. She had been doubly blessed. She had two mothers who had loved her—loved her all her life.

"Father," she said simply, "thank you for knowing us. For loving us. For being concerned and powerful, and willing and able to act on our behalf. For being *real*. Amen." She wasn't sure if Catherine and Anne would understand her prayer, but she knew that the Father did. Her heart was finally home. She was free to live without bitterness, pain, or guilt.

Chapter Thirty-three

The sun was so benevolent it was hard for Nicole to believe there had ever been a time of storms and gray days, or that winter would come again.

She strolled with Anne through the village of Georgetown, and the two brought the market to a standstill. All wanted to gather and greet the pastor's long-lost daughter, see the story come to life. Even people from outlying settlements had by now heard the tale of the babies being exchanged as infants. All had to approach and see the two young ladies standing side by side. The market and the village observed two girls who shared shy smiles and family heritage so intertwined the telling brought tears to the eyes of those who loved the pastor and his wife.

Anne led Nicole out through the town to the cliff walk, along the steep edge to where the sea stretched out on three sides, burnished mirrors of gold under the noon sun. Nicole spotted fishing boats and men casting nets into the sparkling waters. "My father loves to fish."

"What is our father like?"

"He is not a tall man but strong as an oak. He is the village elder. No, more than that. The fact that we have a village at all, the reason we stayed together and arrived in Louisiana and built our homes, this is because of my father's strength."

Nicole's mind became filled with images of her childhood. There would come a time to speak of her hard times, but not now. She wanted to share everything with Anne, this stranger who was swiftly becoming both a friend and the sister she had never had. But these memories were not fitting for a day of such peace and beauty. So she finished with, "Our father is a great man. And our mother is the woman he deserves as a wife. Kind and gentle and wise. And she is strong too."

"Our parents sound very much the same," Anne said quietly.

"Yes, I see much of Henri in Andrew, it is true. And Catherine and Louise could be sisters. Perhaps this is because they share the gift of faith."

Anne looked over at Nicole. "Is it difficult for you, talking of God?"

"Not so much now. I see how you live this faith of yours, and I see it is what I want for myself." She found herself smiling. "Do you know what surprises me most? How easy it is to talk with you. Not just about God. About anything. I could almost be jealous that your Dr. Mann will soon be taking your time and attention just when I am getting to know you."

Anne led Nicole over to where the massive tree stump formed a comfortable bench for the two of them. "The day I learned that Uncle Charles was going to search for you, I came out here. My grandfather found me."

"He is a wonderful man, Grandfather Price," Nicole murmured, remembering back to the time when she had first met the man who was her grandfather. It was not just his tears that had touched her heart, but his prayer of thankfulness. He had held her as if he had always known her. Strongly, in spite of his weakness, joyous, in spite of his sorrow.

"Oh, I'm so glad you feel so," Anne said, flushing with pleasure. "He found me here and asked me why I was crying. I told him it was because I was afraid you might be found and tear our family apart."

Nicole opened her mouth to speak, but Anne's intensity silenced her before the first word was uttered. Nicole sat and studied Anne's faint air of fragility, her fine-boned features. The raven hair and warm dark eyes suggested a strength that was in truth not really there. She was healthy now, yes, but here was a woman who would never withstand life's harshest winds. Nicole felt her heart flooded with a feeling of protectiveness.

"Grandfather said that I mustn't worry, that God would see us through, and make whatever came a gift. I think I trusted Grandfather more at that moment than I trusted God. But I see now he was right. I feel as though I have gained a sister and a friend."

"Me too," Nicole murmured.

"A sister and a friend," Anne repeated and opened her gaze to Nicole. "You know Dr. Mann and I are to wed in the autumn."

"He is a good man," Nicole answered. "I knew that the first time he cared for young Michel. I could see it in his eyes. His hands. Hear it in his voice."

The color rose and fell in her delicate features. "I was wondering . . . that is, would you . . ."

Nicole reached over and took Anne's hand with her own and waited. It was not for her to press.

Anne took a breath. "Would you be my bridesmaid, Nicole?"

Nicole smelled the scent of lavender water as she reached to embrace her. "I would love it so."

Chapter Thirty-four

Charles found himself amazed at how sweet the earth smelled. And how pleasant it was to weed a garden. Such a simple act, one that was utterly new to him, so alien that John Price had twice chided him for pulling up vegetables with the weeds before going inside for his nap. Charles reveled in the closeness to growing things and the sunlight and the sweat on his brow, and he promised himself that whatever came he would make a garden of his own. Whatever came.

From his position in the front garden, the sun was angled so that Anne and Nicole walked straight into the light. He had opportunity to observe them before they saw him. The two were remarkably similar, yet incredibly different. They walked arm in arm, both looking pleased and bashful at the same time because of their newfound closeness. Anne's fragility was most evident when walking alongside someone as vibrant as Nicole. From the little time he had spent with this young woman, Charles was amazed at how utterly unaware she seemed of her own innate strength, both of spirit and body. She was held from being a beauty only by her sharp-featured strength and determination. Charles shook his head and returned to his spade work. Nicole was indeed a most appealing yet formidable young lady.

The two girls finally spotted him in the front garden and self-consciously dropped arms. "Uncle Charles, what are you doing there?"

"Enjoying myself utterly." He brushed the earth from his hands. "Never knew it could be such a pleasure to till the earth."

Nicole had withdrawn into her natural and mysterious reserve. Charles rose to his feet and lifted his cap, saddened that his presence should draw such a response, but expecting no less.

Anne asked, "Do you know where Father is?"

"He and John Price took your young doctor to visit an ailing parishioner."

Anne turned to Nicole. "Why don't you stay out here and enjoy the warmth," she suggested. "I'll go help Mother with the meal."

"But . . ." Nicole's hand rose and fell, the protest dying before it was formed. Her reluctance showed as she slowly turned toward Charles, her eyes squinting against the sun, her features now strained.

"I would be most grateful," Charles said quietly in his careful French, "if you would join me for a moment."

She nodded assent, but he knew there was no eagerness there.

Charles waited until she was seated before joining her on the kitchen window bench. He started to excuse his dirty hands and knees, but something told him that this was not a time for the usual social courtesies. He waited through a moment of afternoon sunshine and birdsong, then said, "I can well imagine what you must think of me."

"You have no idea," Nicole stated with a firm shake of her head, "what I think. None."

"A young woman makes an impossible journey to find her blood kin," Charles continued, pitching his voice low. He knew that everyone within earshot had a vital interest in what he said, but the French words would provide some measure of privacy. Even without that, though, he found he did not mind. Either he was a part of this family, or he had no business speaking at all. "A man she meets upon the course of her journey, a wealthy man, turns out to be a long-lost relative. He arrives in Georgetown a few days after she returns from a journey of renewal and joy and asks if she might travel with him to England. He explains that he wishes to shower her with wealth and titles, make her his appointed heir, and grant her entry to the highest echelons of society. But the young lady does not think this is a gift. Not at all. This man and his fancy words threaten to shatter the fragile bonds she is building to a mother and sister she only recently met."

So slowly, it seemed to Charles, that she moved against her own will, Nicole's head turned to gaze upon him. He kept his own face pointed toward the sunlight and the garden, and continued, "I represent a threat. It is true." He waited a moment, marveling at this newfound ability to speak the truth, even when it went against his own stated aims. "A threat to the goals you set for yourself at the start of your voyage."

"I am not so sure anymore," Nicole replied, her voice so soft it would have been easy to miss the words entirely, "what my goals were."

"Do you know," Charles said, "I believe we might have found some common ground."

Nicole said nothing, simply watched and waited.

Her patience was as astonishing as her strength, so different from what he had known of the young ladies of London society. A part of him would have argued, cajoled, bribed, or whatever else he could mobilize to impose his will upon her. Charles shut his eyes to the light and the day. She was intelligent, resourceful, strong, wise. What she did not know in the way of etiquette, she could most certainly learn. She was, in all truth, a perfect heiress. Though he had faced incredible odds to finally find her—no, even after all that he could not take credit for discovering her—she had turned out to be far more than he had hoped and dreamed.

With great effort, Charles made himself relax. He could not—would not—do it. Even if it were possible, he could not try. She was a woman in her own right. He had seen from where she had come, the hardships she had endured, the fortitude it had taken to arrive here. If this was her quest, what right or ability did he have to subvert her chosen course?

He was changing as well. His own course was altering. He did not know where he was headed, or what was intended. Only that change had begun. And that he was no longer alone.

He opened his eyes to find her still watching him. "Yes?" he asked.

"I was just thinking," Nicole said, "how strange it was that we would sail together for weeks and only now sit and talk."

"A few months back," Charles said, returning to gaze at the golden afternoon, "I would have said it was a mockery of fate. And use it as a reason to mold my own course, to bend others to my own will and direction."

"And now?"

"Now, yes, now..." A hint of breeze traced its way across his forehead, and Charles found himself recalling a different afternoon, one far grayer with a gale blowing many times greater. Enfolded in the sea and mists of timeless seeking, he had felt upon his face the whisper of something unseen, yet very present. "Now I confess that my own will is but a feeble thing. That there is a power far greater at work. And I need to acknowledge the Source of this greater power. To know His will and what is intended here." He had to smile. "I can scarcely believe I am saying these words."

"And I," Nicole replied quietly, "can hardly believe that I agree with them."

"Two agreements in the same afternoon," Charles said, no mockery to his tone.

"Yes." She turned her own face to the light, leaning against the wall, in comfortable companionship. "I feel as though I am relearning lessons my parents attempted to teach me, but it is only now that I am truly ready to learn. Lessons about one's choices in life, and what it means to begin by making the *one* choice correctly."

"The one choice," Charles murmured.

"Well said. Very well said indeed."

Agreement brought with it an easy silence that was both restful and deep, such that when Nicole spoke again, it was with a new openness. "I have a favor to ask."

"Anything."

"I must ask that you hold it in strictest confidence."

Charles turned to her, though she would not meet his gaze. "As you wish. You have my word."

"My father was named village elder in the year before the expulsion from Acadia. He buried the village treasure upon a hill above Minas. My uncle was assigned to retrieve it and find a way to get it back to Louisiana."

Charles leaned forward in anticipation of providing a service for this remarkable young woman and her family. "Do they wish the items themselves or its value? I could readily arrange for a banker's draft and have it sent to your father through connections in New Orleans."

"I don't know which they would prefer. I will need to discuss it with my uncle." She released a sigh. Then she asked, "You met my parents?"

"I did. And saw your home."

"What did you think?"

"Your mother is a French version of Catherine. Two ladies more similar and yet without common bloodlines I have never before met. It was most remarkable."

"And my father?"

Charles found himself recalling the contrast between his arrival at Plaquemine, with its squalor and tragedy, and the quiet, rock-steady comfort within Vermilionville. And he said with genuine sincerity, "Your father is a king among men."

The day itself seemed to hold its breath. Then Charles was startled by Nicole's slender hand upon his own, light yet incredibly strong, feminine yet marked by toil and affliction. "I have not thanked you," she said, and her voice was low, controlled, "for coming to look for me—no matter the reason. And for arranging passage on your ship. Things could have been so different had our group not been given berth. . . ."

Charles looked at her and met a gaze that was shaped by history and journeys he could not fathom. Eyes as green as the summer, as deep as the oceans he had passed through. And he knew, no matter what might lie ahead, or the distance that might be set between this young lady and himself, he knew with absolute certainty that their lives were bound together. So it now was, and so it would remain.

Chapter Thirty-five

The trail was broad and easy—and surprisingly empty for that time of year. Andrew rode alongside Charles. Ahead of them, the three women sat in the comfort of a new wagon driven by Cyril. John Price had seen them off with fond farewells, even for Charles, and the declaration that though he did not feel up to a journey to Halifax, nonetheless he would be fine there on his own.

The wagon was a marvel, the two seats set upon springs that both steadied the ride and eased the passengers over the bumpy trail. The wagon and horses were gifts from Charles, who had avoided argument by simply going down to the market, making his purchases, and driving them back to the Harrow cottage. How could Andrew protest with all three women exclaiming over the modern features and the new wagon's ease of travel?

The new wagon was piled with items Catherine wanted to take from Georgetown to Cyril and Anne's house in Halifax. It would be their first viewing of the bride-to-be's new home, and Catherine had no intention of arriving empty-handed. And high atop the load rose Charles's own house-warming presents, two handwoven rugs and a trio of quilts made from swatches of velvet crimson and gold and lavender. Charles had found them hanging over a porch rail in Georgetown, and he spent two days convincing the woman to part with them. He'd had to pay a sum that would have fetched a silk coverlet from France, for the woman had crafted them with her own family in mind. But Charles was vastly pleased with his purchases. They suited Anne far more than silk and shone like rainbows in the morning sun.

Andrew told Charles of his joy at being back in the saddle. His journeys on horseback had been few and far between, he explained, restricted to travels with wealthy parishioners who owned more than one horse. Charles had not actually announced that the horses and wagons were Andrew's, since that would have given him an opportunity to refuse the generous gifts.

The three ladies chatted with an animation that matched the birds flitting through the forest and filling the day with their song. There was so much to converse about, years of longing, years of empty places in heart and hearth.

The only cloud upon the day and their

journey was that Nicole did not appear to be the least interested in discussing a life in England. Since their conversation in the garden three afternoons ago, she seemed to be avoiding him—as much as two people could avoid each other in such close confines.

Catherine chose that moment to throw back her head and send a peal of laughter echoing about the treetops. Andrew smiled at his wife and said to Charles, "I have never seen her so happy. We have had a good life, and much joy. But only now, when I hear how lovely it is, do I find that I had missed the laughter that had been lost."

"Andrew, I want you to hear me out without argument." Charles gripped the saddle horn. "I am leaving a sum of money in your name with a banker in Halifax." Charles raised his voice before Andrew could protest. "Don't argue with me, brother!"

Catherine cast a worried glance toward the two, and Andrew gave her a quick up-raised hand in reassurance. "Have your say, then."

Charles continued, his voice sounding hoarse in his ears, "Our mother's will left what money she had of her own to you."

Andrew's head turned so swiftly it caused the horse to neigh and stomp. He patted the steed's neck and muttered, "I knew nothing of this."

"No, nor I, not until our father passed on. He said he had included the inheritance in the moneys he sent to you, so I was to consider the matter settled, if I so wished. Those were his words, and naturally I wished for nothing else. I had no intention of righting any wrong that might have been done to you." The last words barely could pass the constriction in his chest and throat.

"Charles, I assure you, there is no need—"

"Hear me out. I beg you." He took a deep breath. "You are not young anymore. And I will not leave this continent without knowing you have what is rightfully yours. I will not, do you hear me?"

"There is no need to shout, brother. I am right here beside you."

"I will not hear of it," Charles repeated more quietly. "You cannot be both a leatherworker and a pastor, not at your age. I realize you will not accept my money. So take what is yours by birth, by a legally binding will laying out our mother's express wishes."

Andrew reached over and gripped his brother's arm. "I accept, and with an overfull heart. Thank you, dear brother."

"But . . ." Charles shook his head in bewilderment. "Why now, when before you would not even let me discuss it?"

"Because before it was offered as a bribe. You wished to gain something from me. It was not a gift, as it is now."

"True. That is true," Charles nodded gravely.

"Charles, I wish you could see what changes the Lord is working in you."

Charles looked up at a slender ribbon of blue framed by trees so tall they seemed almost able to touch the clouds. "I tell you, brother, all I see is the lack in me."

"The Lord himself said," Andrew continued, "it is easier for a camel to pass through the eye of a needle than a rich man to enter heaven. And yet you are making those steps and growing inwardly in truth and righteousness."

"Only because I was broken upon the sea and the bayou and the trail," Charles confessed quietly. He realized the wagon had slowed, and all were now watching and listening. "Only because I was brought face-to-face with just how hollow my existence has been."

Nicole found it easier to remain behind her reserve and observe all the joyful activities from a safe distance.

The days in Halifax were nothing if not wondrous. Charles took for them the entire top floor of the city's finest hotel. Nicole knew Andrew accepted the invitation because of her. He and Catherine wanted her to have an opportunity to see just exactly what it was that awaited her in England. Here it was on display, at least hints of what could be for her. The entire city seemed to gather to pay Charles homage. He refused invitations on a daily basis, brought by emissaries from merchants and government alike.

The ease Charles showed with Andrew was translated to a similar level of comfort with Guy Belleveau. When the two had met, despite their differing cultures and their nations having been enemies, there was a remarkable acceptance on both sides. Nicole tested it by confessing to her uncle Guy that she had told Charles of their need to get the treasure back to Vermilionville. Guy had not seemed to mind her sharing the village's secret at all; in fact, he had seemed to accept both her admission and Charles's own offer of help as a gift from God. The two men had spent much time together, speaking of both the situation here and the one in Louisiana. Guy eventually had accepted Charles's loan of horses and wagon and set off for Minas.

One afternoon the governor himself had come to their hotel, arriving in a carriage more elaborate than anything Nicole had ever seen, drawn by four matched geldings and accompanied by three aides in long coats with velvet borders. She saw the uncertainty in Andrew's face when Charles introduced them and drew his brother over to sit with the governor. Nicole remained at a distance, and she observed the familiarity with which Charles moved in the circle of power and influence. She was quickly picking up enough English to follow much of what was being said. She felt herself drawn by the allure of Charles's world. She sensed something within herself, so new she could not name it. And she knew that it could be very easy to accept Charles's offer and travel with him to England and wealth and fame. Very easy indeed.

Anne and Catherine were busy with plans for the coming marriage. Nicole had been included whenever she wished to join. She sensed Catherine's desire to draw her closer still and felt she understood the older woman's uncertainty and pain. She yearned to know her mother better, and her father, though the familiar titles rested uneasy on her heart, as though even thinking them in relation to two who were not Henri and Louise was somehow disrespectful to the memory of Henri and Louise.

Impossible choices. Whatever she did, it meant a loss. And this ultimate result of any decision she could make was far easier for her to see than possible rewards. What to do? Nicole sat in the hotel lobby's far corner, sheltered by heavy drapes drawn back from the tall front windows, and watched Charles with the entourage of power and privilege. What to do?

A whisper of memory, a smiling bearded face above a stocky body, a seminarian who was both a stranger and a friend saying simply, *Make the first choice*. Yes. Choose rightly in the beginning, and all else would come clear.

Nicole closed her eyes, in the finest surroundings she had ever known, with people rushing about, and servants ready to leap at her call. And she prayed. *I want only your will, my Lord. I want to please you. Please show me what your choice for me is. I do not know my way forward. Everything seems right, and everything seems wrong. What do you want me to do?*

When she lifted her head, Catherine was

standing before her, watching her with a smile. "Am I disturbing you?" she wondered.

"No, please join me," she said, motioning to the chair beside her. "I was praying," she added slowly.

"Oh," Catherine said, "I'm so glad."

Nicole could not return the warm smile, for the moment was too open and honest. "I don't know what to do," she murmured sorrowfully.

Catherine leaned toward her. "Nicole, sometimes the greatest moments of my life have been masked by impossible questions."

"You may call me Elspeth if you wish. It's all right. Really."

"Elspeth." Catherine's smile wobbled a bit at the edges. "No, Andrew and I have discussed this. You should hold to the name that is yours by heritage. In my heart you will always be my Elspeth, but you are also the lovely Nicole, raised by Henri and Louise. As part of this legacy, I will call you by that name."

Nicole stared at the woman, this stranger she felt impossibly close to, whose very presence was enough to make her want to burst into tears. She managed, "Thank you."

Catherine reached for Nicole's hand, then hesitated and let it fall back into her lap.

"You and I have talked about our histories, about some similarities but mostly about the differences. Though there were times when I was sure I could not bear the loss of my own flesh and blood a single day longer, I have found life to be good. There have been so many blessings I wake up some nights fearing that I have let some slip. That I have not been thankful enough. That I have forgotten to cherish something to its fullest."

The words opened a thousand doors, revealing not just a woman, but a heart and a soul. Nicole did not know why she felt such an urge to weep. But she would not allow herself to lose any of this moment in tears.

Catherine seemed unaware of the effect of her words. "Part of learning to count my blessings is accepting that many of them I would not have chosen if it had been left to me. I must first give up any attempt to compare what was with what might have been. By accepting God as my Shepherd, I must also accept the path He sets me upon—and the blessings from whatever circumstances of life."

Nicole found herself unable to more than nod. But she was sure Catherine did not see this, for sorrow was etched so deeply upon the woman's features that it was unlikely she was noticing anything beyond her own inner thoughts.

There was a long moment of silence, punctuated by the noise and bustle in the hotel's lobby. Finally Catherine said in a voice so quiet the words could easily have been lost entirely, "It also means that I must accept His will when it comes to those I love."

Nicole wanted to protest, to say something comforting in the face of the obvious pain Catherine was feeling. But she could not speak. Catherine went on, speaking to the hands in her lap, "What I am trying to say, my dear, is that if you feel it is your destiny to go back to England with Charles, then know you shall travel with my blessing." The final word quavered, and a single tear traced its way unnoticed down Catherine's face. She repeated, more unsteadily still, "You will always be in my heart and my prayers, wherever you go."

Nicole closed her eyes, desperate for answers she knew she could not find for herself. She felt as though her heart were crying out with a voice attempting to shake the heavens with its strength, *Tell me what to do.*

When Guy and his sons returned from

Minas, they reported the good news that the long-hidden treasure had been found. Accompanied by Catherine, Emilie, Anne, Nicole, Charles, and Andrew, the adventurers went straight to the bank. Charles hefted one of the filthy sacks, brushed off as much dirt as he could, and carried it through the bank's main lobby and up the stairs to the senior official's office. Guy followed with the second one. The sacks had to be carried from underneath, for the burlap had rotted and the seams were splitting. Charles only noticed how dirty he had become when the banker's aide protested as the sacks were deposited upon the table's polished surface. The banker waved the aide outside and carefully used his letter opener to split the seams. The rest of the group crowded into the office, craning to see what the sacks held.

Together the three men separated the treasure into two piles. The larger by far was made up of plate, most of which was silver. The smaller was coinage drawn from a vast array of denominations and countries. There were gold Louis, sovereigns, ducats, even a few pesos from the most southern colonies. Charles watched Nicole's uncle separate the coins and heard his murmurs of delight. The man had probably never seen so much money in one place before.

"My friend," Charles said to Guy, speaking slow and careful French so the banker also might follow his words, "I am happy to say that it looks as though you have considerable wealth here." Charles paused to look once more over the pile of money. "I cannot say for certain," he continued, "but I would estimate you must have at least two hundred gold sovereigns' worth of coinage alone."

Charles began scooping up the coins and settling them into the astounded banker's hands. Charles continued, "I would suggest you pack up the plates and return them to the people of Vermilionville to keep as part of their heritage. Would you not agree, sir?"

"M-most assuredly," the banker stammered in broken French.

"Then you will have your people count this coinage and issue a draft forthwith," Charles instructed. "I will add to this my own promise of assistance to Henri."

"What promise was this, m'sieur?" Guy asked.

"A long story, one for another time." He gave Nicole a deep look, one that only added to the tumult in her mind and heart. Then Charles instructed the banker, "Make it for one thousand sovereigns even, and a second draft for an additional fifty sovereigns to Guy Belleveau." To the gasps of the gathered clan, Charles hastened to add, "I would be most deeply grateful if you would please accept this gift, m'sieur. I feel certain Henri would agree that part of the money owed to your clan should be used to help you settle here in Acadia."

Charles waited as Guy stammered his astonished thanks, then continued in English, "I have been doing some thinking, and I have an announcement to make."

He had the attention of everyone in the room as he walked over to take a place between Catherine and Anne. He directed his words to the younger of the two. "I have found passage upon a swift ship bound for England."

"Must you go so soon, brother?" Andrew asked, his voice full of genuine regret.

"I must," Charles said, touched deeply by Andrew's care for him. "I have already been away far too long."

"When do you depart?"

"In three days." He pressed through the murmur of protest, saying to Anne, "I am deeply sorry to miss your coming wedding, my dear. But I have been giving thought to a suitable wedding present."

"But the lovely carpets—and quilts. It is not necessary for you to do more."

"Oh, but it is." He paused long enough

for Catherine to translate for those who spoke no English, then said, "My contract with Captain Dillon's ship continues through the end of this sailing season. But because I have found this passage back to England, I no longer personally require its service. I would therefore like to order the captain south, with all possible dispatch."

Anne's hands flew to her mouth. Charles was rewarded with a second gasp from Catherine, and a third from Nicole when the words were translated and the realization dawned. He went on, "I will invite Henri and Louise to travel north. They will be required to spend the winter here. But if they wish to avail themselves of it, I will arrange for the earliest possible passage for them back to Vermilionville in the spring."

Anne said nothing, and nothing was required. The look in her eyes was the finest expression of gratitude Charles could ever want.

Chapter Thirty-six

That night they celebrated with a rather boisterous meal in Cyril and Anne's new house. Tables were borrowed from the doctor's office, benches from the waiting area, plates and silverware from the hotel. There was much laughter and translations that got started and never finished and delightful horseplay among Guy's younger children. Charles felt a deep contentment and sense of satisfaction as he sat and laughed and talked with these, his family and new friends. It was a gift, not just for the night but for all the departures and farewells to come.

As though in confirmation of that gift, Nicole chose to walk alongside him back to the hotel. Her first comment, when night and a few paces distanced them from the others, was, "You knew that if my parents came up from Vermilionville, I would have to stay."

"I sensed that you were leaning in this direction already," Charles responded quietly.

Candlelight from a passing window painted Nicole's features with warm hues. "It must have been hard for you."

"In truth," Charles confessed, "I have seldom known anything to feel more right."

The silence was as comfortable as the

night breeze, and after a half dozen paces, Nicole asked, "May I take your arm, Uncle Charles?"

"I would be most honored."

She slipped her arm through his and said, "Until you said you were sending for my parents, I did not know what I was to do. It seemed as though all I could see before me was what I would lose. Every choice was wrong."

"Does that mean you were tempted by my offer?"

"Very." Though the night was warm, he could feel her shiver. "So much so that it frightened me."

"Perhaps," Charles ventured, "it is possible for you to do both."

"How—what do you mean?"

"Stay the winter here with your families," he said carefully. "Then you could come join me in England in the spring."

He dared not look at her for fear he had been too bold. Finally she replied, "I will think on this. And pray about it."

And once again Charles felt a sense of reward, a true and lasting rightness. "I can ask," he replied, "for nothing more."

———— ❧ ————

The comfort of the crackling fire warmed more than the body as Nicole sat sipping hot cider from a heavy mug. Anne had gone for a walk with her fiancé. Her wedding date had been postponed. They would wait for Henri and Louise, however long it might take them to make the journey. Cyril had not complained about the postponement, knowing how much the presence of her other parents would mean to his bride. But he told her with serious countenance that if God answered his prayers, there would never be a ship to make this journey in a shorter time.

Nicole thought how wonderful it was for Anne to be looking toward her wedding day. What if she had agreed to marry Jean Dupree? For the first time Nicole truly realized what a dreadful mistake that would have been. Only God had saved her from it, at a time when she really didn't know Him.

Andrew had come into the sitting room of their hotel suite and was quietly watching Nicole. He asked through Catherine, "Are you weary?"

Nicole hid a yawn behind her hand. But at the same time that her body was urging her toward bed, she felt strangely refreshed. Perhaps it was because the inner struggle was over. Because she had stopped trying to figure everything out on her own. "Yes, I'm tired. But Mama must be more so."

"I am exhausted, I will admit," Catherine acknowledged from the other side of the fireplace. The warm glow in her eyes was more than reflection from the coals. "I don't think it was the journey itself as much as all the excitement since our arrival. I've never had so many things happen in such short order. So much coming and going."

She stopped to translate for her husband, who said, "I do hope Charles's return journey will go more smoothly than the voyage over." Andrew hesitated, then asked gently, "Might we ask if you have reached any decision?"

Nicole dropped her gaze and looked down at the cider swirling about the bottom of her cup.

"You are leaning toward his offer?" asked Catherine in a small voice.

Nicole looked over at Catherine for a long moment, then said, "I am." She had to admit it. She was leaning in that direction—unless God clearly gave her reason to change her course. "But not until the spring, so that I can be here to greet Louise and Henri and join in Anne's wedding."

Catherine stared down at her cup but made no outward sign of distress. Nicole was thankful that there was no emotional protest. Perhaps her mother had known for some time that this was a likely eventuality.

"It is reasonable," suggested Andrew. "A few short months ago I would have fought against it. But now—with the change in your uncle Charles, I have not the same fears."

This time it was Catherine who nodded.

"Papa, have you ever considered going back?" Nicole asked suddenly. "I'm certain the estate is large enough for two, and Uncle Charles would gladly share now. You could be the local vicar if you wished and . . ."

Andrew held up a hand. "God has called me here," he said simply. "To the colonies. If He ever wants me in a different place, I'm sure He will let me know."

Catherine's weak smile held a hint of relief. Nicole knew her roots here went deep.

"I am happy to accept the bequest from Charles. It will make things much easier for your mother," Andrew continued. "And I confess that I will not miss the leatherwork. Especially in the dead of winter. And we do have a Georgetown cobbler now, so my hands are no longer needed."

"I still have much praying to do," Nicole reminded them. "As I said, I have not given Uncle Charles a firm yes."

Andrew straightened from his place in

the doorway. "We will all pray," he assured her. "I think a good time to start is now." He crossed the room to kneel on the floor between them, taking a hand of each in his own. Nicole looked at each face, feeling a calmness and a peace she had never felt before. Whatever happened in her future, she could depend on one certainty. With two sets of parents praying, she was sure God would show her the way.

Chapter Thirty-seven

The morning of departure was one of billowing clouds and a strong wind from the land, as though heaven and earth were joined to hasten his sailing. Charles stood at dockside, surrounded by his family he had not even known a half year previous. And yet these were now unbelievably precious to him.

His brother stood before him, the wind blowing strands of graying hair from beneath the hat. Charles studied the silver threads and wondered with a pang in his heart if there were more permanent farewells to come. "Andrew," he confessed, "I do not know if I have the strength for this."

Catherine pushed past her husband and

held Charles in a warm embrace. "Who ever would have thought this moment would so pierce my heart?"

He clenched his jaw against the pain of another separation. He said to Andrew over Catherine's head, "Help me, brother."

"It is hard to think of it just now," Andrew said with a deep sigh, "but we must all remember that no parting is final within God's family."

The words were enough to unlock the band that had tightened around his chest. Charles took the day's first easy breath and returned Catherine's embrace. "I will miss you, dear sister," he said as she stepped back.

Andrew motioned for the two young women to join them, and together they clustered upon the quayside. The wind whistled around them, the waves crashed against the stone wall, and gulls swooped and soared over the little group. Charles bowed his head with the others and listened as Andrew called for God's blessing upon the journey and the homecoming. And when the words stopped, Charles found his own waiting and gave voice to his first spoken prayer. "Father, I see now more than ever my own weakness, my own needs. I ask for your blessing upon these good people, and upon me as well. Whatever it is that I should do, whatever it is that awaits me, help me to journey into the future as your servant."

The hugs and the farewells were swift in joining and slow in ending. Nicole's embrace was without words, but Charles did not need any. *Whatever is right*, he prayed silently as he released her.

Charles felt as though he and Andrew both were seeking to delay not only the departure but maybe time itself in the strength of that last clasping of arms and meeting of hearts.

Finally Charles climbed into the waiting skiff and stood amidships as the oarsmen made for the waiting vessel. The farewells and waves continued on until the calls grew fainter than the gulls. The last voice he heard clearly was that of his beloved brother. Andrew's final words, lofted upon the wind, seemed to be borne from heaven itself.

"Go with God!"

Children's Books by Janette Oke

Making Memories
Spunky's Camping Adventure
Spunky's Circus Adventure
Spunky's First Christmas

CLASSIC CHILDREN'S STORIES

Spunky's Diary
New Kid in Town
The Prodigal Cat
Ducktails
The Impatient Turtle
A Cote of Many Colors
A Prairie Dog Town
Maury Had a Little Lamb
Trouble in a Fur Coat
This Little Pig
Pordy's Prickly Problem
Who's New at the Zoo?